Common sense urged Blythe to be the one to turn her back.

But reckless curiosity, the kind that came from too many sleepless nights spent allowing self-doubt to cripple her, had her doing the opposite instead.

Stretching, she stood and crossed to him. With her heart beating in her chest like a trapped hummingbird, she moved closer to him, with their gazes still locked.

In unison, they moved backward, around the corner and out of view of the sofa. No words were spoken as he took her hand and pulled her close, up against him.

She kissed him first, standing up on her toes and arching her body into his. He deepened the kiss, letting her feel the heat of his own desire. She was glad to learn it burned as hot as her own.

Books by Karen Whiddon

HARLEQUIN NOCTURNE

SILHOUETTE NOCTURNE

HARLEQUIN ROMANTIC SUSPENSE

SILHOUETTE ROMANTIC SUSPENSE

*The Pack
**The Cordasic Legacy

Other titles by this author available in ebook format.

KAREN WHIDDON

started weaving fanciful tales for her younger brothers at the age of eleven. Amid the Catskill Mountains of New York, then the Rocky Mountains of Colorado, she fueled her imagination with the natural beauty that surrounded her. Karen now lives in north Texas, where she shares her life with her very own hero of a husband and three doting dogs. Also an entrepreneur, she divides her time between the business she started and writing. You can email Karen at KWhiddon1@aol.com or write to her at P.O. Box 820807, Fort Worth, TX 76182. Fans of her writing can also check out her website, www.karenwhiddon.com.

THE LOST
WOLF'S DESTINY

—

KAREN WHIDDON

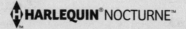

Recycling programs
for this product may
not exist in your area.

ISBN-13: 978-0-373-88577-0

THE LOST WOLF'S DESTINY

Copyright © 2013 by Karen Whiddon

All rights reserved. Except for use in any review, the reproduction or
utilization of this work in whole or in part in any form by any electronic,
mechanical or other means, now known or hereafter invented, including
xerography, photocopying and recording, or in any information storage
or retrieval system, is forbidden without the written permission of the
publisher, Harlequin Enterprises Limited, 225 Duncan Mill Road,
Don Mills, Ontario, Canada M3B 3K9.

This is a work of fiction. Names, characters, places and incidents are
either the product of the author's imagination or are used fictitiously,
and any resemblance to actual persons, living or dead, business
establishments, events or locales is entirely coincidental.

This edition published by arrangement with Harlequin Books S.A.

For questions and comments about the quality of this book,
please contact us at CustomerService@Harlequin.com.

® and TM are trademarks of Harlequin Enterprises Limited or its
corporate affiliates. Trademarks indicated with ® are registered in the
United States Patent and Trademark Office, the Canadian Trade Marks
Office and in other countries.

Printed in U.S.A.

Dear Reader,

Most of us have suffered some kind of pain in our lives. We wear scars that cannot be seen on the outside. Some of us become bitter and remain mired in the wounds inflicted in the past, unable to heal or grow. Others manage to move past the hard lessons learned by cruelty. Forgiveness is a gift you give yourself. The person who hurt you may not know or care that you've managed to forgive them, but inside the damage does not continue to fester and cause you harm.

Sometimes in real life, there are people whose damage I can see but cannot heal. So I turn to my writing, to fiction, where all scars can be erased by the healing power of love. This story is about such a man, once broken and made to believe he was less than garbage. As he finds his destiny, so can you, if only you remain open to the endless possibilities out there. I wish you joy in reading this story, and hope and, most of all, love.

Karen Whiddon

To all the broken people out there. You know who you are. I'm hoping you healed, rose above your past and learned from other's mistakes.
Special thanks to my bestie and critique partner Anna Adams, for going above and beyond helping me make this book the best it could possibly be. Your help and amazingly sharp eye are appreciated more than you know.

Chapter 1

The instant Lucas Kenyon heard the man's cultured, sanctimonious voice on the six o'clock evening news, his blood froze. Despite not having seen the speaker for fifteen years, he shuddered. He knew that voice, knew it too damn well. Even after fifteen years, it still haunted his nightmares.

Up until this past January, he'd assiduously avoided anything to do with The Church of Sanctuary and its leader. If something came on the news, he'd changed the channel. Newspaper or magazine articles were tossed, unread. He'd wanted no reminders of his painful past.

But the time had come to face his demons. Lucas had never in his life made a New Year's resolution. This year, he had. No more would he bury himself in work and avoidance.

"What the hell?" he muttered, grabbing the remote and turning up the volume.

The man, Jacob Gideon—Lucas refused to think of him

as his father—smiled benevolently. "We can heal young Hailey, I promise you that." His tone reverberated with the sincerity of his conviction. "Faith works through my hands."

Faith? Try *murder.* Un-freaking-believable. Briefly, Lucas closed his eyes, allowing the long-ago grief and pain and shame to wash over him. On some inner level he'd known. After all, Jacob had killed once in the name of his faith. Lucas had no doubt the man would do it again.

If he hadn't already. Lucas cursed. No wonder the voice of his conscience had gotten so loud he'd been unable to drown it out.

As the man spoke again, Lucas snapped out of it. What Jacob was suggesting—no, *stating*—was more than wrong, more than an outright lie.

Of course, Jacob spoke as if he really meant his own nonsense. Lucas made a sound of pure disgust. Jacob had always believed he was an angel appointed from up high who had somehow misplaced his wings.

As if angels killed. Though thinking about how Lucifer actually had been a fallen angel, Lucas supposed it was possible. Jacob always had styled himself as if he sat on the other side of God.

His father looked sincere and kind, but Lucas knew better. Jacob was pure evil. Studying the man, he shook his head. Jacob looked eerily the same, as if selling his soul to the devil had granted him eternal youth. He was more than dangerous. He was deadly. No one knew that better than Lucas. After all, Jacob had been hunting him for the past fifteen years.

With narrowed eyes, Lucas watched the rest of the news segment, wincing as a fragile little girl with a heart-shaped face smiled painfully at the reporter. Something about her delicate vulnerability reminded Lucas of the child he'd once been, and the other. The twin he'd lost. The sister Jacob had killed.

As the camera narrowed in on a woman—her mother?— Lucas moved closer to the television. The sight of this unknown woman—as defenseless as her daughter—hit him like a sucker punch to the gut. Her brownish-blond hair as fine as spun silk, creamy porcelain skin and long-lashed green eyes, made her a beautiful mystery that interested him far more than his father's manipulative faux spiritual healings. She was, Lucas thought, both lovely and otherworldly, in a way neither he nor Jacob Gideon would be able to resist—for reasons as different as they were themselves.

This was partly what interested him, or at least that was what he told himself. True, she was gorgeous, but around her he could see the faint hint of an aura. An aura that meant she was like him. He'd learned there were others, of course, and how to recognize them, even though he stayed away from them like he stayed away from Jacob.

Until now, as far as he knew, no others of his kind had fallen into Jacob Gideon's clutches. Of course, if they had, he wouldn't have noticed. A shudder racked him, of guilt and grief and sorrow at the knowledge that his years of avoidance might have enabled Jacob to snare another Shifter. Lucas had personal experience with what would happen to any soul so unlucky.

He closed his eyes. Though it had been fifteen years, he still fought the lasting effect of those inner wounds. This woman, whoever she was, was making a terrible mistake. Jacob would torment her the same way he'd tortured his own son, under the guise of doing his idea of the Lord's work. That was awful enough.

Ah, but it didn't stop there. Worse, far worse, was the fact that her little girl would be in even greater danger, de-

spite Jacob's claims of being able to heal her. Neither she
nor her mother would ever be heard from again, once Jacob
had them locked away in the compound known as Sanctuary, an enclave of his faithful on thirty acres in the West
Texas desert. Both of them would probably end up dead.

Jacob had killed once before, many years ago. No doubt
he'd have no qualms about doing so again.

The woman came on again, her clear, melodic tone pro-
fessing what sounded like sincere hope that Jacob Gideon
and his Sanctuary church would be able to help her daughter. Standing frozen, Lucas couldn't evade or avoid the pain
and the longing and the need in her voice for her daughter
to be healed. The emotion touched him deep inside.

While he wrangled with the unexpected rush of emotion, his inner wolf came awake, paying attention to the
woman's words. This, too, was odd, as the beast had never
before shown interest in any female. Concentrating on listening, he pushed his wolf back down, trying to figure out
what drove the woman to ask for Jacob's help.

She was desperate, he understood. She had to be to
agree to something as far-fetched as Jacob's outrageous
claims. His stomach heaved and he swallowed back bile.
He hadn't expected this when he'd decided to avoid having anything to do with Jacob and his Sanctuary.

The question was, what was he going to do about it?

Dragging his hand through his hair, Lucas stood trans-
fixed in front of his TV, even as the footage moved away
from the woman and child and back to the news reporter.
Finally, a commercial came on. The report had ended. As
he clicked the remote and turned the television off, reality sank in.

Jacob Gideon had finally gotten his claws into another
Shape-shifter. As far as Lucas knew, there hadn't been
any other victims since him and Lilly, which had led to his

own escape so long ago. Since that fateful day, the image of his beloved sister's lifeless body had haunted his every waking moment, as well as his dreams.

And this? He couldn't hide from the truth. Unless he did something right now, he'd have to live with another innocent's death on his conscience.

Which would be, of course, completely unacceptable.

Furious, he snarled an unintelligible curse, stopping himself just short of hurling the remote at the flat screen.

He could no longer remain hidden; the revenge he'd spent half his life dreaming about would finally be a possibility. After all, he was no longer a frightened teenager. He had to return to Sanctuary and save the Shape-shifter woman and her daughter.

Because he knew in his heart of hearts if he didn't, he'd be just as bad—just as horrible, foul and evil—as the man he'd once called Father.

Blythe Daphne smiled wanly at the television camera, loathing that she had to beg for sympathy and invite ridicule. She'd do anything—absolutely anything—to help her daughter, Hailey. This was her last resort.

Proof positive stood a few feet away, flanking Hailey's tiny body. Jacob Gideon, leader of a religious group called Sanctuary and renowned faith healer. Despite the fact that he was human and she and Hailey were not, she wanted to believe him. Though she'd be careful he never learned the truth about her daughter's nature, Blythe supposed faith was faith and healing was healing. Her daughter could use healthy doses of both.

Hailey had been born with a defective heart. She hadn't been expected to live a week, never mind five years. Surgery couldn't repair it and since Hailey was a Halfling, the wait for a compatible heart transplant was unfathomable. Halflings, the Pack doctors said, didn't have these sorts of problems. None of them were able to explain Hailey's condition. And, since Blythe knew very little beyond the basic dry medical information she'd been given about the sperm donor who was technically Hailey's father, she couldn't explain it, either. But she loved her baby girl more than life itself.

Despite her grim prognosis, Hailey fought and lived and grew. Her caramel-colored eyes sparkled with joy and love. Together, they celebrated each birthday almost defiantly, Hailey still standing, as though her little spirit refused to give up. And if her daughter wouldn't admit defeat, then how could her mother?

Blythe had started an all-out campaign to find a way to save her daughter. When conventional medicine, both human and Pack, had failed, she'd turned to the internet, trying everything except what seemed dangerous. Each obscure cure grew stranger and more expensive than the last. None of them made the slightest difference.

Finally, having read about him extensively, she'd arrived at one of Jacob Gideon's Power of Faith seminars. Jacob Gideon was confident. Taking hold of Blythe's hand, he'd gazed into her eyes and promised he could heal Hailey, as long as the two of them were willing to stay at his West Texas compound, Sanctuary.

That's when Blythe had balked. Something about Jacob Gideon agitated her inner wolf. Hailey, however, acted as sweet toward him as she did everyone else.

Torn, Blythe hadn't been able to make up her mind. Sensing this, perhaps, Jacob had contacted the press, no doubt using them as a means to sway her as well as gain publicity for his church. So far, she'd been interviewed for two national news stories. They'd run on consecutive days, and she suspected they'd be presented as if she'd already agreed to travel to Sanctuary while in reality she still struggled to make up her mind.

Every instinct she possessed urged her to run away as fast as she could. Only the tiniest bit of hope kept her considering it. How could she not try something that might— no matter how remote the chance—save her daughter's life?

While the media was around, Jacob seemed sincere. He gave grand speeches, making Blythe believe all over again. After all, the Pack had a Healer. She'd long ago placed Hailey's name on the waiting list.

If the Pack had a person who could heal, why would things be any different for humans? The more Jacob promised to help them, the more desperately she clung to the flicker of hope that he could.

Hailey shouldn't be sick, but she was. An ordinary man shouldn't be able to heal, but maybe he'd been graced with the same kind of gift that the Pack Healer, Samantha, had been given.

Taking a deep breath, Blythe made her decision. "I'm honored to accept your kind offer to help my little girl. I'm willing to go with you to Sanctuary so you can heal her."

The media greeted the news with applause.

Jacob Gideon simply inclined his head and smiled. "Wonderful." Beaming at her, he crouched down and took Hailey's small hand. "Your mother loves you very much, doesn't she?"

Smiling, Hailey nodded vigorously, even as she clung to Blythe's pant leg.

Apparently satisfied, Jacob pushed to his feet. "Blythe, I want you to be certain this is what you want. You do understand that you must forsake the rest of the world for a minimum of thirty days?"

She nodded, keeping a smile on her face despite the

fact that his insistence on this was the only thing that truly bothered her. Why so long and why only there? Healers healed. Right then, right now. Under normal circumstances, she would have told him no, thank you, and taken her leave. She'd seen the pitying glances from the reporters and their camera crews. This, she could live with. None of them understood her determination to save her little girl and prove all the doctors wrong. They'd given Hailey less than a year to live. Blythe planned to ensure she had a lifetime.

No matter what it took.

"Are you certain you comprehend this?" Jacob pressed.

"I understand," she said smoothly, her smile wearing a bit thin. "I just need to go home and pack a few things—"

"No need," Jacob interrupted, the sincerity in his voice making her feel a bit better. "You can spend tomorrow shopping, since I have a few more services scheduled before we return. But really, there's no need to buy much. Everything you require will be provided to you at Sanctuary."

She nodded, clinging to hope. This was it then—her last possible chance to back out. But why would she, when this man might be her only chance to help Hailey? She'd done her research. Just because she was desperate didn't mean she was a fool. Though a lot of people—for example, most of the general public—likened the close-knit community of Sanctuary to a cult, no one had reported anything negative. Jacob Gideon had broken no laws and was not on the government's radar for any he might potentially break in the future.

Once Blythe had established that, she'd turned away from the negative and began looking for the positive. Exactly forty-two people, all alive and breathing, claimed Jacob Gideon and his principals had cured them from a terminal illness. Blythe had managed to speak to several of them personally, and had been granted permission to review their medical records, as well. Contrary to their various doctors' dire expectations, each and every one of these people had finally been given a clean bill of health, which they all attributed to Jacob Gideon.

Maybe—just maybe—Jacob's Sanctuary and the power of faith could heal Hailey. The sheer magnitude of having actual hope made Blythe catch her breath.

A normal heart. Pink-tinged skin and tons of energy. This was what she wanted for Hailey. She'd sell her soul in order to get that.

Glancing again at the man she'd heard described as everything from the right hand of God to an angel on earth, she smiled. You never knew from where help might come.

The next day, while Jacob preached, she and Hailey had a girls' day out. They ate breakfast out, shopped, caught the newest animated movie and had a lovely early dinner at a pizza place. By the time they got back to the hotel, both of them were exhausted.

They'd barely made it to their room when someone knocked on the door. Blythe opened it to find Jacob Gideon standing in the hall, flanked by his entourage.

"Are you ready to go now?" he asked, one silver brow lifted, his expression kind and concerned.

Slowly, she nodded, her heart skipping a beat.

Giving her a half bow, he stepped aside, waving her on. "This way, please."

She and Hailey gathered up their bags and followed one of his people outside.

He'd come in a limo—long, black and mysterious. When his driver opened the door, Jacob indicated she and Hailey should climb inside.

Clutching her daughter's hand, Blythe only hesitated briefly before doing as he'd asked. Jacob got in after and took the seat directly opposite her, his expression calm, as though he was inwardly reflecting. His impeccably groomed silver hair matched the winter frost of his eyes.

Inside the darkly luxurious vehicle, Blythe felt uncomfortable, out of place. Jacob looked larger than life, at ease in his surroundings. Catching her eye, he flashed a reassuring smile. Rather than feeling at ease, she pressed her hand to her stomach, trying to smother her sudden doubt. Was she doing the right thing?

Inhaling deeply, she inwardly chanted her new mantra. *Anything to give Hailey a chance. Anything.*

The drive to the compound/ranch/whatever seemed to take forever. She'd known it would be a long ride. Afraid that she and Hailey would be subjected to hours of Jacob's glib patter, she was pleasantly surprised when he got out a laptop computer and began working, ignoring them.

Hailey, whose only signs of her illness so far had been the bruising and a bit of breathlessness and fatigue, curled up at Blythe's side and promptly fell asleep. Evidently she didn't share her mother's misgivings. This, too, gave Blythe hope. Hailey might be young, but she was a pretty good judge of character.

After three hours had passed, Blythe began to regret drinking that diet cola earlier. Determined not to draw attention to herself, she crossed her legs and tried not to squirm. Surely sooner or later Jacob would have to stop, right?

Finally, when she thought her bladder might explode, she reached over and touched his arm. She must have surprised him, because he recoiled and his lips curled in a snarl. Then, so quickly that she might have imagined it, the almost feral look vanished and the pleasant, benign fatherly figure was back.

"Yes, child?" His voice boomed, filling the small space.

Hailey stirred, whimpering.

"I need…" Blythe licked her lips, her mouth suddenly dry. "That is, could we please stop so I can use the restroom?"

"Of course, of course." Still sounding too hearty, Jacob rapped on the glass partition and ordered the driver to find a gas station or fast food place so that their guest could take care of her bodily functions.

The odd phrasing sent a prickle of alarm up Blythe's spine. Why did he make it sound as if normal human needs were somehow beneath him?

Misgivings swamped her. Maybe, just maybe, this had been a bad idea. She shouldn't have let herself be bulldozed. She should have insisted she take her own car and meet him there at a future date. That way, she'd have had a method of escape.

Escape. She grimaced at her own foolishness. As if she'd need that. She was going with Jacob Gideon because he'd graciously agreed to help her daughter. Without asking anything of Blythe but her time. He was a good man, a healer. If he acted a bit odd, she'd have to put that down to his lofty calling. She really needed to put her strange misgivings aside and have the necessary faith to let him do his thing.

Nothing ventured, nothing gained.

Once they parked, she helped her little girl out of the car and stretched. Hand in hand, they hurried toward the restroom. Inside the little convenience store, Blythe bought Hailey a juice and some animal crackers. She got herself a bottle of water and, as a last minute afterthought, picked up one for Jacob and the driver, too.

Back in the car, Jacob accepted the drink and thanked her, then put the bottle aside and never even looked at it again. Blythe caught herself wondering if he had some kind of superhuman ability to withstand thirst and then giggled softly at the notion. She must be more exhausted than she'd thought.

"Do you find something about me amusing, Ms. Daphne?" He sounded deeply concerned. As she raised her head to look at him, he gave her a self-deprecating, worried smile.

"Of course not." Guilt stabbed her. "I'm just overly tired.

He nodded. He didn't ask her to explain and she didn't offer. As a matter of fact, for the rest of the trip, when Jacob did raise his head from his work, he barely glanced at Blythe. Instead, he studied Hailey, his patrician features soft with compassion. Blythe appreciated his concern, and took his kindness to heart. Even while Hailey slept, Jacob continually watched her. Which Blythe supposed was only natural, since she was the one he would be healing.

Faith. Shiny and bright. She clung to that, holding her little girl close.

After sleeping for several hours, Hailey stirred and woke, one pale cheek red where she'd been sleeping on it. "Mama, are we there yet?" she asked, shifting her tiny body restlessly, trying to kick at nothing.

"Not yet, honey." Blythe did her best to soothe her daughter. From past experience, unless she could divert Hailey with food, something to drink and entertainment— whether a toy or television—Hailey would begin to act out.

Since Blythe had only juice, she knew it would be rough going. Once or twice, she looked up from her efforts to keep Hailey occupied to find Jacob watching, a sympathetic expression on his face.

The last few hours of the drive began to feel like torture. Bored and whiny, Hailey appeared to be trying her best to ruffle the older man's feathers while Blythe caught herself holding her breath. Blythe wondered if a man like Jacob would have patience for an exhausted, cranky five-year-old.

To her surprise, he did. To Blythe's relief, Jacob appeared indulgent, long-suffering and patient. As he answered her daughter's nonstop, rapid-fire questions, she began to relax the tiniest bit, allowing herself to feel a warm, fuzzy glow. Maybe, just maybe, all her worries had been for nothing.

"Don't worry," Jacob said, directing the comment at Blythe as he handed Hailey a pad of paper and a pen so she could draw. "There are many small children in my congregation."

Then Jacob smiled at her. Blythe found herself smiling right back. That was one thing. Ever since she'd purposely wandered into one of his mega services, she'd liked him. Even though he wasn't Pack—a Shape-shifter like her and Hailey—she hoped and prayed and believed he'd be able to help her Halfling daughter with the faulty heart.

Finally, Hailey dozed off, giving both Blythe and Jacob a rest.

After what felt like an eternity, they arrived at Jacob's compound—Sanctuary, she reminded herself—well after dark. Huge gates, which must have been modeled after someone's idea of the biblical gates to heaven, blocked their way. They were lit up by floodlights and when the driver punched a code into a box, the gates swung open slowly.

"We're here," Jacob boomed, once again waking Hailey, who began to sniffle.

"Shh, sweetheart. We're at the ranch," Blythe soothed.

At the word *ranch,* the five-year-old's eyes opened wide. "With horses and cows and cowboys?" she asked. "Will I get to see them?"

Jacob made a sound low in his throat. Both Blythe and Hailey looked at him, waiting for an answer.

"You're in the West Texas desert, child," he finally said, his voice calm although a bit condescending. "It's summer, you know. So hot that we can barely go outside."

Hailey squinted up at him. "No horses or cows?"

"No. You won't be seeing any livestock here."

His door opened, the driver standing woodenly at attention. Jacob glanced at Blythe. The icy flatness of his gaze surprised her, especially after all the warmth he'd shown during the ride. "My people will tend to you and your child. I will see you again tomorrow morning."

Without waiting for her answer, he climbed from the car and back stiff, head up, he strode away. He didn't look back. Then he was gone. Just like that.

Lucas didn't sleep well. That night for the first time in a decade or more, the old nightmares returned with hurricane force, as if they'd never left. He woke aching, hurting as though he'd just been beaten. Though his body still bore numerous scars from that time, he'd trained himself not to see them at all. He didn't allow himself to relive the beatings and the torture.

Thus far, his method of self-hypnosis had worked. Avoidance enabled him to try and forget, to move forward with his life, even if doing so meant he had to steer clear of facing up to his past.

Until today. Hearing that man's voice again—Jacob Gideon's—had brought the past rushing right back at him. And realizing the woman and her daughter were in danger had awakened some primal instinct he'd long since forgotten he'd ever possessed.

Apparently, facing up to his past meant making retribution. He hadn't been able to save his sister. But maybe, just maybe, saving Jacob's newest victims might help patch that jagged scar in his soul.

So he found himself awake at first dawn. Shaky from lack of sleep and still seething with a peculiar sort of fury, he pushed himself out of bed and began to plan his trip. A journey back to his own personal hell.

He had a choice, he knew. He could turn his back, as he once had for the sake of his own sanity. He could remain here in Seattle or retreat to his mountain cabin up high in the Colorado woods, and pretend he wasn't worried about the beautiful Shifter woman and her little girl's fate.

That would be both a lie and cowardly. Whatever else he might be, he was not that. After suffering tremendous guilt from failing to save Lilly, fifteen-year-old Lucas had managed to escape Jacob's long arm. He'd run away, far, far away from the monster who'd raised him. Now the time had finally come to go back and confront the beast.

No longer a child, he had to stand up, not only for himself, but for the helpless child or—God help him—the woman Jacob might at this moment be setting up for torture.

Confronting his past. He gave a bitter laugh, though there was no one to hear him. This wasn't what he'd imagined when he'd stood on his mountain gazing at the moon and made his promise.

Part of him refused to believe he was actually going back. Once, he'd sworn he would never return. He'd moved as far away as he could—in both climate and attitude. As a teen on the run, he'd learned how to live among Seattle's active underground. With a change of hair and name, no one had connected him.

In the years since, he'd grown up, moved on and made a life of his own. After going to work for a custom-home builder as a teen, he'd discovered he had a knack for installing tile, and parlayed that into a successful flooring business.

It would run just fine if he took a few weeks off. His employees all knew he was due for a vacation anyway. Ever since buying his mountain cabin, he'd managed periodic escapes, reveling in the solitude.

Though the thought of entering the state of Texas made his stomach clench, Lucas mapped out the route in his head, since he knew the directions by heart.

Now he just needed a plan. After all, he couldn't simply show up at Sanctuary and demand that the woman and her daughter leave with him. First off, Jacob would want to capture him, too. Even if Lucas managed to avoid Jacob and bluff his way in, he'd never get within ten feet of Jacob's newest prizes.

Grimly, he considered his options. He'd come up with something. After all, he was facing a long drive. Either he'd figure out some kind of plan, or he'd have to wing it.

He blinked, once again assaulted by the image of his sister's beaten, lifeless body. Not having a plan didn't end up well where Jacob was concerned. Lucas had failed once. He would not fail again. This time, if anyone was going to die, it would be Jacob.

Chapter 2

Though it was dark, the main house of Jacob Gideon's ranch was well lit, lined with soft, flattering floodlights that looked less like a prison's than tastefully done architectural highlights. The building, a series of interesting curves and angles, appeared to be made of a soft golden-colored stucco that blended with the desert landscape. Blythe hadn't expected to find it so warm and welcoming. She'd thought it might be more austere, like a convent or a monastery.

Groggy and out of sorts, Hailey refused to walk, so Blythe carried her. She could do this since her daughter had such a slight body. Hailey wasn't anywhere near the size of a normal five-year-old girl, a fact that pained Blythe. Once Jacob healed her, then surely Hailey would bloom and grow.

The woman who led Blythe and Hailey to their room was soft-spoken and seemed kind. She appeared fairly young and, to Blythe's curious eye, normal. No long, prairie-type skirt or pale, downtrodden expression. Instead, she spoke in a quiet, East Coast accented voice as she explained a little about life at Sanctuary.

"You both are honored visitors here," she said, smiling as Hailey tried to disappear by hiding her face behind Blythe's neck. "And though your room might seem small and plain, I promise you it will be comfortable. We don't go much for luxuries at Sanctuary."

Trying not to show her exhaustion, Blythe nodded. "We just need showers and a good night's rest."

"No problem," the woman said. "I'm Ginger, by the way. Is it all right if I call you Blythe?"

"Of course." From somewhere, Blythe dredged up a smile.

They traveled down a long, dimly lit hall. Keeping with the building's exterior, the glazed terra-cotta flooring and Spanish-style decorations brought to mind an upscale hotel rather than a ranch house or, as some had claimed, a cult headquarters where women were kept prisoner.

Maybe it was the exhaustion, but Blythe relaxed somewhat as they took an elevator to the second floor.

"Here we are." Stopping in front of a door marked with a large number seven, Ginger unlocked it and pushed it open.

Wearily, Blythe trudged past her, still carrying her exhausted daughter. The room was small, but looked clean. There was a double bed, a nightstand, one chair and a dresser. She placed Hailey, who had nearly drifted back to sleep, on the bed and turned to inspect the rest of it. There wasn't much more. A doorway led to an equally spartan bathroom.

"There you go," Ginger said brightly. "You'll find a supply of clothing and undergarments in the dresser, as well as pajamas."

Blythe frowned. While Jacob had said they didn't need to bring anything, she'd anticipated making a stop along the way to purchase a few clothing items.

Taking a step forward, she opened the top drawer. Inside, she found several neatly folded T-shirts and pairs of jeans, all in her size. In the drawer below were similar things for Hailey, again in the right size.

"Everything you need," Ginger said.

"How'd you know the size?" Blythe blurted out, not sure whether to be amazed or creeped out.

Ginger shrugged. "Mr. Gideon is a good guesser."

"But—"

Stifling a yawn, Ginger ratcheted her smile up a notch. "If you don't mind, Jacob would like to meet with you before you rest for the night." She glanced at Hailey, who, with her sagging eyelids and drowsy expression, was clearly exhausted. "I'd be happy to stay here with your daughter if you'd like."

Blythe frowned. This was odd, considering she'd just spent several hours with Jacob in the limo. After a moment of hesitation, Blythe tried to stall. "Do you think it can wait until the morning?"

"Oh, I don't think so." Her smile was sweet. "We generally don't refuse Jacob when he asks for something. But don't worry. He won't meet with you for long. I promise I'll take good care of your little one while you're gone."

Though no doubt the woman meant well, a shiver of warning skittered across Blythe's spine. They generally didn't refuse Jacob when he asked for something? What the heck did *that* mean?

"No." Reaching a decision, Blythe spoke in a sweet voice, though firmly. "I'd rather take her with me."

"Really?" Ginger cocked her head. "That's hardly fair to her, is it? Look how sleepy that poor baby is."

"Hailey," Blythe said, pushing back mild panic and hating the way she felt out of control. "Her name is Hailey."

Ginger acknowledged the introduction with a shy dip of her chin. "Of course. And I do think it'd be best if we let her rest. Just one moment. I'll have someone else come and take you to Jacob."

She removed a walkie-talkie from her belt and spoke a few words into it. "There we are. Savannah will be here shortly."

Struggling not to let exhaustion claim her, which was no doubt why she'd overreacted, Blythe nodded. "Have you been here long?" she asked.

Immediately, Ginger's friendly smile vanished. "Excuse me a second," she said, ducking out into the hallway without answering.

Surprised, Blythe didn't move. Was there some rule about asking personal questions? That would not only be weird, but more cultlike than she cared for. When this Savannah person arrived, she'd ask her the same thing and see if she got a similar reaction.

A moment later Ginger returned, accompanied by a short, older woman with long, frizzy hair that looked as if she hadn't combed it in days. She wore no makeup on her lined face and no jewelry. With her stooped shoulders and listless movements, she looked every bit as weary as Blythe felt.

Her faded blue gaze skittered over Blythe as she entered the room. "Come with me, please."

For a split second, Blythe considered refusing to go. Instead, she swallowed back her questions. She'd committed to this. She trusted Jacob Gideon and, by default, his people. She'd need to learn to deal with her misgivings.

After a final glance at Hailey, she turned to follow the older woman. Ginger stopped her. "Wait just a second."

She held out some papers on a clipboard. "I need you to sign here, please. This simply states that I've delivered you to your room."

Enough was enough. Who needed to have a room delivery signed? "I don't make a habit of signing papers without reading them," Blythe said. "Leave them and I'll sign them later, after I've had time to go over them."

Ginger's crestfallen expression didn't change Blythe's mind.

"I'm sorry." Squinting tiredly at her, Blythe accepted the clipboard and tossed it on the bed. "I promise I'll look at it when I get back."

"Very well." Ginger smiled softly. "I'll wait here and watch over your child. We can go over the paperwork together when you return. I do need to have it signed before I go back to my regular duties."

Again Blythe found this weird. But then again, what did she know? She'd never been inside a religious compound before.

Once she was out in the hall, Savannah grunted. "Follow me, please," she said. Trudging along a few steps ahead, she picked up her pace each time Blythe hurried to catch up.

Exhaustion forgotten, Blythe grabbed her arm. "Wait up."

The other woman rounded on her, her expression panicked. "Don't touch me," she yelped, jerking her arm away. Then, shaking her head and muttering under her breath, she took off again.

Stopping short, heart pounding in her chest, Blythe stared at Savannah's retreating back. Enough was enough. These people were definitely strange, bordering on scary. No way was she going anywhere without Hailey.

She turned, intending to head back to her room.

She'd barely taken a few steps when Savannah came rushing back. "I'm sorry. Please accept my apology," she said, the words running together without any real trace of contrition. "I'm new here and I've had a rough time before all this. I really don't want to blow it."

That explained a lot. Still wary, though no longer verging on the edge of panic, Blythe nodded. "Apology accepted. Lead the way." Following Savannah again, this time she knew better than to speak.

Finally, they reached the end of a long hallway and stopped in front of the last room. Double doors where the others were all single, these were made of some dark wood like mahogany or cherry. No mere knob here, but an elaborate pewter handle, which made for an overall effect of understated luxury. More like a corporate CEO than a preacher, but then what did she know? Most churches, especially the mega ones like Sanctuary, were run like profitable businesses.

"Knock twice and go in when he says to," Savannah said, her voice once again devoid of inflection. She moved away, heading back up the hall with her head and neck forward, her motions reminiscent of a plow horse struggling against the harness.

Still unsettled, Blythe watched her until she disappeared around a corner. Then, turning and facing the door, she lifted her fist and knocked.

"Come in."

At his invitation, she turned the handle, wondering at her sudden urge to see him again. He was so kind, so warm and reassuring. Stepping into the room on carpet so plush her feet appeared to sink into quicksand, she moved toward where Jacob waited for her behind a massive cherrywood desk.

"You wanted to see me?" Though she hated the feeling

of being summoned before the lord of the manor, she kept her tone and her expression pleasant. After all, this man only wanted to help her precious child.

He stood, indicating two overstuffed chairs near a fireplace. "Please, take a seat."

Once she had, again feeling suffocated by the eerie feeling of sinking into the upholstery, he went to a coffee machine on a side table, one of those fancy ones that made single servings. "Would you like something to drink?" he asked. "I have decaf and regular, as well as several varieties of tea."

"Decaf, please." While he busied himself making their coffees, she studied the room. It was beautifully—and from the looks of it, professionally—decorated, but devoid of personality. Much like a hotel room, the furnishings and artwork gave no hint whatsoever of Jacob's character.

When he returned with their coffees on a round silver tray, along with various kinds of sweetener packets, he placed them on a table in front of them and took a seat in the other chair. He appeared the benevolent older gentleman, concerned about her well-being.

She accepted her drink, after adding a bit of sugar and stirring. Taking a sip, she glanced up to find him watching her with an intensity that added to her discomfort.

"Jacob, I'm really tired," she said gently. "And I find Savannah and Ginger a bit odd, to say the least."

He grimaced, appearing instantly concerned. "Savannah is new to us. Before she came here, she suffered greatly. Please don't take her behavior personally. She means well."

Inhaling, Blythe nodded. "She explained that."

"Now about Ginger?" He leaned forward. "What is your concern with her? I chose her to help you because she genuinely loves children. I thought she'd be a good choice to watch over Hailey when you couldn't."

Once again, Jacob was the voice of reason. She relaxed back into the softness of the chair. "I'm guessing there must be something you forgot to tell me in the car?"

One eyebrow winged up. "Not exactly. I wanted to speak with you away from your little girl."

"Hailey," she said, wondering why she felt this fierce compulsion to make everyone use her daughter's name. Humanizing her, possibly. Just in case doing so might make her caregivers try even harder for her. Another bit of paranoid foolishness, she supposed.

"Yes, Hailey." His mild tone contained a hint of reprimand.

This time, rather than respond, she sipped from her coffee and waited for him to tell her what he wanted.

Instead, he leaned forward and, staring intently at her, asked her if she liked animals. It took every bit of self-control she possessed not to jump up and ask him to please cut to the chase.

"I do," she nodded, her expression tight, deciding to respond in kind. "Do you have any pets?"

"No. But I wasn't talking about pets." Again he drank from his cup. "I'm asking about wild animals."

Stranger and stranger. "Okay." She didn't know what else to say.

"Specifically, wolves," he drawled. "Are you fond of wolves?"

She stiffened. Instantly on alert, she forced herself to try to appear indifferent. "They're all right. Why do you ask?"

His smile seemed knowing. "No reason. I find them to be beautiful. Wild and fierce."

If he thought she would reveal her true nature as a Shape-shifter, he was wrong. And there was no possible way he could know. Not only were there Pack laws about this sort of thing, but no one revealed their true nature to humans without a damn good reason.

"Lovely artwork," she commented, gesturing toward the wall, hoping to change the subject. "But I don't see any personal pictures. You know, photographs of your family. Do you have any children?"

He looked nonplussed. "No," he answered. "I was widowed a long time ago."

Draining her cup, she set it down on the table with a loud clatter and waited with barely concealed impatience for him to come out with whatever he was trying to say.

Instead he placed his own cup down and pushed to his feet. "You do understand that we will have to do numerous tests on your daughter?"

"Tests? What for? She's had enough tests. Why would a faith healer need tests?"

He regarded her with a patient smile, as though humoring her. "I understand. But we still must do tests in order to learn where to focus our healing energies."

Crossing her arms, she shook her head. "I'll be happy to furnish you with the results of everything she's already had done. But no new tests."

For a moment something dark blackened his kind eyes. Then he dipped his chin, as if disappointed. Maybe she'd imagined it. "As you wish, Ms. Daphne. We'll speak more on this later."

Once Jacob turned away, Savannah materialized. She might have even been standing in a shadowed corner of the room. "Come with me," she said.

"Thank you for your time," Jacob said, clearly dismissing her.

Pushing to her feet, her unease settling like a sour ball in her stomach, Blythe left.

Once they reached her room, Savannah opened the door and stepped aside. As soon as Blythe entered, she came back, pulling the door closed behind her.

"See, I told you it wouldn't take long," Ginger said softly, smiling. "Your daughter didn't even wake up while you were gone."

"Hailey," Blythe corrected automatically. "And she's ill. Can you make sure we're not disturbed in the morning? I want to make sure she gets her rest."

At the question, the younger woman's smile faded. Pointing to what looked like a walkie-talkie sitting on the nightstand, she backed away. "Use that if you need me for anything. There are all the necessary toiletries in the bathroom. Now, have a good night's rest, okay? I'll see you in the morning."

Again without answering Blythe's request, she'd made her own demands. Then, before Blythe could question or acknowledge, Ginger stepped out into the hall and closed the door.

Pushing away the doubts and fears that threatened to overwhelm her, Blythe gently shook her little girl awake.

"Sweetheart, we need to clean up," she murmured. "Then we'll get you into your pajamas."

Still half asleep, Hailey nodded. Blythe shepherded her into the bathroom and began filling the tub.

As the water rose, Hailey blinked. "I don't wanna take a bath," she protested. "I'm hungry and thirsty and I want to eat and then play."

Her droopy eyes and flushed face told a different story. "You need a bath," Blythe said, her voice firm. "After we're both clean, I'll see what I can find for us to eat, okay?" After all, if there was nothing in the room, she could use the walkie-talkie to call Ginger.

Only partially mollified, Hailey nodded.

Later, after they were both clean and dressed in brand-new, soft cotton pajamas in exactly the right sizes, Blythe located a small refrigerator, partially hidden underneath the desk with a curiously lightweight chair. Inside she found juice, water and diet cola, as well as various healthy snacks. She grabbed a roll of string cheese and a bottle of water and carried it to Hailey.

While her daughter ate her snack, Blythe turned down the bed. The sheets appeared to be of a good quality and looked as though they'd been pressed.

Impressed, she shook her head. This place could pass for a hotel or resort, if not for the weird attitudes.

"Is it dark outside, Mommy?" Hailey asked, stifling a yawn.

"Yes, baby." Blythe answered automatically, turning back the comforter and patting the bed. "Let's try to get some sleep so we're rested in the morning. We've got to be wide-awake so the nice man can try and help you."

Hailey's eyelids were already drooping. "Okay," she murmured, crawling up and laying her head on the pillow. "Cover me up, please," she ordered.

Climbing in beside her daughter, Blythe smiled. "I'll cover us both." She leaned over and kissed Hailey's baby-soft cheek. "I love you, sweetheart."

"I love you, too, Mama."

Heart full, vowing to dream of hope, Blythe clicked off the light.

Damn. Guilt and shock and yes, the ever-present simmering flame of anger filled Lucas. The place still looked the same, he thought, coasting slowly past the immense wrought iron gates as though he merely a curious biker, riding the back roads on his Harley. Pushing away the instinctive dread that coalesced in his gut, he studied the deceptively peaceful house through the black iron fence.

And he forced himself to remember the exact layout of Sanctuary. As if he could ever forget. That particular image was burned in his brain.

The urge struck him, hard and fast and furious, to give his bike the gas, spinning the wheels, and roar off into the sunset. Of course, he wouldn't. He couldn't. It was time he paid back the debt he'd incurred fifteen years ago by failing his sister.

Continuing on, his powerful motorcycle rumbling beneath him, he circled the western edge of the property. Either Jacob had gotten careless, or he truly wasn't worried about intruders, because here the fence was gone. From the looks of the deteriorating rubble, it had come down years ago.

Once, there had been perimeter cameras, and barbed wire, and patrolling guards. Despite all that, Lucas had managed to escape, his desperation and sorrow fueling him.

Then, the place had been a veritable fortress. Now, fifteen years later, apparently Jacob had no such worries, whether about people escaping or breaking in. Which meant either he had all of his followers completely brainwashed or he hadn't managed to snag another abomination, as he'd called Lucas.

Until now. Until the little girl and her beautiful mother. They were like him, which was why they were in such grave danger.

He sighed. Somehow, Jacob had convinced them to come willingly, unaware of what kind of a monster the publicly pious man truly was. Lucas could well imagine the spiel, the honeyed lies flowing freely as Jacob promised healing and hope for the clearly exhausted mother and her seriously ill child.

Again, Lucas saw the woman's face, as clear in his mind as if he knew her. Once more, his wolf came alert, the strong tug of something—attraction?—apparently affecting not only the man, but the beast, as well. Not good. And not only irrelevant to his mission, but a distraction he didn't need or want. He had revenge on his mind, not lust.

Shaking his head, he forced his thoughts back to Jacob Gideon, the devil incarnate. Who knew what Jacob really meant to do, what experiments and torture he planned to inflict on the helpless small child, all in the guise of healing? If they were anything like what he'd done to Lucas, his own son, and to Lilly, his own daughter, they would be brutal. Truth be told, after seeing how delicate and weak the little girl appeared to be, Lucas doubted she'd be able to survive. His sister certainly hadn't.

Pushing away the still-raw wound, he wondered what Jacob planned to do with the mother once he killed her child? A grieving mother would not only understand the depths of his betrayal, but would crave vengeance, no matter what the cost. Grimacing, he didn't want to imagine the special something Jacob had planned for her, as well. No matter what she was, Jacob couldn't help but notice her startling beauty.

Growling low in his throat, Lucas again pushed back his wolf. He had a job to do, and perhaps his wolf self would be helpful in that. Either way, no matter what, Lucas knew he had to get them out. As quickly as possible.

He made one more slow circle around the ranch, just to make sure. Sanctuary was unguarded. Good for him, bad for Jacob. But then again, he reminded himself, who the hell would really want to break *in* to Sanctuary? Especially if they'd never been given a reason?

Again Lucas pictured the small girl's wan face and her mother's tired, hopeful beauty. His fists clenched. He had to save them. He would save them, no matter what the personal cost.

It had taken him three days to make the drive. But then, he didn't know exactly when the woman and her child had arrived here. If it had been directly after the newscast, that would mean they'd been under Jacob's roof for seventy-two hours. Who knew what had already happened to them? He'd seen the look of desperation in the mother's eyes. She'd obviously tried everything and was now reduced to grasping at straws. Jacob Gideon's blatant brand of faith healing drew only the truly hopeless or the truly lost.

He wondered if she'd yet begun to figure out how things went. They'd probably had enough time to realize they weren't exactly guests, but prisoners. And that Jacob might not be the benevolent prophet of God that he claimed to be.

He had one plan. Break in. Find the woman and her child. Get them out. And annihilate anyone who stood in his way.

Savagely, he realized he actually hoped that Jacob decided to stand in his way.

The woman might not believe him, but he'd have to take that chance.

His motorcycle, which had long been his primary form of transportation, wouldn't work for getting them out. He'd need something larger, a car or truck or van.

He'd deal with that later. Right now, he'd gotten the lay of the land.

Driving past the gate for the last time, he gunned the motor and headed into town and the motel room he'd reserved by phone. He'd come back tonight under cover of darkness, go in and take a closer look.

Briefly, it occurred to Lucas that Jacob might have set a

tràp for him, using the woman and child as a lure to bring in his prodigal son. But as soon as he had this thought, he dismissed it. Too many years had passed and for all Jacob knew, Lucas was dead. Not once in all that time had Lucas attempted to make contact with the man who'd raised him. Despite the evidence of his bruised and battered young body, he hadn't even gone to the authorities and reported Jacob for child abuse. He'd suspected they wouldn't believe him or, if they did, Jacob's silver tongue and powerful influence would convince them otherwise.

Full of guilt and sorrow, all Lucas had cared about was putting as much distance as possible between himself and Sanctuary and the man who had killed his twin sister.

After parking in front of his rustic motel room, he checked in and received his key. Next to the motel, a flashing neon sign advertised a café. His stomach growled. He needed meat, lots of it, red beef, hamburger or steaks, something with lots of protein to feed the animal inside him.

Using his key, he unlocked his room door and went inside. The musty odor of stale cigarette smoke mingled with the lingering smell of bleach. The scents, no matter how offensive, barely registered.

Because he suddenly realized he did have an amendment to his plan. Pretty much foolproof. Because no matter what Jacob might or might not expect from Lucas, he wouldn't expect him to return as a wolf, the very thing that made him a demon in Jacob's eyes.

Inside, Lucas's wolf growled with approval. Decision made, he turned around and left the room to head toward the café. Now he would eat to make sure he was strong enough for the change. After, he might try to catch a few hours of shut-eye before nightfall.

Tonight, he'd return to the place that haunted his nightmares. Tonight, he would change and let his inner beast free. And this time, he would succeed.

He nearly laughed out loud. The irony of the situation wasn't lost on him. It was fitting he go there as wolf. With his amplified senses—especially scent and night vision—he'd have the advantage. Jacob might have put the woman and her daughter out there as bait, using them to lure his son back. Or he might not. Either way, Lucas would find them and set them free. And in the process, he'd find a way to expose Jacob Gideon for what he truly was.

Once Lucas was done, once he got the woman and her daughter out, he'd make sure Jacob never hurt anyone else ever again.

Chapter 3

The next morning, after a fitful night trying to sleep, Blythe rose before dawn, craving coffee. The nightstand clock showed it was a little after five. A search of the room revealed no small coffeepot, like the ones in some hotels, so she reluctantly gave up on that idea.

Since Hailey was still sleeping, she moved quietly, aware her daughter needed all the rest she could get. The bad heart made Hailey tire quickly and suddenly. She'd collapsed a few times, unable to catch her breath. Each time that had happened, Blythe felt her own chest constrict, the horrible aching fear for Hailey, her frustration that she could do nothing to help her baby girl.

Crossing to the dresser, she took a T-shirt and undergarments, plus a pair of jeans. The idea that the clothing—all exactly the right size—had been purchased with her in mind, made her wonder. What if Jacob didn't want guests to have their own things because he was trying to break the guests' connections to the outside world?

As soon as she had the thought, she shied away from it. Her only concern had to be for any chance to heal Hailey.

Ah, well. She supposed this was their way of attempting to make her feel welcome.

Once inside the bathroom, she quietly closed the door and located a fluffy white towel. One thing she was learning about Jacob Gideon's Sanctuary was that he didn't skimp on luxuries.

Turning on the shower, she stepped under the hot spray with a sigh. The water felt good and she let herself relax.

Once she was clean, she dried herself off and brushed her teeth. She towel dried her hair as best she could, not wanting to use the blow-dryer that had been so thoughtfully provided, in case the noise woke Hailey.

She had a bit of her own makeup that she'd brought with her in her purse, so she applied that. Finally, she considered herself ready to face the day. Opening the door, she went to wake her daughter.

But the bed was empty. Hailey was gone.

Stunned, Blythe stood for a moment in shock. How could this be? She'd heard nothing, and surely Hailey would have screamed if some stranger had entered the room and taken her. Wouldn't she?

Why? Why would anyone take her baby? What the hell had she done? She should never have come here.

Cursing under her breath, Blythe rushed to the door and tried the knob. Locked.

Damn them.

"Help!" she shouted, pounding on the door with her fists. "Help!"

But no one came. She hit the door until her fists were bruised. She kicked, pummeled and body slammed it, but the thick wood held.

Then she remembered the walkie-talkie. That girl—

what was her name?—Ginger, had said to use it if she needed anything.

Scooping it up off the nightstand, Blythe flicked it on. "Ginger?" Her voice vibrated with barely contained fury. "Ginger, come in."

Nothing but static answered her. Desperate now, she tried every channel, and when she received the same lack of response, she tried again. Her inner wolf snarled in fury.

She barely restrained herself from slamming the useless piece of equipment into the wall. Finally, she tossed it on the bed, crossed to the window and drew back the curtains. To her relief, there were no metal bars on the window. At least she wasn't in that much of a cage.

But a closer examination revealed that the windows did not open. Effectively, she was trapped inside the room.

That was what they thought. Seething, she searched the room for a heavy object she could use to smash the glass. They'd taken her daughter. For what reason, she didn't know, nor did it matter. The abduction, the locked room, the stupid walkie-talkie that didn't work—none of it made sense.

But Hailey, Hailey. Even if they needed to take her somewhere alone to heal her, why would they steal her away like this, without consulting her mother?

Hefting the weight of the chair, which was too light-weight, she roamed the room, her blood humming with an adrenaline-fueled combination of fury and fear.

The lamp was also useless. She couldn't lift the desk. No doubt her captors had thought of all this, planning the furnishing of the little cell carefully.

Then she spotted the mini refrigerator. Lifting it a few inches off the ground, she realized she might have to struggle to lift it, but since it was the heaviest thing she'd found, it would have to do.

Sliding it out from under the desk, she unplugged it, then hefted it in her arms and carried it over toward the window.

She braced herself and heaved the fridge at the window.

It hit, bounced back toward her and dropped to the floor, the door flying open and bottles of juice and water going everywhere. Blythe stepped over the mess. The window looked the same.

With maybe a tiny crack, a chip, where the edge of the mini fridge had hit.

Wondering if the noise would alert someone that she was trying to escape, she took the cheap, lightweight desk chair and wedged it under the door handle. It might not be good for breaking glass, but at least it would deter entry into the room for a little while. Because there was no way in hell she would let anyone stop her.

She had to save Hailey. No matter what.

Resolute, determined, she bent over, scooped the fridge up, and heaved it again, aiming roughly for the same spot.

Success! This time the window shattered.

But not neatly, not the way windows broke in movies. Instead, there was a ragged hole in the middle, with jagged shards of glass sticking out everywhere.

Carefully, she knocked them out until the window opening appeared both safe and large enough for her to climb through.

Heart still hammering in her chest, she peered out. And remembered that she was on the second floor. She'd have to climb out and let herself hang from the ledge and drop to the ground, hoping she didn't break a leg or any other body part.

Climbing up, she scanned the outside area, trying to see in the predawn darkness beyond the glow cast from the outside landscaping lights.

As far as she could tell, no one was out there. But then, even if someone was, she would still do it. No way was she staying locked in the room while they had her baby.

Once she was free, she planned to change to wolf form and go hunting.

Knocking away the last remaining shards of glass, she gripped the windowsill, feeling slivers cut into her palm.

Slowly she swung her legs up and over, scrabbling for purchase on the stucco, until she hung all the way out, unsure exactly how far up she was from the ground.

Then she let go and fell.

In his wolf form, Lucas had spent hours cautiously roaming Sanctuary, keeping low to the ground and staying in the shadows. He saw no guards, no hint of heightened security. Letting his nose guide him, he followed the scents, almost netting a plump rabbit for his dinner, but he'd already eaten in the café.

Oddly enough, the only scents he detected were those of wildlife. Almost as if the people who lived within the luxurious stucco house never set foot outside.

This would not have surprised him. In fact, he wouldn't be shocked at all to learn Jacob kept them all prisoners, or so brainwashed they didn't take a single step anywhere without his approval.

The night had edged its way toward morning and the sky had begun to lighten. Lucas drew closer to the sprawling house. Sanctuary's inhabitants still slept, and all remained quiet.

As he debated leaving so he could shift back to his human form, a light came on in a room on the second floor.

He froze, half expecting someone with a high-powered rifle to appear and start taking potshots at him.

Belly low to the ground, he backed up, keeping to the

edge of the landscape lights, until he felt confident he couldn't be seen.

The drapes remained drawn and nothing else happened. He'd just about started to lose interest when the curtains flew open and *she* stood there in plain view.

His heart skipped a beat. *Her.* The woman he'd come to rescue, the mother of the little girl. The one who was like him.

While he'd watched, she disappeared from view. Pulse racing, he waited, hoping she'd reappear. Instead, a few minutes later, she threw something at the glass, something large and heavy, obviously attempting to break it.

Lucas bared his teeth. Jacob must have locked her in. But she was getting out, using whatever means necessary to make an exit. Lucas approved.

The ever-present desert wind had ruffled his fur as he'd watched and waited, heart pounding in expectation. Again, she'd heaved something at the window. This time, the glass shattered. He'd held his breath while she picked the shards clean, climbed up on the windowsill and let herself hang. She let go a second later.

Watching closely, he'd felt relief when she climbed to her feet, apparently unhurt. He saw no sign of her child. What had happened to the little girl? Surely she wouldn't just leave her there, would she?

She took a few steps toward him, obviously unable to see very well in the darkness. When she moved outside of the perimeter of landscape lights, she stopped and began shedding her clothes. What the…his heart stuttered. Had she already gone mad, after such a short time with Jacob?

Then she dropped to all fours, completely naked. Watching, he cocked his lupine head, puzzled. And then…and then…the air around her changed. A thousand tiny pin-pricks of lights danced in the atmosphere, circling her, surrounding her. The hair on his back rose as he realized what he was witnessing.

He was watching her change.

The intimacy of the act was not lost on him. Thirty years old and he'd never seen another being go from human to wolf. This was by choice.

Others hunted in packs. Lucas hunted alone. Despite numerous invitations to join the huge, global Pack of Shapeshifters, he trusted no one. He'd declined and mostly they'd left him alone.

Exactly the way he preferred.

Now this. Was this how he'd appear to others? He'd never seen anything so amazing.

A moment later, the sparkling lights faded away and she stood in the darkness, muzzle raised to the sky, a wolf with a shining pelt of pure white. He sucked in his breath. Unusual, even he knew.

As his human self had reacted to her face, even on the television, his wolf self responded even more strongly to her in lupine form. He fought back the urge to bound over to her and begin the elaborate play that would mark the beginning of the mating ritual. Mating?

He'd have to let her know he was there, at least. If he was going to help this woman, he'd have to make her aware of his presence.

Moving quietly, carefully, he circled around, making sure he stood upwind of her, letting the breeze carry him to her sensitive nose. He could tell the instant she scented him—her entire body went still, ears pricked forward. And then she swung her head around and, with her superior lupine night vision, spotted him.

She growled, low in her throat, a warning.

To show her he was no threat, he did not move. Though he refused to adopt a submissive posture—he submitted to no one—he was careful not to make direct eye contact and he kept his head low.

Slowly, she circled around him, taking in his scent. He knew she'd be able to detect his human aspect, and would discern that he was not fully wolf, not a wild animal that had happened upon her by accident. No, she'd realize he was a Shape-shifter and had come here on purpose.

After she'd taken his measure at a distance of a few feet, she came closer. Her hackles were raised, though his had settled.

He let her get close, keeping his stance relaxed, neither threatening nor subservient, just friendly.

When she ran, at first he did not follow. But, when he realized she was heading for the front of Sanctuary, he knew he had to stop her.

Though she couldn't open the door, there were windows. If she got inside as a wolf, they'd slaughter her. He understood she wanted to get to her daughter, but this was not the way. Unfortunately, he couldn't speak and explain. Instead, he ran full out, slamming into her hard enough to send her flying.

Snarling, she leaped to her feet, going on the offensive. But rather than attacking him, she tried to dodge him in order to get past.

The sky continued to lighten. Soon, the sun would rise over the horizon, making them easy to pick off with a high-powered rifle. He knew this. Unfortunately, she did not.

They battled again and again. He, careful not to draw blood. She, not caring in her desperation. She came at him again and again. But he blocked her every time.

After a few moments of this, she spun away and ran in the opposite direction.

Stunned, at first he didn't follow. Belatedly he realized

she was running away from him, when he'd come all this way to save her.

He barely caught up with her. They crossed the boundary of the land, reached the road and she swerved. Running parallel to the street, she headed toward town. Soon she'd find where he'd parked his bike, hidden away from any headlights under some tumbleweeds and brush.

Had she thought this out, her escape? She had no clothes and when she changed back to human, she'd need something with which to cover herself. As a stark-naked female out in the wee hours of the morning, she would be placing herself in grave danger.

Any moment now, she'd be at the mound that hid his bike. He barked at her, once, a warning. To his surprise, she slowed her pace, first from an all-out run down to a lope, then a trot. And finally, she stopped and faced him.

When he caught up to her, he sat, keeping a few feet between them, not wanting to encroach on her space.

Shaking herself all over, as though removing water from her fur, she made a sound between a growl and a whine, and initiated the change back to human. Pausing for a second, aware he always changed back to a man fully aroused, Lucas did the same.

As soon as he was human again, he turned his back to her and crossed to his bike to retrieve his clothing. But before he could put it on, he heard her behind him and turned, shielding himself with his clothes.

"Who are you? I don't have time for this." Standing tall with her hands on her well-shaped hips, she vibrated with rage and seemed completely unashamed of her nakedness. Worse, she either didn't see or didn't care that when he'd shifted back to human, he was completely aroused. It was always this way with him. He didn't know if this was normal among his kind, or if he was some sort of aberration. He'd never cared enough to find out.

Having the most beautiful woman he'd ever seen face him unclothed only made things worse. Holding his clothing in front of his arousal, he literally had to clench his hands into fists to keep from reaching out and yanking her to him.

"Are you with them?" she snarled. "Working for that damn Sanctuary? My daughter might be in danger. I've got to get her back."

"I don't work for them. I came to help you. I'm on your side," he said, wincing at the cliché and wishing his voice sounded less husky and more authoritative.

"Are you? Then you'd better talk," she ordered. "And quickly. I need help. Jacob Gideon has taken my daughter."

"I thought he would."

Scowling at him, she shook her head and began backing away. "You work for him, don't you?"

"No." He snarled the word. "But I'm well aware of what he's like."

"Do you have a phone?" she asked, holding out her hand. "I need to call the authorities and get them out here. I want my daughter and I want her now."

"It's not going to do any good," he told her, realizing she wouldn't believe him. "Here." He tossed her his T-shirt. "Put this on and let me get dressed and then we'll talk."

Though she caught it easily, she made no move to pull it over her head. Instead, she stood glaring at him with suspicion.

Hell. With a shrug, he turned his back to her and yanked on his shorts and then his jeans, wincing as he tried to tug the zipper up over his swollen body. When he turned back, she still clutched his T-shirt, quietly watching him dress.

With a shrug, he uncovered the motorcycle.

When he'd finished, he looked up to find she finally wore his shirt. On her, it was as long as a minidress, covering her, though the thin cotton did little to hide her lush shape or her engorged nipples.

Damn. What the hell was wrong with him? What was it about this woman that made him want her so intensely?

He indicated his bike. "If it's all the same to you, I'd rather have our discussion as far from here as possible. Pretty soon his goons are going to realize you've escaped and come looking. I'm thinking you don't want to be found. At least, not yet."

What he'd thought was calm rationality clearly enraged her. "Are you crazy? Since you were on the property, you must be one of Jacob's men. What'd he do, tell you to persuade me to leave my daughter? I won't."

"You can't get her back alone. Jacob has hundreds of loyal followers. They will stop you. In fact, they might hurt you. We need to go get reinforcements."

"There's no way I'm walking away and leaving Hailey in danger. Look, I just escaped. Jacob has no guards—at least none that I could see."

The sun rose, bathing them with bright yellow light. Lucas winced. "Jacob is no fool. If he went through so much trouble to get your little girl, he's not going to let you take her back without a battle. Look, I promise you I know what I'm talking about. I escaped from there once myself. If you go back on your own, they might kill you. And that would leave your kid with no one to fight for her. Is that what you want?"

She wavered, clearly not understanding. "I'd like to call the police. They'll help me."

"No, they won't. Jacob has the entire town in his pocket. And I didn't bring my cell with me."

"What are you saying?" she cried, her narrowed gaze

telling him she didn't believe him. "You honestly expect me to just take your word and believe that there's no hope?"

"Oh, there's hope." Once again, he indicated his motorcycle. "But you're going to have to come with me. Evading capture is the only way you're going to get your daughter back."

Though she still appeared unconvinced, she finally dipped her chin in answer. "I don't trust you," she said. "But I'm going to go with you. At least until I can get reinforcements, like the sheriff's department. Let's go."

He liked the way she made decisions quickly, without wasting precious time agonizing over the pros and cons.

Climbing on his bike, he motioned for her to get on behind him. Once she had, he tried like hell not to think about how she was naked underneath his T-shirt, and that the heat of her body pressing against him was only separated by cloth.

He turned the ignition and the Harley roared to life. The vibration against his already-aroused body made him clench his teeth.

"Hold on," he told her, the wind carrying his words away. Once she'd wrapped her arms around his middle, he took off, heading for his motel and hoping like hell no one had seen them.

While they rode, Blythe tried to calm her rising panic. Not for herself, but for Hailey. She still didn't understand why Jacob Gideon's people had locked her in a room to begin with. And then stolen her daughter. Why take Hailey like that? He'd promised to heal her, not hurt her. And he'd done so publicly, which also made no sense.

On top of that, with her arms wrapped around the muscular chest of a large and dangerously handsome man, she had to wonder. Where had he come from? She had to consider the possibility that he worked for Jacob and had been sent to keep her away from her daughter.

Her companion drove the big motorcycle competently, but then he had the look of a man who knew how to do most everything well. Tall and well built, he moved with a grace that told her he was at home in his own body.

Still, for him to appear out of nowhere, just when she was making her escape… She had to wonder. Could he be trusted? Since she'd already made one huge error in judgment by trusting Jacob Gideon, she wasn't sure she hadn't just made another.

Reminding herself that he was Pack, like her, and therefore most likely on her side, helped slightly. With all the craziness that was going on, she might need the help of more of her own kind. The Pack had a group of people called the Pack Protectors. She might have to call on them to help save Hailey. After all, who knew what the faith healer had planned? She was certain whatever it was, it wasn't good.

Her panic began to build. Hailey needed certain medications. Would Jacob's people remember to give them to her? She knew if she kept thinking along those lines, she'd be reduced to an ineffectual, panicked mess. She needed to try and remain as calm and clearheaded as possible if she wanted to succeed in rescuing her baby.

Finally, they coasted to a stop in front of an L-shaped, wooden motel that had seen better days. She took a deep breath. Hopping down from the bike, she pulled the large cotton T-shirt down and eyed him. "I asked you to take me to the sheriff's office and you bring me to a motel. You'd better give me a damn good reason not to start screaming for help."

Her passionate speech didn't seem to faze him.

"I'm Lucas Kenyon," he told her, the rumble of his deep

voice oddly reassuring and dangerous at the same time. "Formerly Luke Gideon. And I promise I'll explain everything."

Stunned, she gaped at him. "But he said he had no children."

"He would." He grimaced.

"You're his…son?"

"Not anymore." Crossing to a room, he used his key and opened the door. "Come inside, please. I'll tell you everything."

She hesitated. She no longer trusted anyone with any connection whatsoever to Jacob Gideon, Pack or human. Especially his son.

"There's a phone inside that you can use. I promise I won't hurt you," Lucas said, clearly misinterpreting the reason she wavered.

"I didn't think you would," she told him, pushing past him. "But I'm calling the sheriff before I listen to anything you have to say. I want my daughter back."

Once she was inside, he closed the door behind her. "Go ahead and call," he said. When she reached for the telephone on the nightstand, he grabbed a cell phone off the dresser. "Use this instead. He can't trace you that way," he told her, by way of explanation. "It's disposable. I've got several others just like it."

Accepting his phone, she eyed him and then she punched in 911. When a woman answered, Blythe tried to speak calmly, so she'd be clearly understood. "I need help. Jacob Gideon over at Sanctuary has taken my daughter. She's only five. He took her without my permission."

To her shock and disbelief, the operator chuckled. "You know, he just called in. He said you'd say something like that."

Confused, Blythe looked at her companion. Although he

couldn't hear the other end of the conversation, his expression appeared resigned. "I'm saying it because it's true."

"Oh, I know Jacob. He'd never do something like that. He told us there'd been a little misunderstanding."

"This is *not* a misunderstanding," Blythe interrupted. "He took my daughter. I need you people to help me get her back."

The woman continued on as though Blythe hadn't spoken.

"I know who you are. You're the lady we saw on TV the other day. You brought your little girl here so Jacob could heal her. You just need to calm down and let him do his work."

"Calm down?" Blythe could hear her voice rising as it began to dawn on her that she really was on her own. This Lucas was right. No one else was going to help her save Hailey. Still, she had to try. "Let me talk to your supervisor."

She swore she could almost hear the woman shaking her head. "He won't be in until later this morning. Around nine. You'll have to call back then. Why don't you just phone Jacob and give him a chance to explain? He told me to tell you it's a big misunderstanding and that you should come back right away."

"He told you?"

"Of course." The woman sounded smug. "Everyone around these parts is on very good terms with Jacob Gideon. Go back. Talk to him."

Go back? Give Jacob a call… This was surreal. Blythe looked up and saw from Lucas's glum expression that this was exactly as he'd expected. Which meant…what? That he was in on it? Or that he was a really good judge of what Jacob Gideon would do.

Gripping the cell phone, her hand sweaty, she said the

only thing she could think of. "I don't have his phone number."

"Let me give it to you." Suddenly solicitous, the dispatcher rattled it off, which Blythe repeated out loud so Lucas could write it down on a small pad of paper beside the hotel phone.

Once she was certain he'd gotten it, stunned and feeling as if she'd been run over by a semitruck, Blythe ended the call.

She stared at the cell phone, suppressing the urge to fling it against the wall. "Hailey is dangerously ill." Biting down on her fury, she spun to face him.

"I'm not sure what just happened," she began, seething.

"I told you he has them all in his pocket," Lucas said, his voice sounding both resigned and angry. "You'll have to get help from far away from this area to find someone he hasn't corrupted."

As she continued to eye him, she couldn't find even the slightest resemblance between this man and the preacher. Where Jacob was slender and average height, Lucas stood well over six feet with a muscular build. Even their facial structures were different. Jacob had meaty features, with a bulbous nose. Lucas's were patrician, as if they'd been carved from marble.

"You say you're his son," she said, in a tone that was not quite believing. "Yet not only do you not resemble him in the slightest, but you sound like you don't like him, either."

He shook his head, his ruggedly handsome features impassive. "As I said, I'm not his son any longer. As far as I'm concerned, that part of me died fifteen years ago, when I escaped Sanctuary roughly the same way you did."

Crud. Suddenly dizzy, Blythe sat on the edge of the

bed. "I don't give a damn about you or your father, but you'd better tell me anything that will help me find a way to rescue my daughter."

Chapter 4

Lucas began to talk. He told her an abbreviated version of the truth, though he said nothing about Lilly and how Jacob had killed her right in front of him. That part of his past was his own private shame, which he would always bear alone. As he spoke, choosing his words with care, he watched her closely. While he didn't want to send her into shock, she needed to know what she faced.

"My mother must have been a Shifter, because Jacob is human. I don't actually know what happened to her, because I remember absolutely nothing about her. Long story short, Jacob caught me changing into a wolf. He viewed this as a sign from his God that I was a demon, and he set about trying to purge my body and—as he said—make me holy again."

Swallowing, he pushed away the image of his vibrant sister, beaten and lifeless. "His methods were horrific. I believe he would eventually have killed me. I managed to escape, and I ran. I haven't seen him since. It's been fifteen years now."

Watching him, her eyes, a shocking shade of green, went soft with sympathy. "You must have been very young."

"Fifteen." While he tried to factually relay his horrific past without growing emotional, his wolf reacted with hers on another, more primal level. Though he knew she had to be aware of this, externally she showed no reaction.

Was this how it was normally between Shifters, he wondered? At the thought, a wild sense of longing possessed him, something unwanted and unwarranted, and which he promptly pushed away.

"That's it. When I saw you and your little girl on the news, with him promising he could heal her, I knew I had to come and stop him. I drove from Seattle."

She nodded.

Watching the emotions trace across her beautiful face—shock and horror and revulsion—he stopped talking. There were no more words he could say without revealing the most important part of all. His sister's death.

Silence. He waited, almost defiantly, for her reaction. Half of him expected condemnation, as if all of what had happened had been his fault, as if he'd somehow deserved the actions of the so-called pious man of God.

He also feared she would panic, because in revealing his past, he'd also revealed what Jacob had in mind for her little girl.

As Lucas talked, Blythe found herself listening in a sort of horrified fugue state. Disbelief, shock and terror for Hailey mingled with revulsion that a so-called man of God could do such things to his own son.

And what about her daughter? If Lucas was right, she'd delivered her baby girl into the clutches of a madman.

When he finally finished, the silence rang with a thousand questions, none of which she expected him to be able to answer.

"Why?" she finally asked. "Even if you being able to shift was—is—out of the ordinary, you're his son. Throughout history, other parents have learned to deal with that. What would drive him to…recoil from you like that? Why would any father do such a thing to his own child?"

"I've asked myself that very same question a hundred times. I don't know that I can explain the unexplainable. But as far as I can tell, it's because of his belief system. In his narrow-minded view, such a thing as a Shape-shifter cannot exist. I'm a werewolf, he said. He honestly believed—believes—that I have a demon inside me."

"That you come from hell," she said, still unable to entirely wrap her mind around the idea.

He nodded. "Yes."

"But since he's human, that means your mother…"

"She must have been a full-blood. But she died when I was born and he destroyed everything of hers. I've never even seen a picture."

"Seriously?" Again, such a thing was beyond her comprehension.

He shrugged once more, as if it didn't matter. "Yes. I know nothing about her."

"Then you had no one to teach you to…"

A shadow crossed his face. She got a sense that there was more, that he hadn't told her everything. But she didn't press him, not now. Hellhounds, he'd already revealed so much horror, the thought that there might be more was staggering.

"The first time I felt the urge to shift, I freaked out." He sounded rueful, speaking of something that broke every Pack law she could think of regarding children. The first change should be a special thing, guided with a loving hand. Like Hailey's would be, if she lived that long.

Blythe clenched her fists. Though she felt sorry for this man, listening to him talk about the past wasn't going to help save Hailey.

He cocked his head. "You must be wondering how all this relates to your daughter," he said, as if he'd read her mind.

Masking her inner turmoil with what she hoped passed for calmness, she nodded. "Yes. Yes, I am. Tell me. What do you think your father—"

"Jacob."

She acknowledged the difference with a dip of her chin. "What does Jacob want with my daughter?"

Instead of answering, he asked another question. "Does he know you're a Shape-shifter?"

"No, of course not." Puzzled, she frowned. "Why would I tell him something like that? He's human. You know the law."

"Since I'm not actually part of your Pack, no, I don't. But no matter. I think Jacob has somehow learned that you and your child are like me—Shape-shifters. Since he believes these powers came from a demon, he's on a holy mission to wipe out the evil. He intends to cure your daughter—not of her physical ailment, but her spiritual one. Even if it kills her."

For a split second, she couldn't breathe. Couldn't think, couldn't move, couldn't even swallow. "Then we've got to go help her," she finally managed. "Now."

Expression grim, he shook his head. "You heard what happened when you tried to call the police. He's got the entire area in his pocket."

"Then we'll go out farther." Desperate now, she began to pace. "The FBI will help."

"Not if they talk to the local police and are told you're a crackpot."

Stunned, she stared at him. "Are you serious?" she asked. "You really think that's what will happen?"

He nodded.

This was like something out of a nightmare.

"These people really are crazy," she said, trying to keep her hands from trembling. "How is that possible? An entire town..."

"He's a very hypnotic speaker."

She stared at him, letting him see her disbelief. "Are you saying he hypnotizes people?" Then, before he could even answer, she inhaled sharply. "Hellhounds. Are you saying he hypnotized me?" That explanation would certainly clear up a lot of things.

Lucas grimaced. "To be honest with you, I don't know. It's entirely possible."

She took a deep breath and released it. "It sounds like you think no one is going to help me."

The wry grimace he made didn't make her feel any better. "At least no humans will. What about your Pack?"

"I don't know. I'll call them." She grabbed the cell phone and then stared at it in frustration. "I'm not sure I know the number. It's stored in my cell, which he took from me."

"So it appears you're on your own," he said, without inflection.

His lack of emotion was beginning to get to her. She glared at him, determination and ferocity coursing through her. "Then I'll do it by myself. I have to get my daughter out. I don't care if I need to rip out some throats to do it."

As another Shifter, no matter what his upbringing, she believed Lucas would understand. When in their wolf form, they all retained their human intellect. This made them deadly fighters when they needed to be.

His face a stony mask, he shook his head. "You're not alone," he said. "I'll help you."

"Look," she said. "I'm grateful, but you have to understand I don't trust anyone involved in any way with Jacob Gideon and his Sanctuary."

"I'm not involved with them." He glared at her. "I told you, I drove all the way here from Seattle to help you."

"Assuming I believe you, I have to ask you why. We're total strangers. Why do you care what happens to us?"

"It's more than just you. What that man did to me and mine should never be done to anyone else."

She opened her mouth to respond, and then closed it. The cold fury shimmering in his dark blue eyes made her shiver.

"And to answer your question as to why, it's time he was stopped. For good. No matter what the cost, I will help you save your daughter. And then, I'll make sure Jacob Gideon doesn't hurt any other Shifters. Ever again."

Oddly enough, this fierce resolve decided her. "All right. Thank you. I accept your offer of help."

"Good." Something in his grim tone told her he hadn't actually given her a choice. "They won't be expecting two of us. You need to get ready."

"Get ready?" Incredulous, she could only stare. "I'm chomping at the bit. The sooner I can get Hailey away from that monster, the better."

"Good. Because we're going to go in and get her out. No matter what."

She nodded. "When?"

He glanced at her, his jaw set. "Tonight."

As a slow, fierce smile broke out over Blythe's expressive face, something intense flared inside Lucas. What the hell? Pushing it away, he dragged his gaze away from the hope shining in her emerald-green eyes and forced himself to focus. He wondered if she understood the risks she'd be taking. If caught, and especially if Jacob learned she was also a Shape-shifter, she'd be subjecting not only her daughter, but herself to unspeakable acts of torture.

By the end, she'd be longing for death.

He considered telling her more than the bare bones, but in the end, decided not to. The knowledge would change nothing. Like him, she had no choice.

"What time?" she asked, raising her chin in a way that told him she was a woman of courage, a mother willing to fight tooth and nail for her child.

"We'll use the darkness to provide cover. Until then, you're going to have to stay hidden. If I know Jacob, he will have told the locals some preposterous story about you, and they'll be on the lookout to have you arrested and brought in."

Her eyes widened in fresh shock, making him inwardly wince. Every truth he had to throw out to her was like feeding a wolf a poisoned bone. But she needed to understand just how much of a monster they were dealing with.

"Arrest me for what?"

Grimly, he ticked the possibilities off on his fingers. "Child abuse, child molestation, attempting to sell your daughter, trying to prostitute her to pedophiles—he'll come up with the worst possible story and make them believe it."

She swallowed hard. "But none of that is true. He'd have no proof."

"It doesn't make any difference. What does matter is that he will have convinced everyone that he took your daughter away for her own good. That you are a danger to her. I promise you, they will believe him."

Crossing her arms, her expression radiating darkness, she dropped into the dingy motel chair. "I'll kill him."

"No, you won't." Though if the truth were to be told, he'd been aching to take the man out himself ever since the news story had aired. But the repercussions would be tremendous. "Making him pay will have to wait. First, we're going to rescue your kid and get away. After that, I'll figure out a way to expose him, so he can't do this to anyone else."

"Hailey," she said. "Her name is Hailey." There was both strength and delicacy in her face. "Inside there, in Sanctuary, they kept trying to depersonalize her and I instinctively kept insisting on giving them her name. At the time, I didn't understand why. Unfortunately, I do now."

Eyeing her, he felt it again: the rush of attraction that was not only inappropriate, but dangerous. He wondered if Blythe even realized how beautiful she was. On the heels of that thought came another, one he'd considered earlier and had forgotten.

For as long as Lucas had known him, Jacob had always had a weakness for the ladies. If worst came to worst, there was the possibility that they could use that against him. Lucas decided not to mention it to Blythe yet. Hopefully, it wouldn't come to that.

Her stomach growled, making him smile, even as she gave him an apologetic look. "Sorry," she said. "I should have gone hunting earlier."

"When was the last time you ate?"

She thought for a moment. "On the drive down here yesterday."

"Yesterday? I saw the story on the news a few days ago. I would have thought you'd have been here longer."

"Nope. Jacob had a few more appearances scheduled, so Hailey and I spent the day shopping, eating out, and we saw a movie," she said. "I had a few misgivings, and apparently for good reason. I so badly wanted to have hope. Instead, I should have trusted my instincts." Sighing, she glanced away. "Look what happened. I haven't even been here twenty-four hours and already my baby is in danger."

"Don't worry," he spoke with more confidence than he felt. "We'll get her out. In the meantime, I'll go fetch us something to eat."

She nodded listlessly, so he left her there.

Later, he returned with a couple of breakfast burritos and coffees, as well as a change of clothes for her that he grabbed at the local big box store. She ate with a mechanical precision that told him she was already working on a rudimentary plan.

"Maybe you should tell me," she said, blotting her mouth with a napkin. She'd missed a crumb, and he found himself aching to lick it off her lips, which shocked him.

What the hell was wrong with him? With difficulty, he tried to focus on her words. "Tell you what?"

"What I should expect to find when we get into Sanctuary." Mouth a thin line, she leaned forward. "I need to be prepared."

"No," he said, as gently as he could. "You don't. Let's leave it at that."

Her gaze locked with his, the determination in her expression twisting his gut. But finally she nodded. "You're right. I need to concentrate on getting Hailey out."

"Yes."

"But after…"

"One day at a time," he told her. "That's how we're going to get through this. One day at a time."

Though she nodded, she got up and began to pace the confines of the small hotel room, her lithe grace reminding him more of a trapped panther than a wolf. Even in the artificial light, her hair gleamed like strands of luxurious silk.

Watching her, he tried to throttle the dizzying current of desire racing through him. This both infuriated and intrigued him, because despite his instinctive reaction to her when he'd seen her on the television, he hadn't expected to want her. More than that, actually. He hadn't thought he'd crave her the way he did.

He needed to get a grip. For someone who always prided himself on being in control, he felt perilously close to completely losing it.

"I wonder, have you always known?" he asked her, more to distract them both than anything else.

She stopped pacing, swiveling her head around to look at him, sending her long hair whipping around her shoulders. "Have I always known what?"

Feeling foolish, now he regretted asking. Almost. "What you were. A Shape-shifter. When was the first time you changed into a wolf? How old were you?"

As distractions went, it worked. Head cocked, she stared at him, the expression in her vivid green eyes making it clear she was trying to decide if he was messing with her or telling the truth.

"I really want to know," he added, his voice a bit huskier than he'd have preferred, but sincere all the same.

"I was ten," she said. "Most of us are ten or eleven when we shift for the first time. Once in a while it happens to someone much younger, but that's the general age."

"I see." Truthfully, he hadn't known.

"You had no one to guide you at all, did you?" she finally asked. "Because your mother died and you were all alone, except for that crazy man who raised you."

He doubted his careless shrug fooled her. "I had no idea. The first few times I had the urge to shift, I panicked. I

was eleven and I didn't know what was wrong with me."
He and Lilly had shared that sense of fear. But of course,
he didn't mention that to Blythe.

"Did you go to your father?"

He winced, this time unable to hide it. "No. I couldn't.
Even though I was still relatively normal, I couldn't fail
to notice how rigid the lines were for him. I think I instinctively knew he would recoil from me in disgust and
horror."

The sympathy on her beautiful face completely pissed
him off. He didn't want her pity, or anyone else's, for that
matter. That was part of the reason he'd avoided his own
kind all these years. He was what he was and damned if
he'd make apologies for it.

With difficulty, he managed to rein in his emotions.
None of this was her fault. In truth, he didn't understand
the way she made him feel, the things she made him want.
Desire was both the least and the greatest of these.

What he was about to tell her was private—he'd never
shared it with another human being, with the exception of
the one person he'd let Jacob destroy.

But Jacob had her daughter. If anyone deserved to know,
it was Blythe. He'd have to be careful in how he told it, because Lilly had been with him then. Lilly had always been
with him. He and his twin had been exceptionally close.

"I was out in the desert near Sanctuary," he began, hoping like hell he didn't slip up. He had to tell the story as if
he'd been alone. "I liked to go on long hikes in those days.
It was a way for me to think. The urge to change had been
coming more and more frequently, which terrified me. But
so far I'd been successful in fighting it off. Not this time."

He took a long pull on his coffee, considering his next
words.

To her credit, she simply waited, her eyes vivid-green as

she watched him through her long lashes. She was quiet, rather than peppering him with questions. This, he appreciated.

After a moment, he continued. "This time, when the urge to change hit me, the need was like never before. Fierce and compelling. I fell to my knees and tried to fight, but something else took over my body and I couldn't. Before I knew what happened, my clothes were torn and tattered and I shape-shifted into a wolf."

"You should have had someone there to help guide you," she said softly. "It's always like that, the first time."

He shrugged, careful to keep his face expressionless. His memories of that day were still vivid, though they mostly consisted of watching what had happened to his sister as she went through her first change. They'd been frightened and exhilarated, amazed and shocked.

When they'd changed back, they'd each managed to do so far enough away from the other that they were able to hide their nakedness until they got dressed.

It was all new and strange and a continuous learning process. But they'd had each other and so they'd learned to cope.

"It was a long time ago. But I was in an animal frenzy after that. As wolf, I ran and hunted, when I was human again, I got dressed in my shredded and tattered clothes and returned home. I vowed that one time would be it and I'd never let it happen again."

"And of course it did," she said, her expression soft and understanding.

He nearly told her then, nearly revealed the truth of the horror that had happened to his twin so many years ago. But at the last moment, he reined himself in. They were strangers, after all. He would do his best to help her and her daughter, after which he doubted he'd ever see her again. He wasn't the kind of guy women depended on.

Still, he had to tell her part of the truth, just so she really understood what kind of monster she was up against.

"I went as long as I could before changing again. Each time, I came away convinced something was wrong with me." He shrugged, to show her it no longer mattered. "I started being more diligent about attending Jacob's services. I tried to be kinder, more studious. In short, I thought if I somehow atoned for whatever sin made me this way, I could be normal again."

He didn't tell her this had been Lilly's idea. She'd been convinced that their shape-shifting abilities were some form of punishment, doled out from an angry God. Jacob's God. Lucas had gone along with her, because when she was happy, he was, too.

Lost in his memories, he became aware Blythe was speaking. "You only wanted to be normal. When in fact, all along, you were perfectly ordinary, at least for our kind."

He said the first thing that came to mind. "You sound sad."

"Of course I do." Frowning, she shook her head. "Jacob had to have known this would happen. When he married your mother, she would have told him. We're always allowed to tell our mates. He should have taken steps to ensure you were educated in the ways of the Pack."

"I'm not sure he knew." Aware of the bitter twist to his mouth, he looked away, unable to bear the pity he was sure to see in her eyes. "Or if he once had known, he made himself forget. That would be the only explanation for how he reacted once he learned the truth about us."

"Us?"

Damn. Swallowing hard, he gestured at nothing. "You know what I mean. Our kind. Us."

After a moment, she nodded, seeming to accept this explanation. He'd slipped. He needed to be careful.

Because in addition to what had happened to his sister, there was more, much more, that he didn't tell her. How he'd tried to run away, to stay wolf forever. He'd thought that would make his life easier. And it might have, though he never got a chance to find out. No matter how hard he'd tried to stay in his wolf form, eventually he'd always changed back to man.

She shifted restlessly. "If you don't mind telling me, how exactly did your fath—I mean Jacob—find out what you were? I assume you didn't tell him."

"He became curious and I was careless. He followed me one day. He was careful to stay hidden so I didn't see him. He watched while I changed." He shook his head, the images as fresh as though they had occurred yesterday. He'd stick to the details whenever possible...more or less. "Full of self-righteous rage, he ran at me when I was still wolf."

Narrowing her eyes, she continued to watch him. "He's lucky you didn't attack him."

"Maybe."

Because of Lucas's paralyzing fear, Jacob had caught them both. After ordering his twin children to be led away in chains, he'd locked them in one of the unfinished basement rooms, eerily reminiscent to Lucas's young mind of a dungeon. "Jacob screamed, called me a worthless dog, demon-spawn and evil."

"What did he do after that?" she asked.

He took a deep breath, well aware that what he was about to say would barely skirt the edges of what had happened. It wasn't even the worst of it. "He beat me to within an inch of my life."

"While you were still wolf?"

He nodded. "While I was still a wolf."

"And of course you changed back." It wasn't a question. She knew, as he had not, that all Shifters changed back to their original form when they were hurt or wounded. He was aware of that now, of course.

"I changed back. My father was convinced a demon had possessed me. He was determined to rid me of it, no matter what the cost. Even if it killed me."

She made a sound. He could see in her face that she was tempted to offer comfort. Appalled, he made a gesture, warding her off.

"I'm fine," he said. "That's all in the past anyway. The only reason I'm even telling you all this is so you can understand what he wants to do to Hailey."

Her eyes widened. Glancing at her watch, she cursed. "He's had all day."

Sensing her panic, he acted instinctively, reaching out and gently squeezing her shoulder. "Don't worry. I'm relatively sure he's still studying her to make sure she is what he thinks."

"Relatively isn't good enough," she snarled. "If he lays one hand on her, I'll—" Visibly collected herself, she inhaled sharply. "I'm not going to give him a chance to hurt her."

"*We're* not," he said. "Remember, you aren't alone in this."

She gave him such an odd look he realized that, despite everything, she hadn't actually considered them a team.

Chapter 5

Blythe tried to nap in preparation for the late night ahead, but with her hyperawareness of Lucas in the bed next to her, she couldn't sleep. Instead, she lay there wide-awake, her heart pounding as she continually replayed the events leading up to Jacob's abduction of her daughter.

All because she'd foolishly allowed herself to hope.

She thought she'd been so careful, especially when the media got involved. She hadn't even considered that Jacob would be able to use that same media against her, making all sorts of outrageous claims to prevent her from getting Hailey back.

Finally, she fell into a sort of restless slumber, devoid of dreams. When she woke an hour later, she found Lucas sitting in the chair by the desk watching her.

The instant her gaze connected with his, she felt a jolt of heat, low in her belly. Even as she blinked, trying to acclimate herself, he pushed to his feet and moved away, clearly ill at ease. With his back to her, he peered out the window, silent, his entire demeanor stiff. If he had felt the same thing she had, evidently it made him no happier than it did her.

Bad timing.

Still, she could not look away. Eyeing him, again she was struck by his rugged masculinity. She couldn't help but wonder again how someone like Jacob could have fathered a son who looked like Lucas.

"We should eat something," he told her, his voice husky with sleep. "I'll go get us a couple of burgers and bring them back. I still don't want to take a chance that you might be seen, just in case Jacob has started spreading any lies."

Though she hated having to stay hidden, it only made sense. "Sounds good." She pushed up off the bed and headed for the bathroom. "I'm going to take a quick shower while you're gone."

Jerking his head in a nod, he headed toward the door, moving so fast she had to blink. It wasn't as if she was going to start stripping off her clothes on the way.

And even if she had, what did it matter? They were Shifters. Though he wasn't Pack, Lucas had to get used to acting like one sooner or later.

Once in the shower, she turned the spray to hot and, using the shampoo and conditioner the motel provided, she got herself clean. Glad of the change of clothes, she dressed.

When she emerged from the bathroom about fifteen minutes later, Lucas had returned. The tantalizing smell of hamburgers and French fries made her mouth water.

He glanced up, took in her freshly scrubbed face and wet hair, and nodded, his bland expression revealing nothing. "Dig in."

She dropped into the chair opposite him and did as ordered. The first bite of the thick hamburger almost made her hum with pleasure. "This couldn't have been fast food," she said, once she'd swallowed. After her shower, change of clothes and now an excellent meal, she felt better than she should. She felt she ought to be suffering until she had Hailey back. "It tastes too good."

"It's a local place, right around the corner," he told her. "Called Stripers. I used to eat there as a boy. They're known in these parts for their burgers."

This, she could believe. Giving up all attempts at eating with decorum, she tucked into her meal with gusto.

They ate in companionable—or at least it felt like it to her—silence, both so fixated on the explosion of beef and mushroom and cheese and onion, they couldn't talk.

Only when she'd finished the burger and was down to two thick French fries, did she take a breath. "I needed that," she told him, smiling. "Thanks."

He nodded, shifting in his chair as though her appreciation made him uncomfortable. "Better to go in well fed so our strength is fortified," he said. "After this, I'm going to go trade the motorcycle in for a pickup truck. Though I hate to let the bike go, it isn't practical for a rescue. I need something that can accommodate all three of us."

Gratified—and a bit stunned—that he would do something like this for a total stranger, she only nodded.

After they'd eaten, he left, promising to return as soon as possible. "I'm going to head to a used car lot in the next town over."

Once he'd gone, she paced, missing Hailey and worrying about her. She wished she had something to occupy herself—no, she wished she could call the police and, accompanied by sirens and uniformed officers with badges and guns, march into Sanctuary and reclaim her daughter.

Since she couldn't, she had no choice but to wait.

Roughly ninety minutes later, the rumble of an engine outside the room announced Lucas's return. She peered out through the curtains, taking care not to be seen in case it was someone else.

When Lucas climbed out of the large white pickup, she breathed a sigh of relief and hurried to open the door.

"Check it out," he said, sounding pleased. "I traded the bike in for this. It's a Ford F-250, and it's got four-wheel drive and a V-8 engine. It's perfect for everything we need."

"It looks great," she said. "And thank you."

He nodded, appearing to understand that she spoke from the heart. There weren't enough words to express how much she appreciated his help.

Since they still had a few hours until sunset, he clicked on the TV. The evening news was just beginning and they both watched in silence.

Lucas got up and turned it off when the news was over. "At least no mention was made of you, Hailey, or even Jacob and Sanctuary."

"That's good, right?" she asked.

"So far, yes. Though this news isn't local, it's national," he said. "Plus I really think Jacob's going to keep this as quiet as possible. At least until he needs to do damage control."

She considered this carefully. "Then maybe I should go to the media first. If I beat him to it—"

"He'll already have a cover story," Lucas said as he grimaced. "I'm sorry, but I've already given you some examples. It won't be good."

Reluctantly, she let that particular spark of hope die, aware that he was probably right.

"I'm thinking Jacob won't expect us to go on the offensive," she said, glancing at him for confirmation.

"Probably not." Hands behind his head, he stretched, drawing her gaze to the way his T-shirt fit snugly over his muscular chest. Her mouth went dry. The instant she realized what she was doing, she spun away, red-faced and inexplicably furious.

How could she be so shallow that she could admire and even lust after a man when her daughter was missing? What was wrong with her?

Something must have shown in her expression. Lucas uncoiled himself from the chair. "My turn for a shower," he said. He disappeared inside the bathroom, closing the door behind him with a click.

Once he was gone, she took several deep breaths. To her relief, a bit of the tension coiled inside her eased. She felt as if she had herself completely under control by the time he emerged from the bathroom.

Though a moment ago she'd convinced herself that he made too big of a deal about her nakedness, when he appeared in the bathroom door wearing only a pair of low slung jeans, she felt dizzy. To her relief, he shrugged into a button-down shirt. She couldn't seem to drag her eyes away as she watched him fasten every single button.

"Do you want to play cards?" he asked, dropping a brand-new deck onto the table. "I found these in one of the dresser drawers."

"Sure, why not?"

They amused themselves by playing poker. Focusing on her hand, Blythe managed not to stare too long at the fine hairs on his muscular arm, or marvel at the elegant fingers that seemed out of place on such a large hand.

Finally, the sun set.

"Let's go," she said, after she'd peered out the window for the fifth time.

"Give it a few more minutes," he replied. "We need full darkness."

Ignoring him, she opened the door. "Come on. If I have to wait here another minute, I'll go crazy. If you need it to be darker, then you can drive slowly."

Shooting her a quick look, he got up. Evidently, his nerves weren't as on edge as hers. Though they'd discussed various scenarios, they didn't have a concrete plan. She figured they'd simply wing it, play it by ear.

Leaving the room, they hopped in the truck and rode back to the compound. The huge gates were closed. There were no signs of activity as they circled around, nothing to indicate Jacob was in any way concerned that Blythe might return and demand her daughter.

No doubt if he even considered this possibility, it would give him great amusement. She curled her hands into fists, leashing her simmering fury. If she could have gotten hold of Jacob Gideon at that moment, she'd have torn him to pieces.

When Lucas came to a stop in the same location he had before, she climbed out as soon as he killed the engine.

"Help me hide the truck," he said.

After she assisted dragging several large pieces of brush around the vehicle, she glanced at the flat empty fields. "Human or wolf?" she asked. "I'm thinking we'd be safer as wolves."

"But what about your daughter? How can we get her out if we're in our wolf forms?"

"She knows me as wolf," she said, grinning at the memory. "I can carry her on my back. That's how we accustom young Shifters to what they are."

He considered for a moment. She couldn't read the expression on his chiseled features. "Wolf it is," he finally said. "It'll be easier to make an escape that way."

* * *

Something about the way he held himself—aloof, almost uncertain—told her that perhaps he wasn't quite used to shifting with others. She knew she shouldn't be surprised, after all that he'd told her. He hadn't had the traditional bonding experience that being part of the Pack comprised. But still, he was a man now. Who among their kind would choose to be alone when they had other options?

Apparently Lucas Kenyon.

"You'll get used to it," she told him, throwing the words over her shoulder as she turned away to remove her clothing.

"Catch." He'd tossed her a backpack. Waiting until she'd caught it, he smiled before stripping off his own clothes.

Though she knew she should have looked away, she couldn't. She tried not to stare, honest to hounds she tried to not even look, but she'd never seen a man so beautiful and so perfectly made. His muscular shoulders and chest gave way to a flat, chiseled stomach and…more.

Feeling the rush of heat, she swallowed hard. This was ridiculous. They'd come to rescue Hailey. Nothing more. Snarling at herself under her breath, she yanked off her clothing as fast as she could and dropped to all fours to initiate the change.

Beside her, she sensed him doing the same. As her bones changed and lengthened, she tried to blot from her mind the image of Lucas naked. Once fully wolf, she knew it would no longer matter.

When she opened her eyes again as wolf, she put her nose to the ground and sniffed. When human, sight was the primary sense she used. As wolf, sight came a distant second or third after scent and sound. Her nose was a thousand times more sensitive, as were her ears. In fact, the world was a much richer place when she walked it in her wolf form.

A large black wolf stood next to her. Lucas. They touched noses, getting each other's scent, and then they were off. Loping across the desert, with the wind and the moonlight to guide them.

When they reached the perimeter of Sanctuary, they slowed in unison. Lucas whined, pawing the ground to communicate his unease. This she understood, for tonight the house had an eerie feel, almost as though it was alive and could sense them.

As wolf, she trusted such instincts.

Glancing at Lucas, she saw he, too, had stopped. As he stared at the structure with his snout raised to scent the wind, she saw how beautiful he was as wolf. Masculine. Dark to her light.

Then she noticed the raised fur on his back. Her own hackles went up in response. *Danger.*

Keeping low to the ground, he moved first. She followed. No matter what the risk, she had to find Hailey and get her out. But how would they get inside? Though she hadn't been able to explore during her brief stay, she'd bet the place was kept locked up tighter than Fort Knox.

Lucas ran to a ground-level window and tapped it sideways with his nose. It moved only a fraction of an inch, but this gave him enough room to use his entire snout and even his paws.

When he'd created an opening large enough for them to fit inside, he glanced back at her. Then, moving quickly, he slipped inside.

She didn't even hesitate before following.

Once she went through the opening, she stumbled and fell a foot or so onto what felt like a metal slab. The smell of soap or detergent and bleach hit her sensitive nose hard enough to make her sneeze.

As her eyes adjusted to the darkness, she realized why the window had been left unlocked. They were in what obviously was the laundry room, which reminded her of something she'd expect to find in a hotel.

Industrial-size washers and dryers lined one wall. The metal slab underneath the window was a commercial ironing press, which she imagined would generate a lot of heat. Thus the need to open the window.

Lucas waited near the closed doorway, head cocked as he listened for any hint they might have been discovered. Then he reached up, took the doorknob in his mouth and turned it, backing toward her and pulling the door open.

Successful, he slipped out into the hall, Blythe right behind him.

They saw no one, and in fact all the doors were closed. Every now and then she caught a whiff of something—a woman's faded perfume, the smell of cooked meat, which made her mouth water—but nothing she recognized as her daughter's scent. Or even Jacob Gideon's, for that matter.

Strange. They continued on. Lucas dropped back and let her lead, reminding her that he wasn't familiar with Hailey's scent. Only she could track her daughter that way.

Yet she wasn't having any luck.

She was thorough, pausing at each closed door, putting her nose to the small opening below it and breathing in.

They swept the entire first floor, glad of the darkness, without finding even the smallest trace of her little girl. The stairs beckoned, and these were dimly lit with small lights set into a recessed panel below each step.

Her sense of unease growing, she bounded up the staircase. If she remembered right, her old room was this way.

Though she doubted they'd have brought Hailey back there, especially with a broken window, she had to check.

But first, she inspected each and every door along the hall. Though she had no way to communicate with him, she couldn't help but wonder if Lucas noticed the same thing she had. The house seemed completely empty of people, at least judging from the lack of human smells.

She didn't understand this. Surely they hadn't evacuated. This had to be some sort of a trap.

Backing away, she touched her nose to Lucas's flank to communicate her unease. He growled low in his throat, pushing past her toward the last set of doors at the end of the hall.

She recognized the place from before. Double doors made of dark wood. No mere knob here, but an elaborate pewter handle that she thought might be easier for a wolf to open. Whether intentional or not, she didn't know or care. This was Jacob Gideon's room.

Lucas snarled again and, as the scent tickled her nose, she realized there was a very real possibility he might even be inside.

Though fully wolf, various human memories flooded Lucas as he stood in front of the imposing double doors. The heavily polished mahogany represented a thousand horrors from his adolescence. Most of all, they were a blatant symbol of all he had lost. Lilly's absence—even now—had made a permanent hole in his heart.

Beside him, Blythe matched his growl with one of her own. He glanced at her, noting the way the fur on her back had risen, exactly like his own.

Forcing himself to move forward, he bumped one of the doors with his shoulder. It remained solid and unmoving, which meant they had no way to get inside. Even if he stood on his hind legs and reached the handle and managed to turn it, there was no chance he could pull such a heavy door open.

But still he had to try. Maybe if Blythe would help him...

Nudging her with his muzzle, he jumped at the door, trying to communicate without words what he needed her to do.

She followed him over as though she understood. Side by side, they stood on their hind legs and closed their mouths over the long, curled, pewter handle.

Working as though they'd practiced for this moment, they moved it down, simultaneously walking backward on their hind legs.

The door opened.

And as it did, an alarm began to shriek Klaxon tones.

Blythe froze. Growling at her, Lucas continued to pull. Now that the door was open, he needed to take a quick look inside to make sure Hailey wasn't the prize Jacob considered valuable enough to protect with an alarm.

The room was empty, as he'd thought. Nudging her, he turned and took off with her right at his side.

Moving as one, they ran swiftly through the halls, expecting to be confronted at any moment. Miraculously, weirdly, they made it downstairs and to the laundry room without encountering another soul. Despite the awful sound of the alarm, so loud it tore at his supersensitive eardrums, no one emerged from any of the other rooms.

Sanctuary resembled a ghost town. Abandoned and lifeless.

Maybe the place really had been emptied. Still, they couldn't take any chances. Leaping up onto the commercial ironing platform, they went out through the same window by which they'd entered.

As they ran across the land, Lucas kept glancing back over his shoulder, expecting searchlights or gunshots. But nothing happened—no lights came on inside Sanctuary, no voices called out at them to stop and most important, no one shot at them.

Once they reached the place where they'd left their clothes, they stopped and stood, panting. Side by side, both wolves eyed the silent house, snouts lifted to scent the air for anything that might indicate there would be a pursuit.

Instead, they smelled nothing. Saw nothing, heard nothing. It was as if Sanctuary had been empty for years.

Except it hadn't been.

Finally, Blythe whined. Moving away, she turned her back to him, lowering herself to the ground to begin to shape-shift back to human.

Lucas took one last look at the distant compound and then did the same.

The instant the change was complete, Blythe pushed herself up and stalked over to snatch up her clothing. She dressed hurriedly, her jerky movements revealing both anger and fear.

Lucas's problem was a bit more…earthy. Despite his massive arousal, he managed to walk to his clothes and get dressed, as well.

After he was fully clothed, he went to the truck and began pulling away the brush. Blythe stood slender and straight, clearly in the grips of strong emotions as she eyed Jacob's massive house. Her entire body appeared to vibrate.

Lucas saw her pain, her grief at losing her daughter. It was plain in the tears she didn't even seem to know she was crying, and in the harsh set of her feminine jaw.

Lucas watched her for a moment, uncertain how she'd want him to react. He couldn't blame her. After all, they'd found absolutely nothing—no hint of where her little girl had been taken. Hailey might as well have vanished into thin air.

"Are you all right?" he asked, well aware she was not.

"I'm fine," she snarled, sounding anything but. "We didn't get to search every room."

"I know, but the alarm—"

"No one came when it went off," she interrupted him. "And the place does appear empty. I think we should go back in, right now as humans, and tear the place apart until we find Hailey."

He actually considered the idea. "And if she's not there?"

"Then we search for any scrap of information that might tell us where they've taken her."

"I don't think—" He didn't finish whatever he'd been about to say. Instead, he turned around. "We can try. Only I want you to promise me one thing."

Though her belligerent expression told him she wasn't in the mood to make promises she couldn't keep, she jerked her head in a nod. "Come on."

When she started forward, he grabbed her. "Stay behind me," he ordered. "Just in case."

They made it within a few hundred feet of Sanctuary when the sound of gunfire had Lucas knocking her to the ground. "Stay down." Grim, he hoped like hell he could protect her. "I can't even tell where it's coming from."

Several more shots came in rapid succession. "Is that an assault rifle?" Blythe asked, not bothering to mask her horror.

"Possibly." Continuing to stay close to the ground, he indicated the direction they'd come. "We've got to get out of here. We're sitting ducks, since there's nowhere to take cover."

She looked sick to her stomach. "What do you want to do?"

"Make a run for it," he said. "You first. I've got your back."

Standing, she took off, with Lucas right behind her. He ran blindly, wondering if at any moment a shot was going to tear into his back or worse, take Blythe down.

Surprisingly, they made it back to where they'd left the truck.

"I'm sorry," he told her. "But we've got to leave."

Though clearly she didn't want to, she knew he was right. "Fine. Let's go." Continuing to glare at Sanctuary, she wouldn't look at him. "Let's get out of this place."

That, he could agree with. "Come on." He climbed into the truck and turned the key in the ignition. Waiting until she was securely seated beside him, he shifted into gear and they took off.

Back at the motel, she jumped out of the truck and rushed the door, waiting impatiently for him to produce the room key.

"What the hell was that?" She rounded on him a split second after he closed and locked the door. "How can the place be empty? They were there, I swear to you."

"I believe you. Obviously, someone was. They shot at us."

"Then where are the rest of them? Where did they take my Hailey?"

Guilt, that familiar emotion. Fresh and strong and raw. His gaze locked with Blythe's before he pushed it away.

"I don't know," he told her, swearing silently that this time, he wouldn't fail a little girl in danger.

Narrow-eyed, she glared at him. "You know, I can't help but wonder if you're in it with your father. You're the one who suggested we wait till dark. And waiting gave Jacob time to escape."

Though he supposed he couldn't blame her for her thoughts, that didn't stop her accusation from hurting. "I can assure you that I'm not working with that monster."

Without breaking his gaze, she circled around him, her nostrils flaring as though her wolf was trying to break free and take measure of his scent.

He let her. What else could he do? Either she trusted him or she didn't. Her choice. He was here trying to help.

Finally she stopped. "I believe you," she said. "I don't know why, but I do."

He dipped his chin in acknowledgment. "Thank you."

Barely contained panic lurked behind the anger sparking in her eyes. "There's got to be an explanation."

"I'm sure there is." He kept his voice even. "There's no way they evacuated all those people out of Sanctuary in one day."

"All those people? How many are there?"

He crossed his arms. "I'm not sure. It's been a long time since I was last inside those walls. I'd guess he has at least one hundred followers. Maybe more."

"Then where did they go?' she cried. "Wherever it is, they took my daughter with them."

Since he didn't have an answer, he didn't respond.

She began to pace. He stood still, arms crossed, while she flung herself from one end of the room to the other. She looked wild—restless—and her heightened color highlighted her exotic beauty. Even as he couldn't help but admire her lithe, curvy body and high-cheekboned face, he knew she was dangerously close to losing all reason.

He couldn't let that happen. A panic-stricken woman— or man—made bad decisions. Right now the last thing they needed to do was draw attention to themselves.

"Listen to me." Grabbing her arm, he spun her to face him. "Breathe. Deeply. You've got to get yourself under control."

"Why?" Her eyes spit fire at him. "My daughter is missing. They've all disappeared. They've taken her who knows where."

"Listen to me," he began.

"No. You listen to me." Her voice had begun to rise. She was seconds away from full-fledged hysteria. If the other guests at the motel heard a woman screaming and hollering, they'd alert the local police, who, if they recognized Blythe, might report to Jacob Gideon.

So he did the only thing he could think of to distract her. He kissed her, crushing her against him.

Chapter 6

As he slanted his mouth over hers and breathed in her scent, he dimly realized he didn't know how she'd react. If she was truly intent on spiraling out of control, she could fight him, in which case he'd immediately withdraw.

Or she could freeze. Shut down. Turn all that wild fury and panic inward, into self-regret and loathing.

In fact, she did none of those things.

Instead, she focused all of that passion toward him, singeing him so badly he thought they might both go up in flames in a blaze of heat.

Damn. Aroused, on fire, aching, he desired her, this woman he barely knew but with whom he had shared the most intimate of acts—the change from his human form into his wolf.

And now he wanted more. More than wanted, *craved*.

So, of course, he pushed away from her, crossing to the other side of the room and struggling to get his breathing under control.

"What now?" Color high, eyes wild and hair tangled, she taunted him. "I need this. I need you. Hard and fast and deep. Now."

Even as her words inflamed him, he knew he had to stay strong. Instinctively he knew that having sex with her would change things for him forever. He'd been content living his life alone. Safe. Furious with himself and with her, he reined in his temper and his need.

"No." He lifted his head, letting her see in his face how much letting her go had cost him. "This isn't the time or the place. You're hurting. You're fighting feeling powerless. I refuse to take advantage of that."

For a moment, the thudding of his heart in his chest was the only sound he could hear. He thought she might argue—she looked spitting mad as she eyed him, almost as if she wasn't sure if he was serious or completely insane.

Then, just like that, all the air and bravado and anger went out of her. Deflated, she sank back onto the bed and covered her face with her hands. "What are we going to do?" she asked, her voice so low he could barely make out the words. "What on earth are we going to do?"

He thought fast. "I think a confrontation might be in order."

"What?" When she raised her face, twin tear tracks shone silver on her pale cheeks.

Ignoring the sudden tightness in his chest, he continued. "Give old Jacob a call. His biggest weakness is his own ego. Play to that."

She cocked her head, considering. "You might have something there. If I do it right, I might be able to waltz back into Sanctuary under the guise of repentance." Her voice rose with excitement as she gained momentum. "He might even let me see my daughter. Or at least I could find out where he's hiding her."

Horrified, he stood stock-still, frozen, unable to believe her words. "No," he said. "Absolutely not. There's no way I could let you face down the monster who still haunts me all by yourself. Even if I thought you'd be safe, and I don't, there's no way."

"It might be our only hope."

Exasperated, he shook his head. "That's not what I meant when I said force a confrontation. I meant a call only, to see where we stood. Then we could figure out where we need to go next. Maybe a meeting with the two of us, on our terms."

"He'll never agree to that." Stubbornness coloring her expression, he saw that she'd made up her mind.

"Listen, you don't know what he's capable of." Desperate to stop her, he gave her as much of the truth as he could. "He's already killed—I saw him do it. I was there."

Rather than swaying her, his comment only appeared to strengthen her resolve. Lifting her chin higher, she met his gaze. "All the more reason for me to try to get in. I've got to get Hailey away from him."

"But—"

"No buts. I'm going to try it. Either you're with me or against." Though her voice echoed with bravado, he saw the raw hope darkening her eyes.

Though he had a sinking feeling, he finally nodded. "We can try," he said. "Maybe a phone call will be enough. At the very least, maybe you can learn where they all disappeared to."

As her head cleared from the blind desire, Blythe wished Lucas had been right. She wished she'd only been looking for a channel for her mixed-up, crazy emotions. That was part of it, true. But Lucas made her want him, made her want to lose herself in him. Lucas. No other man would have done.

At least that had led to this. Her idea—to contact Jacob and see if she could worm her way back into Sanctuary—was not only more productive, but made more sense. When the idea had occurred to her at first, she'd wanted to reject it out of hand. It was just too risky, too crazy. There wasn't the slightest chance Jacob would believe she wanted to rejoin his little fold, not after she'd busted out the window and called the police.

"I have to give it a try. I don't have my daughter, don't even know where they've taken her, so I have absolutely nothing left to lose."

When he didn't respond, she glanced at him, noting his set face and clamped mouth. He wasn't happy with her decision, but then he didn't have a daughter who'd been taken prisoner.

"Can I borrow your phone?" she asked. Lucas handed it over without commenting. "You said this is untrace-able, right?"

"Yes. Keep it." Gesturing to his backpack, he gave her a grim smile. "I have others."

"Okay, then. Thanks." Taking a deep breath, she dialed the number the police dispatcher had given her. It must have been Jacob's direct line, because she didn't have to go through a secretary to get to him.

He answered with a curt hello.

"Jacob, it's Blythe Daphne," she began.

"I see you broke into my house," he said, without pre-amble. "First you damage a window and leave, then you sneak back in the middle of the night, in your demon form, and roam the halls of my house." He might have been mak-ing a political speech or preaching a sermon.

A chill skittered up her back. She'd much rather hear a

genuine emotion—whether fury or glee. Something, anything, other than this phony banter.

Then his words registered. They'd been wolf when they'd gone back to Sanctuary. Obviously he must have had security cameras.

"You mean as wolves? That's irrelevant."

"Is it?" he asked smoothly. "Then you won't mind telling me about your companion? That particular beast looks very familiar."

As if he could hear them, Lucas shook his head in warning. She inclined her head to show she'd understood. "That's none of your business. Where is Hailey? What have you done with her?"

"Are you upset?" He sounded genuinely surprised. "I don't understand. I told you I would heal her and that's what I'm doing."

"Not without me," she began. "You had her removed from my room while I was showering, without my permission."

"You're the one who broke out of Sanctuary," he spoke patiently, as though addressing a rebellious child. "We would have brought her back to you after she'd finished with her first treatment."

Of course, she knew he was lying. "First off, you don't lock guests in their room. Second, I just plain don't believe you. Bring her back to me now. I've changed my mind. I don't want you to heal her." Since she was trying not to alienate him, she had to bite back the rest of the words trembling on the tip of her tongue. She didn't want him anywhere near her. In fact, she'd didn't want him even breathing the same oxygen as her daughter.

For the space of one heartbeat, then two, there was only silence on the other end of the line. Then he laughed, a dry, humorless sound that made her throat tighten.

"What kind of a mother says something like that?" Now anger—no, righteous indignation—rang in his voice. For the first time she wondered if he was playing to an audience. Or worse, if he was recording their conversation.

"A mother who is worried about her child. Who you've kept from her child, and lied about to the police. You have no right to do anything to Hailey without my permission."

Again the dry laugh. "You gave your permission, remember? Back when you signed the documents consenting to her care."

"I've signed nothing," she said. "So stop acting as if you're in the right."

"But you did," he told her, the smug self-righteous tone making her grit her teeth. "Right after you arrived at Sanctuary. Ginger asked you to read and sign some papers."

"I didn't sign them. And this is irrelevant. Don't try to confuse me. There's nothing you can say that makes me lose sight of my position on this. I want my child. Give her back to me."

"I honestly wouldn't understand your selfishness, if I didn't know you were a demon." Now Jacob's deep voice was tinged with both hurt and self-righteousness. "Either way, I thought we were in sync with this. You want the best chance for your daughter to live. I'm going to make sure she gets it. Are we in agreement on that, at least?"

"I no longer feel you're her best chance. In fact, you might be her worst."

Silence greeted her words. Belatedly, she realized she might have gone too far.

He sighed. "It seems we have a difference of opinion on this. I can—and will—help her. And you do have a choice, you know. You can come back. Let me save you, too. You have a chance to be the kind of supportive mother Hailey needs."

She was too horrified to find her voice. Had Jacob already begun trying to save Hailey in the way Lucas believed he would? If he had, then he'd already started to torture her little girl.

Resolve strengthened, she knew she had to play her part to the hilt. She didn't have to try too hard to sound shocked. "Come back?"

"It's your choice." He sounded so earnest, she almost believed him. Only a monster could come across as being concerned when he was possibly torturing her baby. Now he was offering to torture her, as well.

Swallowing back her revulsion, she played along.

"If I came back willingly, would you keep me locked in?" she asked, trying to sound tearful and repentant, as he seemed to expect.

"It's for your own good."

On the verge of losing patience, she managed to rein herself in. She was close, so close, to getting a chance to be near Hailey. "I am not your prisoner."

"Either way, Ms. Daphne. Your choice. You can come back to Sanctuary and oversee your child's return to health, or stay away. If you come back, I promise I will give you regular updates."

Stunned at the way he made everything sound perfectly reasonable, she found herself at a loss for words. If she spoke, she might wind up making it more difficult to get to Hailey because she was on the verge of announcing her intent to rip this guy's throat out.

"One more thing," he continued. "Your wolf companion. Bring him along. It's been too many years since I've seen him."

Caught by surprise, she gasped. He knew? How had he recognized Lucas's wolf after all these years apart?

"Take all the time you need," he said soothingly. "Then call me and let me know what you decide."

While she was still trying to gather her thoughts so she could make a coherent response, he ended the phone call, his chuckle echoing in her ears.

Staring at the phone, her throat so tight she couldn't speak, she told herself to just breathe. Her eyes filled with tears. Turning away, she rubbed them furiously, not wanting Lucas to see her cry.

"What did he say?" Lucas asked, coming up behind her to put his hand on her shoulder. She almost let herself lean into the touch. Almost. Instead, she moved away, turning to face him and lifting her chin.

"A lot of nothing really," she said, then relayed the rest of the phone call. "I got a feeling he might have been playing from a script or recording the call for his own protection."

"That's possible. Though he generally thinks he's invulnerable, he believes he's doing the right thing. That's what makes him so frightening."

Frightening didn't even begin to cover it. Jacob Gideon—people like him—terrified her. They operated from their own, twisted agenda, and viewed anyone who didn't see things the same way as evil.

And he knew they were Shape-shifters. This made him even more dangerous, especially to Hailey. Blythe realized she'd been hoping all along that Lucas was wrong, that Jacob didn't really believe her little girl to be a demon.

"Now what?" Twisting her hands together, she tried to think of another plan, but came up with nothing. "I'm thinking I should return to Sanctuary. At least there, I'll have a chance to get Hailey out."

"I'm pretty sure they've abandoned the place," he said. "Other than one armed guard, that is."

"Maybe. Maybe not. He did invite me. Why would he do that if no one was there?"

"Good point." Now Lucas began to pace, reminding her of a caged wolf. "What do you want to do?"

He wasn't going to like what she had to say, but she had to say it anyway. "I'm going to have to go back and pretend to agree with his agenda."

"You do realize this means you're going to be tortured?"

"I have no choice if I want to get close enough to Hailey to have a chance to save her," she shot back.

"Call in your Pack," he said, letting her know the full measure of his desperation. "If any situation ever called for you to need their help, it is now."

"I can't," she swallowed. "If I do, they'll want to take her. She's special. The Protectors have tried to make the parents of her kind agree to turn their children over to them."

He gaped at her. "Explain."

"Not now." Impatient and tired, she waved her hand. "I've made my decision. I'm going in."

"Then I'm going with you."

"What?" Staring at him as if she wasn't sure she'd heard correctly, she cocked her head. "Have you lost your mind?"

"No. I'll go in wearing a disguise."

She crossed her arms, glaring at him as if she thought he might be joking. "He'll recognize you," she said. "He already said something about your wolf looking familiar."

From the narrowing of his eyes, she figured she'd surprised him.

"I'll make sure to avoid him. He's got an entire army working for him. Security guards, cooks, housekeepers. I'm sure he doesn't take the time to acquaint himself with every single employee."

"You're being ridiculous," she told him.

"No. I'm not." He dragged his hand through his thick hair, wincing. "I'll shave my head. Wear eyeglasses. That ought to be enough."

Still she shook her head. "Come on. Stop it. You know he's going to figure out who you are."

"I doubt it." Bitterness colored his voice. "The man's so self-absorbed he rarely looks at others. I think it will work."

"And if it doesn't?" she asked softly. "Are you willing to take the chance?"

"Yes."

"I'm not." She sighed. "I really appreciate the offer, but I can't risk it. If you fail, you'll jeopardize everything. I'll go back, alone. Once he knows I came back willingly, I'm hoping he won't see a need to keep me locked up. I'll find Hailey, contact you and you can show up and take us away from there."

"That's an awful lot of what-ifs," he said.

"I'll just have to be a really good actress. If I can convince him that I truly believe he's my last hope for saving my daughter, gaze at him with unadulterated admiration, I think I can convince him."

"And if you can't?"

She looked away, not wanting him to see her unease. "Then you'll have to figure out a way to rescue me."

Without giving him a chance to answer, she hit redial on her phone. Jacob answered on the second ring. "Have you come to a decision?"

"I'd like to apologize," she said stiffly, trying to force warmth into her voice. "I panicked and overreacted. More than anything I want Hailey healed. And I don't want to be on the outside while you do it. I want to witness your miraculous healing myself."

She hoped she wasn't spreading it on too thick.

Apparently not, because when Jacob spoke again, pleasure resonated in his voice. Though for all Blythe knew, he could be playing her the same way she was playing him.

"I'm glad you came around," he said warmly. "Now tell me where you are and I'll send someone to pick you up."

She thought fast. She didn't want to give away her location—and the fact that she was with Lucas. Then she remembered the burgers. Lucas had said it was right around the corner. "I'm outside a hamburger place. Called Stripers."

"Excellent." He practically purred with satisfaction. "Someone will be there in twenty minutes."

Without waiting for a reply, he hung up.

When she looked up, Lucas watched her intently.

"He's picking me up at Stripers," she said, oddly breathless, her heart fluttering like a hummingbird in her chest. "I'm going to walk there now. You stay here."

He nodded, the narrow glint of his gaze telling her he didn't like this one bit. "At the end of the parking lot, turn right. It's around the corner, after the gas station. First, let me program my number into the phone."

Once that had been accomplished, he handed it back. "Try to keep this with you," he said. "I have the number, so if I don't hear from you, I can call you later."

She nodded. "Hopefully he won't take the phone away."

"Why would he? After all, you're supposed to be his honored guest."

Out of words, she nodded again and then turned to go.

"Blythe."

She spun around, the urgency in his voice reflected in her jagged heartbeat.

"Do you know how to handle a pistol?"

Grimacing, she nodded. "I think so. Or at least I used to. I haven't shot one in years, though, so I'm a little rusty."

Crossing to his pack, he removed a small .22 and carried it to her, placing it in her hand. "Take this. The safety is on, but it's fully loaded. Don't be afraid to shoot if you have to."

Accepting it, she turned the small gun over in her hands. The metal felt cool and despite its diminutive size, she figured it would do the job.

"What about you?" she asked. "I don't want to leave you unarmed."

"I'm not. I have two others, though they're quite a bit larger. That one is more of a spare."

"Thank you." Since she didn't have a purse or a backpack, she wasn't sure where to put it. "Do you have a holster or something? It seems dangerous to put this in my pocket."

Looking grim, he rummaged around in his backpack. "Here it is," he said. "This is a leg holster. Your jeans will hide it. Unless they pat you down, they'll never find it."

She held out her hand. "Let me have it. I've got to get going."

Instead of handing it over, he shook his head. "If you've never worn one, I need to show you how. Roll up your jeans."

Without hesitation, she did, staring down at his dark head as he knelt in front of her and strapped on the holster. His fingers were long and elegant and the contrast of his tan skin against her milky whiteness made her feel dizzy.

"There. Let me have the pistol." Once he'd placed the gun in the holster, he latched it into place and pulled her jeans back down. Finally, he stood up, moving back a few paces.

"All right. You're all set to go."

"Thank you. I just want to rescue my daughter," she

told him. "So be ready. Because if I can figure out a way to get her out of there, I'll need you to help us escape."

"I'll be waiting for your call," he said.

"Thank you." Turning to go, she didn't know whether to shake his hand, offer a hug or give him a quick kiss on the cheek. In the end she did none of them. Instead, she lifted her hand in a wave as she headed out the door.

Once outside, she felt exposed and wary. Every instinct on full alert, she forced herself to walk casually, just a regular person out for a stroll. Heading toward the hamburger joint, she had to forcibly restrain herself from constantly looking over her shoulder. She didn't know what she expected—some sort of gangster execution?—but she still didn't trust Jacob Gideon not to end her meddling permanently.

Unless, craving her adoration, he believed he could heal her, too. This was her one advantage, and one she needed to exploit to its fullest.

At the hamburger place, she lingered outside, checking her watch. No matter what happened, she'd soon be with Hailey again. Hailey must be so frightened.

When the black limo pulled up, she got goose bumps. The sight reminded her too much of the initial journey out here, when she'd still believed Jacob Gideon was on her side and only wanted to heal Hailey.

The uniformed driver parked and got out of the car. "Ms. Daphne?" he asked, his formal tone courteous and devoid of inflection. When she answered in the affirmative, he went to the back door and held it open for her.

Heart pounding, she climbed inside. She could do this. She would do this. She could do anything for Hailey's sake. Anything at all.

When they pulled up to the iron gates, she watched as the driver punched in a code for them to open. She didn't understand the whole gated-driveway thing at all. Since the rest of the ranch was not fenced, it didn't make sense, at least from a security standpoint. Maybe it was more about appearance.

As they approached the house, Jacob himself, dressed in jeans and a button-down shirt, came out to greet them. She stared. For the first time since she'd met him, he wasn't surrounded by his usual entourage.

Her chest tightened, but she fought to keep her composure. Everything depended on her convincing this man she truly believed in him and his ability to cure her daughter.

In a split second, she composed her face into a contrite and, hopefully, ashamed expression.

The driver jumped out of the car and hurried to open her door. She pushed herself up as gracefully as possible, and then rushed over to where Jacob stood waiting. For a heartbeat she debated throwing herself into his arms, but at the last minute she couldn't do it.

"I'm so sorry," she managed, choking up. "I don't know what I was thinking." With her emotions so close to the surface, worried she'd never see her daughter again, she began weeping.

"There, there." Putting a fatherly arm around her shoulder, Jacob patted her back. "Everything is going to be all right now that you're back. Little Hailey has been asking about you."

It took every ounce of self-control she possessed not to tense up at the mention of her daughter's name. Clenching her teeth, she nodded. "Thank you so much for giving me a second chance."

He didn't respond. Unwilling to risk letting him see the truth in her eyes, she kept her head down and reduced her crying to a few sniffles. Making a show of wiping her tears, she shuddered. "I'm so exhausted," she said, sagging against him and hoping he'd take the hint.

"I understand," he finally said. "You'll need to get some rest before I allow you to visit with Hailey."

"No," she gasped, snapping her head up before she realized what she was doing. Belatedly, she reschooled her expression into that of a supplicant. "Please let me see her. I've missed her so much."

Stepping back, he stared at her, his expression calculating. "We'll see. She isn't feeling her best. I'll see if her attendants feel she's up to a visitor."

Her heartbeat sped up as fear mingled with rage and churned up her insides. What had he done to her baby girl? She wanted to launch herself at him, using brute force to make him take her to her daughter.

Instead, she lowered her head, as though passively awaiting his decision. She clenched her hands together, hoped he didn't see them trembling. How would she react if he decided not to allow her to see Hailey tonight? Her acting abilities were wearing a bit thin.

"Come with me." Turning, he swept back inside, letting her trail behind him. Two very large men—bodyguards—stepped from the shadows and moved into place alongside him.

This made her want to sneer. Did the great man actually feel so threatened by her, a petite woman with a slender build?

When he led her up the stairs to the same hallway where she'd been before, her heart felt about to explode out of her chest. Finally, at the doorway right before her old room, he stopped and turned to face her.

"We're still repairing the window you broke," he said.

"Please, send me a bill," she told him, her voice purposely wobbling. "I'm very sorry I damaged your property."

Briefly, his expression darkened before he nodded, opening the door. "This is your new room. You will be locked inside until someone comes for you. Do you understand?"

Locked inside. She didn't move. No way was she going in that room without her daughter. "I want…" Swallowing, she remembered that demands had an adverse effect on this man. "Please, may I see my daughter first?"

"I'll let you know," he drawled, clearly relishing her discomfort. "You need a shower and a change of clothes. I can't risk you contaminating her sickroom."

"Sickroom? Hailey isn't susceptible to contamination," she said, her stomach lurching.

"She is now," he told her, gesturing at his two bodyguards. Flanking her, each man gripped her arm and half dragged, half carried her into the room.

Chapter 7

Jacob's words nearly sent Blythe over the edge. Digging her nails into her palms, she struggled not to lose control. Legs weak, fear grabbing her by the throat, she had to fight a compulsion to change into wolf and seize all three men by their throats.

"Wait…" she began, but Jacob had already turned away.

They flung her at the bed. Stumbling, she regained her balance, and rounded on them. Too late. They yanked the door closed. She clearly heard the sound of the door locking behind them. Once again, she was trapped.

She wanted to scream. More than that, she nearly threw herself at the door in frustrated fury. She should have known this would happen. Now she was in exactly the same spot as before.

Except this time she had an ally.

They hadn't searched her. She still had the pistol and the cell. Slowly, she began to pull Lucas's phone from her pocket, and then put it back, just in case there were cameras watching her.

She had to believe there was a chance, however small, that Jacob would relent and take her to see her baby. Hounds help him if he'd harmed even one hair on Hailey's head.

Sitting on the bed, she breathed deeply, striving for calm. To accomplish anything, she needed to stay focused.

Time dragged. Several times, she wanted to phone Lucas, but each time she decided to wait a bit longer. Nothing happened.

Finally, heart heavy, she gave up and called. "I don't think they're going to let me see Hailey."

"I'm not surprised," he said. "It'd be like playing all his cards at one time. He's going to test you, to make sure you're really loyal before he'll let you anywhere near your daughter."

Digesting this, she tried to push away the sickening feeling in her stomach. "When you talk about tests, what do you mean? Because he knows I'm a Shape-shifter. If he believes I'm demonic, too, we know he's going to torture me."

"You've got to hang in there," he said. "Do whatever you have to and try to stay on his good side. That's the only way he's going to let you get anywhere close to Hailey."

A sound from out in the hallway made her jump. "Got to go," she whispered, ending the call and shoving the phone in between the mattress and the box spring. She'd barely sat back up when her door opened. A large man entered, followed by a slender, dark-haired woman wearing glasses. Behind her stood another man, obviously her bodyguards.

"I'm Dr. Silva," she said, her expression cold as she studied Blythe. "Please come with me."

Standing, Blythe stared back. "Are you taking me to see my daughter?"

"Not now." Her thin-lipped attempt at a smile was anything but reassuring. "It's time to run some tests on you."

"Now?" Faking a yawn, Blythe glanced at the clock. "Don't you think this could wait until morning?"

"It cannot." Motioning to the first man, she stepped toward the door. "Bring her along," she said.

Menacingly, he moved toward Blythe, as if he meant to drag or carry her if necessary. "No need," she told him. "I'm going of my own free will. After all, I'll do anything to make Jacob happy." She could only hope her tone sounded sincere. Judging from the sideways look Dr. Silva gave her, she wasn't convinced.

Restless and impatient, Lucas waited for Blythe to phone again. After two hours went by without a call, he debated his next course of action. He couldn't phone her back, because that would risk letting her captors know she had a cell phone.

But damned if he was going to sit around and do nothing but wait while she was in danger.

Cautioning himself to be patient, he considered his next plan of action. Though Blythe had rejected his plan to go in undercover, he had to do something. He couldn't hang around in safety while Blythe had walked straight into danger.

A quick trip to the huge discount store and he had what he needed. A pair of fake eyeglasses, a couple of button-down shirts and khakis, and some dog clippers. He figured he'd give himself a buzz cut, military-style, wear the glasses and dress in the type of clothing he'd never in a million years normally wear.

It was a long shot, but he was betting on the fact that

Jacob Gideon hadn't seen him—at least in his human form—since he'd been fifteen. No way did the thirty-year-old Lucas Kenyon bear any resemblance to the fifteen-year-old Luke Gideon. But just in case—he had to try to remain anonymous as long as possible to have a chance to reach Blythe and her daughter.

A short time later, he rubbed the top of his nearly non-existent hair and grimaced. Dressing in the starchy cotton shirt, he took care to button it up nearly to his neck.

The pressed khaki pants looked cheap, but were in keeping with the type of persona he wanted to project—a man who fit in with Jacob Gideon's followers. Perching the wire-rimmed glasses on his nose, he peered in the mirror with satisfaction. Perfect.

Jacob might believe his son was around since he'd seen the wolf accompanying Blythe, but he couldn't be certain. Fifteen-year-old Luke had favored black leather and torn jeans. Not in a million years would Jacob imagine the rebel boy would look like one of his own.

Now Lucas had to manage to convince one of Jacob's acolytes that he wanted to join the church—full time. He had to get them to let him live at Sanctuary. Or get a job there, somehow. Not only would he have a better chance to gain access to Blythe, but he could find out where Jacob kept Hailey. And where the inhabitants of Sanctuary disappeared to on occasion.

Gaining access to Sanctuary proved easier than he'd hoped. Since most of the locals were either church members or in Jacob's pocket, looking for followers, it wasn't too difficult to offer himself as a prime convert.

Lucas left his truck parked in front of the motel, crammed a baseball cap down on his nearly-naked head and headed outside. Since it was too late for breakfast or even lunch, he chose Suds, the town's only bar. From what he could remember, Jacob had often sent people there to troll for converts. The reasoning seemed obvious—desperate people driven to drink by life's myriad problems would be eager for a solution, especially one as simple as that offered by Jacob Gideon and his church.

Since it was still early, there were only two other people at the bar—both men. Nodding cordially at the bartender, he chose a bar stool in the middle and ordered a beer. Once the bartender brought it, Lucas took a sip and rounded his shoulders, staring morosely at the bottle as though deep in the grip of a profound depression.

The bartender, a young man with long hair and multiple tattoos, barely glanced at him. But the man on Lucas's left got up and came to sit next to him.

"Hey," the man said.

Lucas dipped his chin in greeting and took another swig of his beer.

"Rough day?" the other man asked in a sympathetic voice.

Lucas simply nodded. The other man left him alone for a few minutes, during which Lucas continued to stare morosely at his beer as though deep in thought.

"Are you new in town?" the man finally asked.

Lucas allowed himself a grim nod. "I drove out from Dallas. I'd heard there might be a job here for me." He shrugged. "The job didn't pan out."

"Sorry to hear that." The other man leaned closer and held out his hand. "Mike Fletcher."

"Larry Canyon." Lucas had given a lot of thought to his name. He wanted it to be close enough to reality so he wouldn't forget it, but not so much that it gave him away.

They talked for a few minutes, ordinary small talk two strangers might make in a bar. Through it all, Lucas was careful to keep his shoulders rounded in a defeated slump.

He hoped to convey a man one step away from the end of his rope.

Occasionally, he took a slow pull of his beer, savoring it as though it might be the only one he could afford.

Finally, dragging his hand across his chin, Lucas peered up at Mike. "Do you know of any work here in town?" he asked, putting just the right amount of doubtful hope into his voice.

"What do you do?" Mike seemed genuinely interested, scooting his bar stool a bit too close. Before Lucas could answer, Mike held up his hand, motioning the bartender over. "Another round," he said. "On me."

Lucas squinted at the other man, and kept his mouth shut. Was Mike a nice guy? Or a member of Jacob's brainwashed congregation?

Lucas suspected the latter. "Thanks, man."

Mike took a long drink of his beer. "Everyone can use a friend," he said. "And as a matter of fact, I might know of a job for you. Have you ever heard of a place called Sanctuary?"

Careful to keep his face expressionless, Lucas feigned a look of puzzlement. "I don't think so."

Mike started to explain. "I work security there. The church could always use a good guard. You look like you could do that kind of work," Mike continued. "What are you, six-two?"

"Six-four." Lucas pretended to consider the offer. Even after all these years, he still could spot Jacob's people. "Any idea what they pay?"

"It varies on previous experience," Mike said. "Have you ever done security work?"

Making a quick decision, Lucas nodded. "Once, a few years back. Some fellas were running an illegal gambling operation in Dallas, and I worked security there for a few years. But I can't give them as a reference. It was all under the table."

Mike appeared suitably impressed. "That's probably enough. All we have to do over there at Sanctuary is guard the faithful. It's easy work. Boring, too, but I think you'd be a good fit."

"I'd like to apply," Lucas said.

Matt nodded. "Sure. I can give you the number of my supervisor, Kane. You can call him."

No way in hell was Lucas letting him leave. Not now, not when he was so close. "How about you take me there to meet him?"

Mike cocked his head as if considering. "I guess I can do that," he said, slurring his words.

When they finally got up to leave, Lucas took one look at the other man's unsteady gait and realized Mike had apparently had quite a bit to drink before Lucas arrived. "I'll drive," he said, holding out his hand for the keys. He expected a protest, but after a moment, Mike just nodded and handed them over.

"You're probably right." He smiled a big, goofy grin. "I might have had a few beers too many."

With Mike drunkenly directing, Lucas drove. They pulled up in front of a neat brick home.

"Your boss lives here?" he asked. "I thought everyone who's part of that big church lives there."

"Nah, not everyone." Mike smiled blearily. "Sanctuary is pretty crowded already."

Not wanting to act too interested, Lucas didn't question him. He parked the car, pocketed the keys, and went around to the passenger side to help Mike get out.

But once Lucas yanked open the car door, Mike waved him away. "I'm okay," he said, grinning. He climbed out of the car, but as he took a step, he stumbled.

Luckily, he righted himself.

Shaking his head, Lucas cursed under his breath. If he hadn't been so desperate, he never would have pushed this. Who knew what this man Kane would think, answering his doorbell to find one of his employees drunk on his doorstep, accompanied by a stranger seeking work.

Since he had no choice, Lucas accompanied Mike up the sidewalk and rang the bell.

A dog began barking inside the house.

"That's Duke," Mike said happily. "He's a good dog. Part wolf, I think."

Though Lucas nodded, he was skeptical. A lot of people claimed to have wolf hybrids, but he'd never actually seen one. As far as he could tell, the two species didn't mate. Or if they had, he'd never met one of their offspring. And he was in a position to know.

Inside, a man's voice rumbled, admonishing his pet to be quiet. A second or two later, the door swung open and Lucas stared, shocked.

Because the man standing inside the threshold had a visible aura, which could mean only one thing. Kane, who was head of security for Jacob Gideon, was also a Shapeshifter.

Anticipating some kind of torture chamber, the pristine cleanliness of the modern laboratory surprised Blythe.

"Please sit," Dr. Silva said, fiddling with one of the machines. "Have you ever taken a polygraph before?"

This surprised her. "A lie detector test? No, I haven't."

"All right then. I'll explain how this works."

Blythe held up her hand. "I get it. But can I ask you why?"

Regarding her dispassionately, the other woman frowned. "Dr. Gideon's orders."

This was the first time Blythe had heard the man referred to this way. All of the research she'd done had focused on the size of his congregation and his purportedly amazing healing abilities. "I wasn't aware he was a doctor," she said. "What kind of doctor is he?"

For the first time since she'd made her appearance, Dr. Silva smiled. "He has his doctorate in theology from Southwestern Baptist Theological Seminary in Fort Worth. Not only is he a man of God, but a very well-educated one at that."

Blythe decided it was probably better not to respond. She didn't want to take a chance of ruffling any feathers.

"Please take a seat."

Blythe sat. Careful to keep her face blank, she didn't move as the other woman set electrodes and calibrated the machine. Inside, Blythe was a mess, all jangled nerves and erratic heartbeat. She remembered reading about a way to beat this machine, but it involved a form of self-hypnosis. The key was to believe everything you said was the truth.

She wasn't sure she could do this, but she sure as heck was going to try.

They ran through the baseline questions—simple things like her name and her age, her height and weight. When these were finished and Dr. Silva had made a few more subtle adjustments to the machine, the real queries started in earnest.

At first, these seemed innocuous. "How many children do you have?"

"One." With an effort, she kept herself from sighing.

"What is her name?"

"Hailey?"

And then, "Is she a demon?"

Blythe's heart skipped a beat. "Oh, goodness, no."

"A werewolf, then?"

The hated term made her frown. "No."

"You're lying," Dr. Silva admonished her sternly. "Look at the machine. The line is all over the place."

"I'm not lying," Blythe protested. "I'm wondering what kind of insane questions you're asking me. My little girl is sick. Jacob Gideon—Dr. Gideon—is trying to help her. Why on earth would anyone accuse her of being a were-wolf?"

Her outraged indignation worked. The other woman recoiled at the tone of Blythe's voice. It was clear she'd only been told what exactly to ask, not the reasoning be-hind the questions.

"I'm sorry." A slightly embarrassed smile played over her thin lips. "I was given a list of questions. I have no idea why that one is on there."

As she read the next question, her frown deepened. "This is ridiculous," she finally said. "But I was hired to do as Dr. Gideon wishes. So I'm going to continue with what I have."

Blythe gave her a rueful smile to show she under-stood. At least now she'd made a small connection with this woman. It might come in handy if Jacob tried to do anything worse to her.

Sitting up straight, she took a deep breath and prepared to lie with a straight face and calm demeanor. Hopefully, without getting caught.

Nothing in Kane's expression revealed he'd noticed Lu-cas's aura, though Lucas knew he had. That was one thing he'd learned early on—how Shifters were able to identify each other from their auras, a subtle glow of color sur-rounding them.

Mike pushed his way in front of Lucas, swaying slightly

as he peered up at his boss, slurring his words as he rambled about the reason for their visit tonight.

For a moment, Lucas wasn't sure the other Shifter would let them inside. Though not outwardly hostile, he had an air of wariness around him that was almost palpable. Finally, shaking his head as though he doubted the wisdom of his decision, he stepped back and invited them in.

Mike staggered over to an overstuffed chair, plopped down and immediately passed out. The entire situation felt extremely awkward, but Lucas couldn't afford to pass up any chance that might gain him entrance into Sanctuary.

Quietly, he explained his situation. He'd come to town hoping to find a job in what he called "computer security," but the lead had turned out to be bogus. So when Mike had mentioned there might be an opening at a church for the other kind of security, he'd jumped at the chance.

"You do realize he's drunk," Kane asked, casting a disparaging glance at Mike, who'd begun to snore softly.

"I know." Lucas summoned up an apologetic smile. "But on the off chance that he wasn't full of crap…"

Now Kane smiled. "Let me get you an application."

After Lucas had filled it out, using the name Larry Canyon, Kane took it and disappeared into a back room. Lucas waited, hoping he appeared patient, though inside he was a jangling mess. More than anything, he'd wanted to jump Kane, pin him to the ground and demand the other Shifter tell him what the hell he was doing working for a man like Jacob Gideon.

Of course, there was always the possibility that Kane didn't know about Hailey.

While Kane did whatever in the back room, Lucas worked on trying to remain calm. If the other man returned with a refusal, Lucas would have no choice but to accept it. Getting in would be easier if he was working for

Kane, but if he had to, he'd find another way. No matter what, he'd find Blythe and Hailey.

They'd be running a background check. Never a problem for him. Due to the kind of life he'd lived, he'd long ago set up two completely different identities. The name he'd given, along with the fictional driver's license and social security number, would reveal completely false information. It would make him appear to be an utterly brilliant, but completely unmotivated, computer hacker. And while it was true he knew his way around computer code, he was nowhere near the level his fake resume claimed.

It also said during college, he'd worked as a bouncer at a few bars around LSU. Perfect for a wannabe security guard.

After letting him cool his heels for a good thirty minutes in the living room with his snoring employee, Kane finally returned. Smiling, the first bit of sincerity he'd shown since they'd arrived, he nodded at Lucas. He carried a manila folder, inside which no doubt, were computer printouts of Lucas's false identity.

"Larry, you're hired," Kane said. "When can you start?"

Though once again he had to stifle the urge to ask the other man how he, as a Shape-shifter, could work for a man who regarded their kind as evil demons, Lucas did not. For all he knew, Kane could be working undercover for the Pack or some such thing. After all, if he were truly a traitor to his own kind, he would have exposed Lucas as a Shifter immediately. The fact that he did not gave Lucas hope. After all, he figured he could use all the help he could get.

He waited for some signal, some sign that Kane knew his true nature, but nothing came.

They discussed salary and hours and then Lucas agreed he would begin work in the morning.

"Be back here at six," Kane said as he walked Lucas toward the door, stopping to try to wake up a sleeping Mike, unsuccessfully. "You'll have to leave him here to sleep it off. You can return his car when you report to work in the morning and someone will give you a ride home."

If things went as Lucas planned, he wouldn't be leaving.

After a restless night of fitful dozing, during which Blythe did not call no matter how many times he rolled over and checked his cell, Lucas rose at four-thirty and showered. He stopped at the local Waffle House for an early breakfast. The only customers there at five-fifteen in the morning were construction workers and road crews. The lone woman in the place, besides the waitresses, was a police officer, who must have had the early shift.

She eyed him with open curiosity the moment he sat down. He made eye contact just once, smiled a quick and friendly smile, and drank his coffee while he waited for his food to arrive.

He also listened to the myriad of conversations around him, waiting for the mention of Blythe's or Hailey's name in the swirl of voices. The two men in the booth across the way obviously also worked security at Sanctuary. Apparently the job was mostly boring, as nothing much ever happened there.

"Bunch of religious nuts ain't gonna try anything," one man said, his lip curling. "All they do is drift around there like ghosts."

Lucas hid his frown. From the sound of it, these men—Jacob's own security force—had no idea that a woman and a child were being held as prisoners there. How was that even possible? Maybe Jacob had his own, handpicked inner circle.

When his eggs and waffles and sausage arrived, Lucas

dug in. Finished, he got his check, tossed a few dollars on the table for a tip, paid and left.

Both of the men stared hard at him, as though he'd done something wrong.

"Good morning," he said, making the effort to be social only because he knew these two would be his coworkers.

One guy dipped his chin in a silent hello while the other guy only stared. They were both human, unlike Kane, who hadn't volunteered any personal information. Nor had he asked any beyond the fake background Lucas had provided.

Outside again, Lucas waited with an eye on the other security guards, to see if he'd somehow betrayed himself. Though as far as he could tell, he'd done nothing to alert them, he'd gotten the sense that they'd fixated on him as a target. Or, as his Shape-shifter half would think, like prey.

The sun had not yet begun to lighten the sky as he stepped outside. He'd walked to Mike's car and put the key in the door when he heard them. They'd exited the Waffle House and were heading toward him.

They could have simply been parked nearby, but Lucas didn't think so. He'd learned to trust his instincts, so he bent over as though he'd dropped his keys and retrieved his pistol from his leg harness.

When he came back up and turned, gun in hand, they were only a few feet away.

Keeping his weapon hidden, he faced them. "Can I help you?"

They stopped. One seemed uncertain. The other moved into an aggressive stance—legs spread apart, chest puffed out, chin thrust forward. He reminded Lucas of a posturing rooster.

"That's Mike's truck," Rooster man said. "What are you doing with it and where's Mike?"

Ah, now he understood. At least they looked out for one another. Quickly, he explained what had happened.

"Mike took you to see Kane?" The two men exchanged a look, which Lucas could only interpret as surprised.

"Yep. And he hired me. In fact," Lucas made a big show out of checking his watch. "I need to be going. Don't want to be late for my first day on the job."

Neither man moved.

With a sigh, Lucas made sure Rooster got a look at his pistol. The instant he did, the other man moved back, both hands up in front of him. "Hey, we don't want no trouble, man."

Lucas nodded pleasantly. He got in the vehicle and, with them still standing there staring, started the car and drove away.

Close call. Had they somehow sensed he was a Shifter, or had their clear suspicion of him been simply because he was driving Mike's truck? For now, Lucas realized he couldn't say anything to Kane. No doubt the other man had his own reasons for keeping silent about his identity. It was, Lucas reflected, a good thing the humans couldn't see auras the way Shifters could.

Apparently the security team due to go on duty at the compound all met at Kane's house. Parking their various vehicles in the street, they rode out to Sanctuary in a white panel van with no windows. The interior had been redone and, instead of bench seating, it had been arranged with one large U-shaped bench seat, against the sides and front, similar to military or prison transport.

Climbing inside, Lucas took a seat near the front, hoping he'd hear any conversation between the driver and the front seat passenger.

The two men from the Waffle House were there. Though they eyed Lucas with unconcealed hostility, they didn't speak. In fact, inside the van there was none of the easy camaraderie Lucas would have expected from a team that had worked together for some time.

Why would Sanctuary be different? While the pay wasn't great, it wasn't horrible, either. From what he'd overheard from the other two earlier, the job was routine, bordering on boring. Was that it? A lack of danger, of excitement? Maybe he'd be able to rectify that soon.

Either that, or this group of men wasn't in Jacob's inner circle.

Mentally shrugging, he settled back in his seat, alert but pretending not to be.

Kane rode shotgun. A guy named Les, another bodyguard judging from his muscular build, drove. Like the men in the back, neither of the two in front spoke.

As they coasted to a stop, Lucas tried to twist around to see. Though the sky had begun to lighten, he couldn't see much. He figured they'd stopped outside the front gate at Sanctuary.

Chapter 8

The rest of the polygraph test was comprised of a mix of questions, from ordinary to completely bizarre. Blythe did her best to answer without inflection, though she wasn't as skilled at controlling her respiration and heartbeat as she would have liked.

For the remainder of the session, Dr. Silva stayed expressionless, once again the controlled, icy woman she'd first appeared to be. Actually Blythe didn't mind; she took her cue from the other woman's actions. She thought she'd done a pretty good job.

Of course, she didn't know for sure since Dr. Silva didn't comment on the results.

Instead, the two goons appeared to lead her back to her room.

"Get some rest," Dr. Silva told her. "There will be more tests later."

Blythe nodded. At this point, she knew better than to

inquire about those. Instead, she asked the only question that mattered. "When will I see my daughter?"

The other woman's dark gaze remained steady, but emotionless. "I don't know, Ms. Daphne. I honestly don't know."

Clenching her jaw, Blythe forced herself to nod. Again, she had to fight the compulsion to shift into wolf and start kicking some ass.

As her guards led her down the hall, Blythe kept her eyes open for the slightest hint of her little girl. At one point, she considered calling out Hailey's name on the off chance she would respond, but thought better of it.

After returning to her room, Blythe listened to the click as they locked the door. Suddenly utterly and completely weary, she went to her mattress to retrieve the cell phone so she could call Lucas and let him know what was happening.

But when she dug under the mattress at the spot where she'd hidden it, the phone wasn't there.

Frantic, she lifted the entire left side, then the right and the bottom. Nothing. Obviously, someone had discovered her hiding place and taken away her only means of contacting someone outside Sanctuary.

She dropped onto the bed, her shoulders slumped, temporarily defeated. Inside, her wolf stirred, reminding her of her inner strength. Failure wasn't even an option.

Too exhausted even to shower, she curled up into a ball and tried to sleep. She had no idea when the next round of tests would come, but they would get her out of this room and maybe closer to her daughter, so she'd welcome them.

She must have fallen asleep. The next thing she knew, a sharp rapping on her door woke her.

Groggy, she sat up and dragged her fingers through her

hair. What she'd give for a rubber band. As she stood, the room spun. She was dizzy. And her arm ached.

Glancing down at herself, she was stunned to find a large bandage around the crook of her arm. What the... She lifted one corner of the bandage and saw a large black-and-blue mark and a puncture wound. Had she been given a shot of some kind? When had this happened?

Abruptly, her door opened. Another bodyguard walked in, followed by Dr. Silva. As Blythe blinked up at the other woman, the second bodyguard came into focus. Arms crossed, he stared directly at her.

Her heart skipped a beat as she recognized who the man with the close-cropped hair and wire-rimmed eyeglasses actually was. Lucas, in one of the worst disguises she'd ever seen, had gotten in.

As their gazes connected, she blinked and looked down, hoping when she raised her head, she'd be hiding her feelings. She couldn't let them know that adrenaline was pumping through her blood like a white-hot jolt of electricity.

He'd gotten in. And he'd clearly taken a job with Jacob Gideon's security force, which gave him the freedom to move around the grounds and building. They could prevail.

While she stood quietly, trying to keep herself still, her inner wolf, energized by her rioting emotions, became a predator preparing to leap out and rip apart its prey. She sensed Lucas's beast responding in kind.

Blythe's heart skipped a beat as she tried to clamp down on her dual nature. The doctor and her machine mustn't know. Somehow, for Hailey's sake, she had to fool them all. She had to appear normal. She had to be strong, no matter what they did to her.

Dr. Silva glanced at her, brows raised.

"Is this going to be painful?" Blythe asked, making her

eyes wide and her voice tremble. Actually, she didn't have to fake the last. Her fierce resolve drove her, and in her determination to endure whatever they might dish out for her daughter's sake, she found a deeper well of strength than she ever would have guessed she possessed.

"Maybe a little," the doctor allowed. "Do you want something to help ease the pain?"

Blythe shook her head no, wincing as the motion made her surroundings appear to move. "I'll be all right." Raising her chin, she stared at the wall and braced herself for whatever was to come.

Eyeing a semi-lucid Blythe, Lucas's first thought was guilt. He reminded himself that he hadn't failed her, at least not yet. He kept his face impassive to mask his concern. What had they done to her? One of her arms sported a huge bandage and she gave every appearance of being drugged.

Every instinct screamed at him to move forward and yank her out of the room into his arms, pulling her close and shielding her with his body as he rounded on the female doctor and demanded answers.

Of course, he could not commit public suicide for both of them, so he stood stock-still and looked down, allowing his senses to absorb every sight, smell, emotion—looking for Hailey, and trying to get a feel for Blythe's well-being.

Meanwhile, a slow rage built inside of him. Mingled with his guilt was a fury he had to suppress.

His wolf had other ideas. The beast snapped his powerful incisors, attempting to surge forth and force the change from human to wolf. Lucas pushed his other self back down into the dark recesses of his psyche. There would be time later. Now, he had to play nice until the right opportunity came along.

It had better be soon, he thought, clenching his jaw so hard his teeth ached.

"It's time for more tests," the doctor, whose name he hadn't gotten, announced.

Swaying on her feet, Blythe nodded.

"I need some assistance here," the doctor barked. "Each of you take one of her arms and help me get her to the lab."

Immediately, Lucas and his coworker, a grim-faced man named Stan, moved to flank Blythe. She didn't resist as they each took her by the arm and half carried, half forced her toward the doorway.

If not for the startled glint of recognition that had flashed into her green eyes, Lucas would have wondered if she'd even recognized him.

Down the hallway they went, toward an elevator. The doctor pressed the button, tapping her toe soundlessly on the carpeted floor as they waited.

Finally, a soft ping sounded and the doors glided open. Moving in unison, Lucas and Stan lifted Blythe into the elevator. The doors closed as the doctor punched a button marked with only an L.

And then they began to move. Down. Past the ground floor and still they kept going. Which made no sense, as Lucas knew from personal experience that Sanctuary did not have a finished basement. All that had been on the lowest level were two large, unfinished rooms, with concrete floors and walls. Back then, the basement had been a dark, dreary place, and where Jacob had often sent Lucas and Lilly as punishment.

Apparently now the basement was used for much, much more. At least that explained where everyone in Sanctuary had disappeared to.

After what seemed like an eternity, the elevator came to a stop. As the doors opened, Lucas dealt with another wave of guilt. He tried not to appear too curious or concerned. Given the way he'd spent the past fifteen years, acting like he didn't give a damn should have been second nature to him. It terrified him that it wasn't.

Gripping Blythe's arm as lightly as he dared and hoping he wasn't accidentally hurting her, he stepped out, following the doctor. Together, he and Stan herded Blythe down the hall. She glided along without looking left or right, her expression blank and unfocused. She'd definitely been drugged.

As they neared a door marked Laboratory, he realized this was a facet of his plan that he hadn't completely thought through. How in the hell could he simply stand by and pretend not to care while they tortured Blythe?

As the doctor opened the door, Blythe coughed softly, making him look. As their gazes connected, a stern expression of warning shone through the grogginess. Then, for just a second, he swore he heard her voice inside his head.

"Don't give yourself away. Hailey matters here. Not me."

Dumbfounded, he jerked his chin in a nod and looked away.

"Gentlemen," the doctor barked. "Do try to keep up."

They were on the move again. Into the laboratory.

As they pushed through the double doors, the first thing that hit him was the odor—strong antiseptic mingled with what smelled like human sweat and chemicals. Through it all, he detected a lingering scent of urine, the same sort of thing he'd gotten when he'd worked in a nursing home in his late teens.

What the hell were they doing here?

Looking around, he saw no other victims, just white-coated lab technicians. And of course, he and Stan and

Blythe and the doctor who clearly ignored her Hippocratic oath to do Jacob Gideon's bidding.

Every nerve jangling, again he glanced at Blythe, striving for casual. She blinked, silently demanding to know if he'd gotten the message.

He gave a slight nod. How on earth she'd managed to communicate to him telepathically was a feat she'd have to explain later. Right now he'd have to work on controlling himself, especially if this lady doctor started hurting Blythe. He honestly didn't know how he'd react.

Think of Hailey. He took a deep breath, reminding himself why they both were here. Saving a little girl trumped enduring anything Jacob Gideon could do to either of them.

Lilly's death had sat like a lead balloon on his conscience for fifteen years. Damned if he'd let any other child come to harm.

His resolve hardened him. No matter what happened now, he'd remember the ultimate goal.

After they released her, and Blythe had folded bonelessly into the chair that the doctor indicated, one of the technicians pressed a button and hand and leg cuffs clicked into place. Once Blythe was strapped in, she didn't struggle.

"You two may leave," the doctor said coolly. "The door will automatically lock behind you. I'll send word when I need you again."

Lucas met Blythe's gaze. Though she revealed nothing on the exterior, her relief and worry flashed in his mind. This time, he didn't react to the intrusion. He got what she was feeling, because he felt exactly the same. Relieved that he wouldn't have to stand by and do nothing while experiments were run on her and worried because he wouldn't know exactly what they were doing to her. Plus enraged, because he had absolutely no control.

Since he had no choice, he turned. Following the other guard's lead, Lucas went to the door. Once outside, he looked at the other man. "So what are we supposed to do now? Guard the door? Or can we return to the room I was told is the break room-slash-command post?"

His companion glanced at his watch and grimaced. "We have to hang around so we can be here the instant she needs us. But I'll tell you this. After they start doing that kind of testing on them, sometimes it's hours before they call you back."

"What kind of testing is that?" Lucas asked, trying to sound as though he didn't really care about the answer.

"I don't know." The other man removed a cigarette from a pack in his shirt pocket, rolling it between his fingers. "They hook them up to machines is what I think. Sometimes I can hear the screams—gives me the creeps."

Lucas didn't have to fake his shudder. The pain of leaving Blythe back there as specific images of his own torture at his father's hands had him wanting to punch something. "What about the legality of this stuff? Do they just assume guys like us won't care?"

"You'd better not care." The other guard's gaze sharpened. "If you want to keep your job, you'll keep your mouth shut." Glancing around, he leaned in closer and lowered his voice. "I heard some guy once tried to go to the police. He disappeared, and no one ever heard from him again."

Lucas jerked his chin in acknowledgment of the subtle threat. "Gotcha." He swallowed hard. "So what are we supposed to do until the doctor calls us again?" With free time, he might be able to find out where they were keeping Hailey.

Again he thought of Blythe, but forced his thoughts

away. He needed to be strong like her and keep his focus on what mattered—Hailey.

This time, when the familiar guilt threatened to envelop him, he was able to resist. Maybe rescuing this child would help him pay back for being unable to save Lilly.

The other guard eyed him. "Are you okay?" he asked, his tone indifferent.

Lucas nodded. "Yeah. Just trying to decide if I have time to grab something to eat."

"Better not. Like I said, it's best to stick around. You never know when something might go wrong and they need you."

Cocking his head, Lucas pretended to consider. "Something goes wrong? What do you mean?"

The other man looked away. "Well…when they start screaming…once in a while, the doctor can't resuscitate them."

Them? How often was Jacob performing this type of testing? And on who? Horrified, Lucas stared. "Are you saying she can *die* in there?" Shades of the past flashed back, haunting him. His sister's lifeless body lying on the floor, him trying to reach her. They'd dragged him away and he'd never gotten the chance to touch Lilly one last time.

"It happens."

"More than once?" Lucas pressed. "How many people go through there?"

"I've seen a few. Hey, I'm sure they're all sick to begin with," his companion said defensively. "This is probably their last hope. I mean, why else would they sign up for the free drug trial?"

Drug trial? Was that what Jacob was telling his employees? Lucas guessed that only Jacob and his doctors knew the truth.

"Well, I don't know about you, but I'm starving," Lucas said, aware the other man would find his self-centered desire for food both familiar and a relief.

"I could eat." His companion glanced at his watch, clearly debating. "Eh, what the hell. We'll just have to be really quick. They usually bring in sandwiches around lunchtime. Let's head on up to the break room and see if they're here yet."

Several other men had already gathered in the small break room, clustered around a short, Hispanic man pushing a tray full of wrapped sandwiches and canned soft drinks.

A few others greeted them. Lucas ignored them, pretending to focus on the food. He snatched the closest sandwich off the tray, along with a can of cola, and retreated out into the hallway. Unwrapping it, he shoved a quarter of it into his mouth, barely chewing. To anyone watching, whether on a security camera or in person, it would appear that he hadn't eaten for days.

In reality, he had better things to do with his time.

The instant he'd finished the sandwich, he drained the cola and tossed the wrapping and the can into the trash bucket near the door. All the others were either eating or bickering over the selections. No one seemed to notice when he slipped away from the break room and down the hall toward the elevator.

If stopped, he had two possible scenarios. He could say he was looking for the bathroom, or—and this one sounded better—he'd been afraid to leave his post for too long.

He made it to the elevator without being accosted. Pressing the button to go to the lowest level, he desperately tried to think of a plan.

Since he already knew where the lab—and Blythe—

were, he needed to explore the rest of this level. If Hailey were here, he would find her.

And then…what? As the elevator coasted to a stop and the doors slid open, he figured he'd have to wing it.

Blythe had no memory of what happened after she started screaming. She remembered a mask coming down over her face, and the next thing she knew, she was back in her room, lying on the bed.

Without Hailey.

Pushing herself up on her elbows, she blinked and tried to stop the room from spinning. Her head pounded and her mouth tasted as if it was full of ashes.

But she'd survived.

Still, what had they done to her? If these tests continued this way, she'd be far too weak to save her little girl.

Then she remembered Lucas was here, and the tightness in her chest eased.

As she stretched, trying to get rid of the pins and needles in her hands, she realized she needed to make a plan to find her daughter. If she didn't, they'd both likely end up dead.

But with her head muzzy, she couldn't think. Weak, exhausted, she abandoned the attempt to figure out a plan of action. Whoever had taken her phone had stolen her only link to Lucas.

She must have dozed off, because when her door opened with a clatter, it took her by surprise. Rubbing at her eyes, she tried to sit up. A burly bodyguard entered, taking up position between her and the door.

Dr. Silva bustled in immediately after.

"More tests?" Blythe asked, her voice barely a whisper.

"Not yet." This time the other woman smiled, which so

transformed her face that Blythe could only stare. "I came here to give you your reward for doing so well earlier."

Reward? Expecting some kind of medication, Blythe waited. She wasn't sure she wanted to take it, especially since she wouldn't put it past them to drug her and knock her out so she'd be less trouble.

"Aren't you even curious?" the doctor asked, her smile broadening.

Blythe licked her dry lips, struggled to focus. "Did you bring me water? Or something to eat?"

"No," Dr. Silva said and waved her hand. "You have all that in the mini fridge in your room. This is something you claim to have wanted, so Jacob is allowing it, this one time. Maybe more, if you continue to cooperate."

Blythe blinked. "All I want is my baby girl."

At her words, the doctor's smile broadened.

Blythe's heart began to pound. Surely they wouldn't be allowing her to see Hailey, would they?

Something must have shown in her expression. Dr. Silva chuckled. "You see, we are not all bad. Everything we do here is for the greater good."

Blythe barely allowed the words to penetrate. No way in hell was she taking a chance of screwing this up. She focused on the doorway, every fiber of her being praying that Hailey would walk into the room. And into her arms.

"Go ahead," Dr. Silva ordered, speaking into a walkie-talkie. "Bring her in."

Her. Blythe could hardly breathe. Wishing, hoping…

Instead of Hailey walking, a second man came in, carrying the five-year-old's limp form. Hailey was clearly unconscious.

Inside, Blythe's wolf roared with rage. Externally, Blythe trembled, aching to reach out for her child, longing to gather her close. Afraid if she did so they'd cruelly snatch her away, she held herself as still as a statue.

After glancing at Dr. Silva and then Blythe, the guard unceremoniously deposited Hailey on the bed.

Unable to help herself, Blythe began weeping. "What have you done to her?" she asked. "Please, Dr. Silva. Do something, anything, to help her."

Instead, Dr. Silva shrugged. "She has had similar tests to you. Though she was not as well behaved, so we had to drug her. We might have given her a bit too much."

Horrified, Blythe sucked in her breath at the doctor's callous admission. "Is she...will she be all right?"

"Probably." Moving toward the doorway, the other woman looked dispassionately at the unconscious child. "I'll leave you now."

Already focusing on smoothing back Hailey's hair from her limp little face, Blythe nodded. "Thank you," she managed, though everything inside her wanted to rage rather than placate.

"Don't get too comfortable," Dr. Silva said, sounding almost normal. "The guards will be posted right outside your door."

Blythe glanced at the two men, wishing desperately that one of them had been Lucas. As she did, she realized the one closest to the doorway had a visible aura, which made him unmistakably Pack.

How was that possible?

As she opened her mouth and then closed it, the man gave a nearly imperceptible shake of his head. *Pack, inside Sanctuary.* Traitor or ally? What could it mean? Did Lucas know?

"You have one hour," the other guard said, before signaling to his companion. "Then we'll be back to collect her."

Hailey moaned, and Blythe gathered her close, her heart aching. She'd give anything, do anything, to protect her child from being hurt.

"Do you understand? One hour."

Though she barely heard him, she managed a nod as she frantically inspected her daughter. The scarlet, irritated skin around her wrists and ankles made her see red. Not only had Hailey's hands and feet been bound, but she'd struggled against her bonds, hard enough to rub her skin raw.

Blythe cursed. Damn Jacob. Damn Sanctuary. She had to get Hailey out of here. Immediately. Right now. But how?

Think. She needed to clear her head and think. One hour. She had one freaking hour. Frantic, Blythe made an attempt to rouse her baby girl. "Hailey, wake up. Mommy's here, sweetheart."

But when her daughter didn't react, Blythe realized whatever they'd used to drug her was too strong. She cursed the missing cell phone, then took a deep breath. She needed to contact Lucas and let him know what had happened. Hopefully they had an ally in the other Shifter who wore the guard's uniform. Lucas would know what to do. She wondered if he was still inside Sanctuary. If he was, how could she contact him, especially since they'd locked her in her room? But Lucas was her only hope. She'd just have to bet he could figure out a way to get them out of here.

Chapter 9

An exploration of one side of the basement—the part he had access to—revealed nothing. More doors, some locked, others not. All of the rooms appeared to be laboratories, though they were all empty. He saw no sign of Hailey, so he had to believe the child was being kept locked in her room, just as Blythe had been. Conceding defeat—for now—he returned to stand outside the still-closed laboratory door. His earlier companion hadn't made it back yet.

Though Lucas kept his walkie-talkie clipped to his belt, no one called him to assist moving Blythe. He wondered what they were doing to her in there, pushing away his jumbled emotions, hating the way he felt so damn powerless.

Kane found him there after what felt like hours.

When the other man—Shifter—appeared, Lucas didn't do anything more than nod a greeting. He wasn't sure what exactly Kane was doing here. Was he working undercover for the Pack or had he simply betrayed his own kind for money?

"The van's parked out front. You can go home now," Kane said, jerking his thumb toward the elevator. As Lucas pushed off from the wall to do exactly that, Kane stopped him.

Leaning in close, he spoke under his breath. "I know why you're here. We need your help. I've got your cell number, so I'll be calling you later."

Raising his voice, Kane inclined his head. "I'm driving the van back out in ten minutes. Be there or get left behind." Then, with one final hard look at Lucas, the other man walked away.

Immediately, Lucas's heart rate kicked into overtime. They had an ally. Maybe, just maybe, the odds were now tipped toward their favor. Wishing he could tell Blythe, he hurried to the elevator, rode it to the surface and strolled casually.

Luckily, all of the men he'd ridden to work with had gotten off at the same time. They all piled back into the van, joking and laughing, talking about getting a beer together before heading home.

Lucas stayed silent, aware he didn't have transportation home from Kane's house. Since he'd driven Mike Fletcher's car to Kane's, he had no way of getting home. He'd have to bum a ride.

But if things went right, he'd be getting Blythe and Hailey out soon.

Even the thought of what could have been happening to Blythe inside the laboratory made Lucas sweat. Dr. Silva worked under instructions from Sanctuary's leader. Jacob was the worst kind of fanatic—he honestly believed wholeheartedly in everything he did. More than once he'd explained to Lucas that a little pain and suffering was nothing if the proper results were achieved in the end. What exactly those results were, Jacob had never revealed.

Regardless, Lucas had reason to know Jacob enjoyed inflicting the suffering more than any so-called cure he could ever claim.

He was glad Kane was going to help them. The sooner, the better. He hated—no, he *despised*—feeling helpless, powerless to do anything other than sit and wait. At least he wouldn't have to stand around and twiddle his thumbs, forced to watch while Dr. Silva tortured Blythe.

Memories of what he'd gone through—and what had happened to his sister—still burned inside him. Finally, the time had come to exact his vengeance and make Jacob pay for what he'd done to Lilly.

Later. First, stopping Jacob from hurting Blythe—and her little girl, Hailey—was all that mattered. Only after they were safe would he go back and make sure Jacob never hurt anyone again.

When they reached Kane's house, Mike surprised Lucas by offering to drive him home. "It's the least I can do, considering how you helped me out last night."

They made small talk on the short drive back to the motel. Lucas noticed Mike didn't ask him to go with him to the bar to meet the others. He guessed Mike wanted to take a break from drinking, which worked out well since Lucas had a lot to do to prepare for Kane's call.

As soon as Mike's taillights turned the corner, Lucas got busy. He needed to get Blythe and Hailey out of Sanctuary and to safety. He'd definitely need to stock up on supplies for where he intended them to stay. While he could make it up the winding mountain roads and long, steep drive-way for supplies if the weather was good, once winter set in, that would be a problem.

With this in mind, he drove to the grocery store and

stocked up on provisions. Bottled water and a lot of non-perishables. If he could, he'd get more once they were on their way, but this would be enough to sustain them while they evaded pursuit.

Finally, he returned to the motel room. Nothing to do now but wait. And think about Blythe. While he'd avoided joining the Pack, he had known his share of women, but he'd always made sure they understood he could only be casual. He'd known many who were beautiful and sexy. Together they'd enjoyed every kind of carnal delight.

None of them affected him the way Blythe did. Just being in the same room with her set his nerves on edge, making him vibrate with a fierce craving unlike any he'd ever felt before. This seriously pissed him off. He didn't need it, not now, not ever. And worse, while she appeared open to a casual sexual relationship, he didn't want that with her. She made him wish for more for the first time in his life.

He couldn't have more. He didn't know how to be a regular guy. He couldn't allow himself to give in to his desire for Blythe. Getting involved with her would be far too dangerous for a man like him, who only wanted to be left alone, as he'd always been.

He didn't know about normal families. He'd never wanted to be part of a couple. He'd pretended to be one of his identities since he was fifteen. How could he know how to be the right man for Blythe? How could he do that to her?

When his phone finally rang, Lucas actually jumped. Swearing, he pressed the answer button, well aware that he couldn't afford to lose focus. Stopping Jacob had to be his only priority.

"It's Kane," the voice said. "If you're ever going to have a chance to get Blythe, it's now. They just brought Hailey to her. They've both been drugged. You have a short time frame. But I'll help you all I can."

Jacob had gotten careless. Either he was really overconfident or he was setting the mother of all traps. A prickle of unease skittered along Lucas's spine. Immediately he discounted it, well aware he had no choice.

Lucas sucked in his breath. "Is Blythe—"

"Conscious? Yes. Her daughter is not. They're only letting them stay together for one hour. How long will it take you to get here?"

Already running for his truck, he answered. "I'm on my way."

The roar of the truck engine nearly drowned Kane out. "I'm sorry," he said, shifting into Drive. "Say that again."

"What's your plan?" Kane asked. "I'm limited in what I can do without blowing my cover."

His cover. That explained a lot.

"I don't know," Lucas admitted. "I'll work something up on the way there. I'll call you when I know more." And he ended the call.

He broke every speed limit, pushing the truck to its limit. He had to come up with a way to get Blythe and Hailey out. It wouldn't be easy, especially since the little girl was unconscious.

All Lucas could picture was the obvious—barge right in, damn them to hell and back, and fight his way to Blythe and Hailey. Which wasn't good, as it could have disastrous results.

Pulling up in front of the massive iron gates, which were closed, he slowed to a crawl. Once again, Sanctuary appeared quiet, as though nothing out of the ordinary ever went on inside.

Shaking his head, he pressed the accelerator and drove around the corner to the spot where the fence ended. He parked facing in, just in case he had to leave the road. Then he killed the headlights.

The instant he did, his cell rang. Odd coincidence, that. Almost as if Kane had eyes on Lucas.

Once again he pushed away his mistrust and answered.

"Well?" Kane asked. "What are you going to do?"

"I'm going in through the kitchen," Lucas said, deciding as he talked. He climbed from the truck and took off toward the back door.

"I've got people watching them," Kane said. "One set of guards has orders to get the kid back to her quarters and the other will be bringing the woman to the lab for more testing."

"I'm nearly there," Lucas told him. "Any way you can provide a distraction?"

"I can try. And Larry?"

Briefly, Lucas remembered he'd used that name. "Yes?"

"Do you have a gun?"

Lucas answered in the affirmative.

"Good," Kane said. "Be prepared to use it." A soft click, and Kane hung up.

Lucas continued on toward the house. He withdrew his pistol, ready for whoever might come at him.

But no one did. Not yet. Had Kane been caught? Was this actually a massive trap? Because he didn't know and because he had no choice, Lucas waited, every nerve ending screaming an alert. He couldn't help but remember how Jacob had always been paranoid about security. There was no reason for him to have changed so much, at least not without a specific reason.

Shaking off an ominous foreboding, he continued around to the delivery entrance. The door was slightly ajar. Still, he saw no sign of movement.

His wolf chose that moment to try to break free. The

beast had been biding his time, but the combination of adrenaline and frustration proved more than he could resist.

He slammed against Lucas's inner barriers with all the force boiling inside human Lucas.

But Lucas batted him away. "Not now," he muttered, more for his benefit than anything else.

Keeping to the shadows, he went inside.

Again, as it had been the day he and Blythe had broken in, the place appeared deserted. No acolytes walked the halls, no students with their heads deep in textbooks. Empty. Which didn't make sense.

He walked on, his feeling of unease deepening. Kane had said Blythe and Hailey were in her room. Which meant the second floor. Choosing to take the stairs rather than be trapped in the elevator, he headed for them.

When he reached the staircase unimpeded, he tightened his grip on his gun and began to climb. All the while, he kept an eye out for Kane—for anyone.

At the top of the stairs was a landing with long halls to the left and to the right. Long, empty halls. The place was a ghost town. It had to be a trap. Still, he turned right and began trying doors.

Though he constantly glanced over his shoulder, he saw no one. Kane had said they'd given Blythe one hour. By that calculation, he had about twenty minutes, give or take.

A shadowy figure at the end of the hallway made him freeze.

"Lucas?" It was Kane. Quickly, he crossed the length of the hall. "Come on. Come with me."

"We're running out of time."

Kane grimaced. "I had to disable the video feed. I've got it looping some old footage so no one gets suspicious. It took me longer than I thought it would."

"Where is she?"

"Follow me." Kane went directly to a door midway down the hall. From inside his pocket, he produced a small silver key.

"In here," he said, unlocking the door.

"Let's get them out," Lucas ordered. "Now." He pushed into the room.

"Lucas?" Blythe breathed his name. He took in the scene—the limp, unresponsive child so still on the bed, and Blythe, so drawn and pale. Instantly, he wanted to gather her in his arms and comfort her.

But there was no time for that. He and Kane exchanged a glance. "You take the girl, I'll take the Blythe," Lucas said. Crossing the room without waiting for an answer, he lifted Blythe in his arms.

"Let's go," he barked, already moving for the door as Kane scooped up the unresponsive child.

Blythe squirmed, trying to help. But when she tried to stand, she apparently didn't have enough strength in her legs.

"That's okay," Lucas told her. "I can carry you." Shifting her, he slung her over his shoulder and headed out with Kane right behind him, carrying Hailey.

They nearly made it.

But the way was blocked by two burly men. Guards. Though they both wore identical menacing expressions, Lucas noted neither of them appeared to be armed.

"Hold up," Kane said, his voice authoritative and calm. "What are you doing away from your assigned perimeter?"

They exchanged glances. "We were told to retrieve the kid."

They were early. Lucas resisted glancing at his watch.

"You were too slow," Kane barked. "I'm taking care of this personally. You're relieved of duty."

The two men exchanged incredulous looks. "Relieved of... What do you mean?"

"Fired." Kane pointed toward the stairs. "Go on, get out of here. You'll be paid two weeks extra for your trouble."

One man started to argue. "But—"

Kane's sharp glare silenced him. "Now. I want you both off the premises."

Grumbling under their breath, the two men took off. Lucas shot Kane a grim look. "Thanks, man."

"Don't mention it," Kane responded. "Let's get out of here."

They made it down the stairs without running into anyone else. Through the kitchen to the back door, which was still wide-open. Once outside, adrenaline enabled Lucas to run, even carrying Blythe, who'd gone totally limp in his arms.

When they reached the truck, Lucas yanked open the passenger door and put her inside. Kane handed Hailey up to her and closed the door. Accepting her daughter, Blythe made a wordless sound of gratitude and held her little girl close.

"Here are her phones—she might need them. Now go," Kane urged Lucas, glancing over his shoulder. "Get the hell out of here."

"What about you?" Lucas asked. "Your cover is probably blown."

"I can take care of myself," Kane growled. "Now go."

Lucas shook his head, then tore around to the driver's side and climbed in. The engine started immediately.

They roared off into the night, still traveling without headlights until he hit the road. Lucas's last glimpse of Kane was in his rearview mirror.

"Thank you," Blythe breathed. "Thank you for giving me my baby back."

He took her hand, holding it tightly, unable to let it go. "I'm glad you're both okay." Understatement of the year. His relief at having her safe defied explanation.

For a few minutes, they clung together in silence.

"My poor Hailey," Blythe finally said. "I don't know what they did to her. We need to get her to a doctor."

"I agree, but not here." Lucas glanced at the motionless child. "I'd like to put as much distance between us and Jacob as humanly possible."

Frowning, she finally agreed.

"I wonder what Jacob's going to do once he finds out we're gone," Blythe said.

"That's why we need to get out of the state. He'll probably contact the local law enforcement."

"Why? What can he possibly say to the police?" Blythe asked, sounding weak. "All you did was rescue me and Hailey. I'll testify to that."

He shot her a grim look as he drove. "Remember, he's got everyone around here in his pocket. Breaking and entering, plus he'll counter with what I told you before—he'll claim you were abusing your little girl or some such nonsense."

"I don't care," Blythe said, briefly closing her eyes as she continually smoothed her daughter's long hair away from her small forehead. "When all of this is over, I promise I will find that Dr. Silva and make her pay."

"And Jacob," Lucas added, sounding equally fierce. "I'm going to make sure he never does something like this again."

She nodded, her attention still focused on Hailey.

"What if she doesn't wake up?'

"She will." He made himself sound certain, though he was anything but. "We're going to be driving like a bat out of hell. I've got a place in the Sangre de Cristo Mountains in Colorado. We'll head there. If she's not stirring by the time we reach the Colorado border, we'll find a doctor. If we do, be prepared to do a lot of explaining."

Again Blythe nodded. "A Pack doctor would be best. As long as they're not affiliated with the Protectors."

Curious, he glanced her way. "Care to explain?"

A look of extreme weariness crossed her face. "Not right now, Lucas. Maybe later."

Though he nodded, he couldn't help but wonder what secret she was hiding. One that she couldn't share with the man who'd just risked his life to save her and her daughter? To cover his irritation, he changed the subject. "We have to get you both out of town before they put out an APB on us."

"An APB?" she said, her voice rising. Little Hailey moved at the sound, the first movement he'd seen at all since they'd left. Even though she'd barely twitched, it gave him hope.

"She's going to be all right," he said, letting his relief show. "It's just a matter of time until she's fully conscious."

Though Blythe looked less certain, she nodded.

Lucas headed west, out of Texas and into New Mexico. The roads were mostly two-lane and there was less traffic here. The more he thought about it, the less likely Jacob would be to put out an APB. He doubted Jacob would want to call too much attention to himself. Therefore, he'd mount a search using his own people rather than risking becoming a story on the evening news.

At least for now. Once he'd exhausted all his resources without finding Blythe and Hailey, that might change. Jacob had no idea to what lengths his son had gone in order to make sure he was never found. And Lucas knew Jacob had searched fifteen years ago. After a few weeks, he'd seen his picture plastered all over the television. Apparently, when a prominent preacher—even one as radical as Jacob Gideon—had a son come up missing, it was newsworthy.

Lucas had found it amusing as he knew Jacob had hated the attention. He liked to control when and how the spotlight shone on him.

Therefore, as long as they got away fast, Lucas figured he and Blythe and little Hailey were safe. By the time Jacob realized he'd need more help than the local police, Lucas would have Blythe and Hailey safely ensconced in his remote cabin two states away. Out of reach.

And even if, by some wild and completely unlikely chance, Jacob managed to track them to Colorado, he'd never find the cabin. Five years ago Lucas had purchased the place with cash, putting it under the name of his tile company in Seattle, founded under his new name Lucas Kenyon. Anyone doing a property search for Luke Gideon wouldn't find a match.

Even better, situated high on a bluff, the house had a panoramic view of both the winding road up the mountain, and the long and narrow driveway leading to the property.

When he'd first bought the place, only privacy and security mattered. Now Blythe and her small daughter had the same need.

His conscience reminded him of Kane. The other Shifter had gone out of his way to help two people who were essentially strangers to him. He could only imagine what would happen to Kane if Jacob learned what he'd done. Even though he'd fired the two guards, Kane wouldn't be safe. Jacob would search for the two missing men in case they'd been the ones who disabled the security feed and helped Blythe and Hailey escape.

As soon as Jacob found Blythe and Hailey gone, he'd be beside himself with rage. Not for the first time, Lucas wondered if he was the only person who realized Jacob was insane.

Still holding Hailey in her arms, Blythe dozed. Lucas kept glancing at her as he drove. Cradling her little girl in her arms, she looked so fragile and so lost. Powerful emotion filled him and he knew he'd protect them both with his life if need be.

Barely an hour had passed when her cell phone rang, jerking her awake. Bleary-eyed, she squinted at it before turning to stare at Lucas with a horrified expression.

"It's Jacob," she said, her voice quivering.

"He has the number because you called him," he told her, keeping his tone calm. "Go ahead and answer. Let's see what the bastard has to say. He can't hurt you now."

Inhaling sharply, she swallowed and said hello, her expression like stone. After a moment, she covered the phone with her hand. "He wants to talk to you. He knows it was you, though he calls you Luke instead of Lucas."

"Good. I'm glad to have the chance to talk to the monster who attacked another defenseless child," he said, holding out his hand for the phone, keeping the other on the steering wheel.

Hand trembling, she passed it to him.

"What do you want, Jacob?"

"Now, is that any way for a son to talk to his father?" Jacob drawled, his carefully modulated tone sending a shudder down Lucas's spine. "Even though you broke into my home and stole from me, I'm offended that you didn't stay to visit. It's been so long since I've seen you. I didn't even know you were alive."

A jumble of emotions—rage, guilt, sorrow, hatred—so consumed him that for a moment he couldn't speak. As he took a deep breath, determined to keep the one thing his father would never take from him again—control—

he realized if he gripped the cell phone any tighter he'd surely crack it.

Running through his mind were a hundred—no, a thousand—ways to respond to the other man's mocking comment.

He said the first one that came to mind. "I didn't come to visit you. You know that. Despite your elaborate precautions, you weren't able to keep me out—or keep Blythe and Hailey in. I took them away, saved them, and I want nothing to do with you. Ever."

"I'm hurt that you can say that." Indignation rang in Jacob's voice. Either he was a very good actor or he truly believed what he was saying.

Lucas believed it was the former. Jacob also didn't acknowledge any reference to Blythe or to Hailey.

"Cut to the chase," Lucas said, unwilling to play even the smallest game with this man, this murderer. "Why are you calling?"

"You know why. I want the child. Bring her back. I wasn't able to help you, but surely I can help her. And her mother. They still have a chance to be free of their demons—unlike you. I must do what I've been called to do."

"Unbelievable." Keeping his icy control, Lucas pressed on the accelerator, watching as the speedometer crept up past eighty. "You tortured me and tried to kill me." He clenched his teeth to keep from mentioning Lilly. He refused to soil her memory by discussing her with this monster. "Why would you even think I'd let you do the same thing to poor Hailey?"

"Because I know what you are." Triumph rang in the older man's voice. "And I call you out, in the name of heaven. You are the spawn of demons."

"So what does that make you?" Lucas couldn't resist taunting his enemy. "I saved two innocents from your hellish grip. You won't be torturing Hailey, or her mother. They're with me, free. Safe. And you'll never find us. So leave us alone."

"Not until you submit to a higher authority." Slipping into what Lucas had always thought of as his preacher voice, Jacob's tone rang with command.

"A higher authority?" Lucas scoffed. "Since you and I both know what you do has absolutely nothing whatsoever to do with God or heaven or anything even remotely good, I'm guessing you mean you? You've always made your own rules." He took a deep breath. "Well, I've got news for you, Jacob. You are not a higher authority and I'll send you straight to hell." He ended the call.

Seething, he glanced over at Blythe and tossed her the phone. "Block his number, please," he said.

She nodded, still eyeing him warily.

"What is it?" he asked. "What's wrong?"

"Nothing," she said automatically, then shook her head. "Your voice… It's just that for a moment, I got a sense that you're hiding something from me."

He felt the impact of her words like a serrated knife straight to the heart. A sick feeling curled inside his gut. "Looks like you're not the only one that has a secret," he finally said. There was only so much he was willing to share of himself. Lilly—and how he'd failed her—was completely off-limits.

"Fine. Whatever." Impasse. She appeared to be equally unwilling to tell her secret.

She took a deep breath. "To be honest, my wolf is disturbed right now. The emotions that your wolf is transmitting…you are scaring me a little."

Startled, he realized his own beast *was* agitated. "Your wolf can sense mine?" he asked. "How is that possible? Is that…normal?"

After a brief hesitation, she nodded. "Sometimes. Especially if two people are really bonded."

Bonded?

Damn. He glanced sideways at her, seeing her exhaustion in the blue hollows under her eyes. Her pale skin looked stark white in the dim light of the dashboard.

Chapter 10

While he struggled to find the right words without hurting her, she gave him a slow smile. "Look, I know we don't really have a relationship," she said, letting him off the hook. "But we have been through a lot together in the short time since we met. Sometimes that's enough to make a bond."

"Right." Noncommittal. Wary. Even though something intense flared inside him.

She lowered her chin. "No worries, I completely understand. You've already done enough. I'll try my best to get out of your life as soon as I can."

Out of his life? How could she not realize that everything had changed, for both of them? She could no more go back to her former life than he could go back to his.

"How are you going to do that?" he asked, curious to hear what she thought. "Are you finally going to get the Pack involved?"

"The Pack?" Judging from her tone, the word tasted sour on her tongue. "No. That's not going to happen."

He glanced at her, surprisingly relieved. What the hell, he might as well give her his opinion. "I have to say I'm glad to hear that. Actually, the Pack seems like another version of Sanctuary."

One corner of her perfect mouth lifted as she shook her head. "Most of the Pack isn't like that at all."

He jumped on her words.

"Most? With the exception being the Pack Protectors?"

Ignoring him, she continued, "Those of us in the Pack don't try to impose one set of beliefs on everyone. The Pack is simply what we are. After all, half of us are wolves. Wolves can't be alone. Even our wild brethren run in packs."

"So you modeled the human Pack after them?"

"I guess you could say that. We change together, run together and hunt together. Cover each other's backs. This is our Pack, a network of our own kind. You'd be surprised how many prominent people are actually Shifters. We look out for each other. And the humans never know."

He considered this. She'd said wolves couldn't be alone, but he had been for most of his life. By choice. He'd never had the slightest inclination to be part of any Pack. Not even now, though he had to admit her simple and eloquent words made him reconsider. Plus, changing with her—he'd never experienced anything quite like it.

Brushing away the unfamiliar—and completely unwelcome—yearning, he glanced at her. "Still, if you do involve this Pack of yours, how will they help you?"

This time when she looked at him, he saw the anger simmering behind the emerald of her eyes. "He must be stopped. They need to know what he did to you. And what he planned to do to Hailey." Again she smoothed back her daughter's hair. The yearning expression on her face left no doubt how much she hoped Hailey would wake up soon.

"Don't involve me. I don't reveal my past to anyone," he said.

"You talked about it with me."

"That's different," he admitted firmly. "I had to in order to make you aware of what Jacob was capable of."

She lifted her chin. "Which would be the exact same reason you'd need to let them know."

"It sounds pointless. If I did talk to them," he said, his tone cautious, "what could they do to stop it? Jacob Gideon and his church of Sanctuary are very powerful."

"They might be in the human world, but the Pack takes acts of violence against Shifters seriously. They'd investigate."

"Which puts us back at square one. You told me the organization that protects the interests of the Pack is called the Protectors. The very same one you're so adamant about not getting involved."

She said nothing, so he continued. "I agree that it's definitely time to expose him," he said. "He can't be allowed to continue doing this to innocent people. Who knows who he could grab next, what other innocent child he'll try to torture and ultimately destroy?"

"Exactly." She sounded relieved. "If he really is on a crusade to destroy our kind, no one can tell how many people he'll hurt—has hurt. I have to let them know," she said.

Torn, he considered for a moment. Part of this was due to his distrust of anything with a group mind-set. Pack or Sanctuary, no matter what Blythe believed, they seemed to be cut from the same cloth, at least to him. Her reluctance to involve these Protectors was another red flag.

Finally, he planned to do it on his own. He really wanted to expose the bastard himself.

Would that selfish desire for revenge be his downfall? Frustrated, he gripped the steering wheel tightly, if only to keep from pounding it. Jacob needed to be brought down. It shouldn't matter who actually did the deed.

Though he hated to admit it, she was right. They did need help. Still, he had to know all the facts.

"Will involving them endanger your daughter?"

She gave him a carefully blank look. "How could it?" This then, was part of her refusal.

"You'll have to be front and center. If there's a media storm, you'll have to be willing to go on camera—and let Hailey go on camera—and say what Jacob has done. You'll need to obtain a lawyer and press charges."

"You're talking like a human." Still not an answer.

"Jacob *is* a human. In order to stop him, you will have to go through human channels. Assuming you don't want him killed."

She looked so shocked he nearly regretted saying the words. But the black thought had been festering inside him for years, churning up his insides. An eye for an eye, he'd often told himself. Jacob's life for Lilly's. Only fitting. Part of his guilt was the knowledge that he should have found a way to kill Jacob years ago and hadn't.

"I'm not a murderer," she said, indignant.

Which only meant she hadn't been pushed to that point. If Jacob had killed or seriously injured Hailey, he had no doubt Blythe would go looking for blood.

"Then be prepared to go through legal channels."

Silence while she considered this. He kept his eyes on the road, taking comfort from knowing they were putting miles between them and Sanctuary. They'd already crossed out of Texas into New Mexico. It wouldn't be too much longer before they reached the Colorado border.

"The Pack will help me find me a lawyer," she said haltingly, making it clear she wasn't fond of the idea.

Ruthlessly, he pressed on. She needed to be clear on what she was letting herself in for. "Are you willing to testify? And let Hailey testify?"

"I don't know." The way her voice broke nearly cracked his heart.

"You'll need to, if you really want him stopped."

"Stop." Her gaze touched on his, pleading with him. "I can't deal with this right now. Maybe later."

Exhaling, he let it go. Before she contacted this Pack of hers, he'd bring it up again.

When he didn't push, she bent over and kissed her sleeping child's forehead. "I just want to concentrate on getting Hailey well. One thing at a time. Then I'll handle all the rest."

The softness in her voice, the love in her expression as she gazed at her daughter…something intense flared inside him. A flash of emotion, so strong he felt it like a punch in the gut.

Mouth dry, he nodded, aware if he spoke, his voice would reveal more than he wanted her to know.

She must have taken his silence for condemnation. She reached out, touching his shoulder, startling him. He stiffened, glancing sideways at her. The fierce determination in her beautiful long-lashed eyes surprised him. "But after, I can promise you this. What that bastard has done will not go unpunished."

"You took the words right out of my mouth," he told her, sounding like he'd swallowed rusty nails. "Because I personally will make sure of that."

Her answering smile sent heat blazing through him.

Again silence fell, though this time he found it companionable. As he drove, finally Blythe fell asleep. Once again alone, Lucas had the entire cab of his pickup to himself. The Colorado border flashed by, making his whole body tighten with relief.

When he reached Walsenburg and saw the familiar turn-off to La Veta and Cuchara, out of habit he glanced again in the rearview mirror. The road stretched out, dark behind him. Fantastic. They were nearly there, with no one following them.

Safe and sound. He'd done it. With help from a Shifter named Kane, but still. Blythe and Hailey were out of Sanctuary, away from the monster masquerading as a man of God.

As the landscape grew more and more familiar, a lightness lifted his spirit. In the seat beside him, Blythe still slept, holding her child close, the shoulder belt across them both. Again, an unwelcome rush of tenderness filled him. This time, he didn't immediately push it away, even though its sharp sweetness made him clench his teeth.

They arrived at the road that led up to the cabin shortly before dawn. Incredibly wired, especially after driving all night, he cracked his window and inhaled the cool crispness of the mountain air.

They had enough provisions for a few days. He still had the ice chest he'd stocked before leaving the motel in Texas. Though Blythe had declined everything but water, after she showered she'd most likely be ready for a hot meal. He knew he would.

"Hey." He gave Blythe's shoulder a gentle nudge. "Wake up. We're nearly there."

He watched her struggle to come up through the layers of sleep. Blearily, she fought to open her eyes, blinking at him, groggy. His chest went tight. No one had the right to look so beautiful and desirable right after waking.

"What's up?" she croaked.

"We're nearly at my cabin. Think hot shower and a hot meal."

But she wasn't listening. She'd refocused her attention back on her daughter. "Has she moved at all?"

Slowly he shook his head. "A little."

"What's wrong with her? She should have at least... she hasn't woken up yet." Barely contained panic edged her quiet voice.

"Give it time."

Her mouth opened and closed. She swallowed hard.

He couldn't help himself, he squeezed her shoulder. "But she has shifted position. That's got to mean something."

"Do you think so?" She raised her face to his. Judging from her expression, hope warred with fear. "How much longer can a drug last?" she asked, worry coloring her tone. "It should be out of her system by now."

"That depends what they gave her and how much. All we can do is watch and wait."

"Is there a doctor nearby you trust? Not only does she take medicine for her heart, but I'm concerned about the impact of the sedative on her."

"Once we get there, I'll make some calls," he promised.

"Thank you." She grimaced and looked away. "I'll never forgive myself if something happens to her because I trusted that man. And he calls us demons?"

"I know," he said, aching for her. "But at least you got her away from him. She's safe now."

Though she nodded, his words didn't seem to bring her any comfort.

They reached the final turnoff. As he swung the truck to the right, his headlights illuminated a huge deer standing by the side of the road. Instantly, his wolf reacted. *Prey!*

Next to him, Blythe let out a low growl. They glanced at each other with sheepish half smiles.

"You're hungry, too," he said, pushing his wolf down.

She nodded. "Sorry. It's been a long couple of days. I'm exhausted and my wolf is very close to freaking out."

Startled, he glanced sideways at her. Before Blythe, he'd never actually talked about his inner beast with anyone else. He couldn't help but wonder if this was what other, more normal Shifters did: incorporate their wolf self into every aspect of their lives.

One thing was for sure. He'd gained so much knowledge about his Shape-shifter nature from talking to Blythe. If they spent a lot of time together, as he suspected they would, he imagined he'd discover a lot more. He needed to learn more, but not just about himself. He wanted to know everything about Blythe. Her favorite color, what kind of music she listened to. What made her laugh. How she sounded, singing in the shower. Every single idiosyncrasy and quirk, habit and flaw. For the first time in his life, he cared enough to want to know about another person.

Shivering, Blythe followed as Lucas carried Hailey inside and placed her on the couch. Blythe covered her with a blanket and watched while Lucas piled logs in the fireplace and worked to get a fire started. The inside of the cabin felt chilly, no surprise as she imagined at this altitude, the Colorado mountain nights would have already begun dipping close to freezing.

After a few minutes, the fire caught. He added wood and soon a good-size blaze was going.

Dusting his hands off on his jeans, Lucas stood. In the dim light, his aura seemed to actually glow. A trick of the fire, she decided. What else could it mean?

Expression shuttered, he glanced at Hailey, who was

still unconscious, then back at Blythe. At first, she thought he'd say something. Instead he simply turned and went back outside to bring in the rest of their things from the truck.

Silently, Blythe watched him go. As she faced her daughter, she fought not to give in to her exhaustion and fear. *Hailey, Hailey, Hailey.* In her mind, she chanted her name over and over, along with a silent prayer. *Wake up, baby girl. Please, wake up.*

Oblivious, Hailey didn't move. Only the slight rise and fall of her small chest gave testimony to the fact that she was alive.

Fear and anger knotted inside Blythe, tangling with remorse. She had no one else to blame. This was her fault. She'd decided to trust Jacob Gideon, to take her defenseless little girl inside Sanctuary. The responsibility belonged to her.

Panic stronger than she'd ever known tightened her throat as she watched her sleeping daughter. Despite Lucas's obvious attempt to soothe her, she knew something wasn't right. It had been hours since they'd escaped from Jacob's compound. Surely the drug should have begun to leave her system by now.

Clearly, they'd given her too much. An overdose.

If Hailey didn't wake up… Terror clawed at Blythe. Breathing in quick, shallow gasps, she forced it back down. She worked to keep her composure. Iron control—that was what she needed now. She'd be of no use to her daughter or anyone if she let hysteria claim her.

Hailey would be fine. Fiercely determined, she squared her shoulders. After all, there quite simply was no other alternative. She couldn't even think about what it would mean if Hailey never regained consciousness. If that happened—it wouldn't, she told herself fiercely—she'd be changing into her wolf and going feral, on a hunting expedition of her own. Jacob—and Dr. Silva, too—would learn the true meaning of hell before she'd finished with them.

Lucas reappeared, dumped their remaining bags on the floor, took one look at her and froze. "Are you all right?" he asked quietly.

Realizing that something must have shown in her face, she looked down. She jerked her head in a nod and swallowed hard before speaking. "I just don't understand why Hailey hasn't begun to stir even a little bit. She needs to show some sort of sign that she'll be able to fully wake."

"She will." He sounded so certain. How could he be that positive? Watching as he turned and went out a back door, she admired and longed for his confidence, even if it was only an act to placate her.

A moment later he returned, carrying logs. "Come on, it will be all right. Don't look so tormented," he said, dumping his armload of firewood in a bucket next to the fireplace. "If she's not better by morning, we'll find a doctor. It's not as bad as you think."

"It seems pretty awful to me," she shot back, her jaw tight. "Not only do I not know what he gave her, but I have no clue how that will impact her already-fragile heart."

He nodded. "Give it time," he countered. "I'm reasonably sure that Jacob wanted her alive a bit longer, so I doubt he gave her anything that would permanently harm her."

That actually made sense. Briefly, she closed her eyes, grabbing on to his words with both hands, as if he'd tossed her a lifeline. When she opened her eyes again, settling on the calm reassurance in his face, she felt slightly better.

"How will I know?" Letting her gaze cling to his, she knew he could see her frustration and the terror she held at bay.

Though his eyes darkened, he didn't look away. He

lifted one shoulder. "Let her wake and then she can tell us how she feels."

Such confidence. Suddenly, fiercely, she prayed he was right. "Thank you," she told him quietly. "Doctor in the morning, if there's been no change."

"Yes."

That said, there was nothing to do but wait. Patience wasn't one of her virtues. She studied her daughter for even the smallest sign she might be on the verge of regaining consciousness.

Every time panic rose, she raised her head and found Lucas watching her. Oddly enough, just the simple act of meeting his blue-eyed gaze was enough to calm her.

"Don't give up hope," he told her, his voice quiet. "Sometimes it takes a full twenty-four hours for the drug to pass from her system."

She didn't ask how he knew this. Hell, she didn't even question why his mere presence had such an effect on her.

Instead, she sat perched on the edge of the couch, watching her baby girl, with the fireplace warming her back. She felt on edge and watchful, hopeful, guilty and terrified all at once.

Every time the tightness in her chest threatened to strangle her, when she thought she couldn't breathe without gasping for air, the sight of Lucas moving around the kitchen grounded her, kept her sane.

Hope. Faith. Things she'd never quite managed to give up on. Ever since her daughter had been born and the doctors had broken the news about her defective heart, she'd found strength and optimism because to do otherwise would be admitting defeat. And where Hailey was concerned, Blythe would never, ever give up.

So she knew her baby girl would wake up. She'd stretch

and yawn and open her beautiful brown eyes and ask for something to eat.

Soon. Just not yet.

For now, Hailey lay limp and unresponsive. Still, the slight rise and fall of her chest reassured Blythe she was alive.

Lucas touched her shoulder, making her jump.

"Sorry," she stammered. "I was lost in my thoughts."

He nodded. "Would you like to put her into bed? I've got a guest room with a nice mattress and a down comforter. She might be more comfortable there."

"No," she said quickly. "I want her where I can see her. I'm sorry, but I'm not ready to let her out of my sight."

"That's understandable." Eyeing her, his expression softened. "You can see her from the kitchen. Why don't you come sit at the table and I'll make you something to eat?"

When she was about to decline, her stomach growled, reminding her she needed nourishment.

"You need to keep up your strength if you want to help Hailey," he added, apparently having noticed her hesitation.

He had a point. And since the cabin was small, the kitchen was close enough that she should be able to hear any sounds Hailey might make.

"All right," she said, pushing to her feet so quickly the room spun. Blinking, she waited for everything to settle.

"Here." He held out his hand. After a split second of hesitation, she took it, sliding her fingers between his, appreciating how secure the grip of his large hand made her feel.

He led her to the kitchen before releasing her. While he rummaged in the cupboard, she took a seat at the table. As she watched him, she noted how he moved around with the ease of long familiarity, opening cabinets and removing various cooking utensils—a stainless steel pot, two bowls and spoons.

"Do you come here often?" she asked, elbows on the table, resting her chin in her hands.

"Yep."

Studying his back, she judged from the shortness of his reply and the sharp tone of his voice that her question made him uncomfortable. Odd, since he'd told her so much about his horrific childhood.

"What do you do for a living?" She figured she had a right to know, since she would be spending some time with him.

"It's a good thing I just completely restocked the place," he said instead of answering her, holding up two cans of what looked like clam chowder. "How does soup sound?"

"Fine." She could eat anything, as long as it filled her belly and provided nourishment. She wouldn't taste it anyway, she thought, with a glance at her child.

Obviously, Lucas didn't understand that his apparent reticence to answer any personal questions only made her more curious to know the answers. Still, since he'd done so much for her and Hailey, she'd save them for another time.

Turning her chair slightly, she returned to keeping a vigilant watch on Hailey. Nothing had changed there, so occasionally she let her gaze drift back to Lucas. He moved with quiet confidence in his tiny kitchen, and she realized she wouldn't be surprised to learn he was a gourmet chef or something. Then she had to shake her head at her overactive imagination. The man was only heating canned soup. Yet...

"Do you cook?" she asked. She found herself holding her breath, wondering if he'd deflect this question, too.

"Cook?" He glanced back over his shoulder, shooting her a smile so brilliant it nearly took her breath away.

Could Lucas know how beautiful he was? Doubtful. He didn't have that sort of self-aware attitude that most great-looking men seemed to have.

Which was good, as she'd never had much patience for that sort of thing.

"I can," he said cautiously. "But since I live alone, I don't usually do much. I might grill a steak every now and then when it's warm out, or make tacos when I'm craving Mexican food, but that's about the extent of it. Why?"

She shrugged, massaging the back of her neck with one hand and trying to relax a little bit. "Just curious."

From the refrigerator, he pulled out a bottle of wine. "It's a pretty decent Riesling," he said. "Would you like some?"

How long had it been since she'd had wine? She couldn't even remember. Halfheartedly, she nodded. "Maybe it will help me relax."

He poured them each a glass and placed the bottle on the table. A moment later he set a steaming bowl of chowder in front of her and her mouth began to water.

"Crackers?" he asked, passing a box of saltines. "Sorry it's nothing fancy, but it's the quickest warm meal I could think of."

"Hailey loves chowder," she said, her throat aching.

"When she wakes up, I'll make her some," he replied, the firm certainty in his voice helping her maintain her equilibrium.

One last glance at Hailey and then she allowed herself to focus on the food, inhaling the delicious aroma. It was hot, but not overly. Just right, actually, and the buttery, creamy taste warmed her mouth and stomach. She ate without regard for decorum, lifting one spoonful after another into her mouth and not stopping until it was gone.

When she'd finally finished, Blythe raised her head and

looked up to see Lucas watching her, his eyes sparkling with amusement. "Do you want mine?" he offered. "The way you devoured that makes me think you're starving."

From somewhere she found a smile to offer him. "No, thank you. Go ahead and eat. I'm full now."

Again she turned to look at her daughter. She felt guilty, allowing herself to partake in a hot meal while Hailey was so out of it.

"Don't do that," Lucas urged, as if he knew. "You can't deny yourself food or sleep or anything. She needs you to be strong. Most likely, she'll be digging into a big bowl of soup by this time tomorrow."

Hounds, she hoped he was right. He had to be. She wouldn't consider any other alternative.

"I know you had some questions for me earlier." He cleared his throat. "And I promise to answer them, but for now I need to inquire about a few things and I'm going to ask you to give me honest answers."

Chapter 11

Honest answers? Blythe drew a blank. "About what?"

"About being a Shifter. And then I'll be happy to answer anything you want to know about me."

Warmth filled her as she realized he was only trying to distract her. Suppressing a smile, she nodded. Right now she actually welcomed the diversion. Anything was better than making herself sick obsessing over Hailey.

"I'm guessing Shape-shifters don't live forever." He pushed his empty bowl away and leaned back in his chair, drawing her gaze to the way his T-shirt stretched across his powerful chest.

"No," she managed, her mouth suddenly dry. "We're mortal, though the only things that can kill us are fire and silver."

He nodded. "Just like the old legends."

"Exactly."

"But we don't get ill like regular people?"

This made her smile slightly. "If by regular people you mean humans, then you're correct. We tend not to catch colds or get the flu or stomach viruses."

When he looked at her daughter, then back at her, she tensed, sensing she might not like what he was going to ask next. "Then why is Hailey so sick?"

Taking a deep breath, she looked down. After a moment or two, she lifted her chin to meet his gaze. "Because she's not a full-blood. She's what's known as a Halfling, the result of a union between a human and a full-blooded Shifter."

Frowning, he looked as if he'd been poleaxed. "Like me," he said quietly.

"Yes. She's a Halfling, just like you are."

"But you're a full-blooded Shifter?"

Slowly she nodded. "Yes." She knew where he was going with this. Though she didn't like talking about it, he deserved to know the truth.

"What happened to her father?" he asked.

Even though she'd known it was coming, she winced, not bothering to hide her slight embarrassment. "I never knew him. I wanted a child and the time in my life was right. The only thing lacking was a man. There was no one in my life, no one like that at least, so I went to a sperm bank."

He looked shocked, which she'd expected. Then he laughed, which she hadn't.

"What's so amusing about that?" she asked crossly.

"I'm sorry." He leaned forward, gaze locked on hers. "I thought I was the only one who couldn't find the right woman and maintain a relationship. I figured that would come with time. But if someone who looks like you can't, either, there's no hope for the rest of us."

Amused, now she laughed, earning a curious look from

him. "I take it you haven't looked in the mirror lately," she said dryly. "I think it's more a matter of the right person not having come along. We're like our wild cousins in that. Like wolves, we find our true mate only once."

"I see," he said, though the cynical note in his tone told her he didn't really believe it.

She wasn't 100 percent certain she did, either.

"Anyway, the end result was I got Hailey." She glanced toward the couch where her daughter still slept. "The doctors knew something was wrong the instant after she was born."

"What exactly is the matter with her?" he asked, his voice gentle as he watched her face. "I saw on the news it was something with her heart."

Though she kept a brave face, she knew he could see the heartbreak in her eyes. "She needs a new heart. Either that, or a visit with the Healer."

"The Healer?" His curious expression told her that this was the first he'd heard of this. "What do you mean?"

Though she raised her chin, she knew her smile was tinged with sadness. "Every few hundred years, a person is born among our kind who can heal Halflings. A long time had passed without one, so long that a lot of the Pack believed it was simply a myth. Then a woman was found, in Texas actually, who turned out to be the Healer. Her name is Samantha."

His skeptical tone matched his expression. "That sounds a lot like the kind of claims Jacob makes. That's how he drew you into his web, by making you believe he could heal your daughter."

Put that way, her hope that Jacob could help her sounded foolish indeed. She shrugged. "She's nothing like Jacob. She's the real deal, and she makes no claims whatsoever. She simply heals."

"How do you know?" He crossed his arms.

"Word of her has spread among our people. As you can imagine, she's in great demand. She spends much of the year traveling the world, visiting the most seriously ill Halflings."

"But you don't know for certain," he persisted. "Whether or not she's real?"

"No." She sighed. "But the Pack comes down hard on charlatans and cheaters. She's considered our most valuable asset. So I have to think she's the genuine thing. A Healer."

"Then your problem is solved. Find her and get her to fix Hailey's heart."

"I wish it were that simple." He didn't know how many sleepless nights she'd prayed for such a thing, hope and possibility making her dizzy as he sat back down. "But because of the demand for her skills, she has a long waiting list. She has a team of people who manage it for her. They say she prioritizes due to seriousness of condition."

"I assume you've already put Hailey on it?"

She nodded. "Yes, of course. I added Hailey to the list four years ago, when she was a year old. Since her condition isn't immediately life threatening, she's not very high as priorities go."

He frowned. "But if it's her heart…"

She nodded, not wanting him to say the actual words. "Yes. In time, it will give out on her."

He pushed up from the chair, towering over her, the picture of masculine strength. The urge to reach out to him, to take whatever comfort she could glean from his broad chest and strong arms, was so powerful she nearly swayed toward him.

He didn't appear to notice. "Then we need to find this

Healer, this Samantha, and make her understand how serious Hailey's condition is."

"Don't you think I've tried," she cried. "You've seen firsthand how far I'm willing to go for my daughter."

Frowning, he stared at her. "What do you mean?"

"I can't find Samantha."

"I don't understand."

"The Pack has many enemies," she said, then sighed. "There are other supernatural beings who are not our allies. So since Samantha is one of our most valuable assets, great precautions are taken to keep her whereabouts secret."

His frown deepened. "When you say other supernatural beings, what exactly do you mean?"

"Let's see. There are Vampires, and Fairies, and the Mer people, to name a few. And the Draconians, and those awful Snake People." As she ticked them off on her fingers, she belatedly realized he might be learning of their existence for the first time.

In fact, he looked downright dizzy. "Are you telling me..."

"Sorry." She reached out and squeezed his arm, by way of apology. "I forget sometimes how much of a sheltered life you've led."

When he laughed she stared at him, wondering if he'd lost his mind. "What's so funny now?" she asked, confused.

"Jacob thinks we Shape-shifters are demons," he said, still chuckling. "Imagine his reaction if he were to find out about all these other creatures."

Shaking her finger at him, she attempted to look stern, which was difficult when she wanted to laugh along with him. "Which is why we must make sure he never learns of their existence. Humans honestly have no idea."

"Someone must have known," he pointed out. "Otherwise all those books about this sort of thing would never have been written."

"Maybe. But I prefer to think that the writers had fantastic imaginations."

"There's that possibility." He didn't sound as if he believed it.

"There's so much you have to learn," she said, sighing. "I hate that your entire heritage was kept from you. That's wrong on so many levels." Though she'd sworn not to, she made up her mind to try and persuade him. He needed the companionship of his own kind.

"You really should consider joining the Pack. You'd have access to so much information, much more than I could ever teach you. We have libraries online and videos you can borrow, and—"

"Nope," he interrupted. "That's not for me."

Both disappointed and unsurprised, she nodded. "I understand."

"Do you?" He appeared unconvinced. "I doubt that."

She shook her head, recognizing the emotion flickering in the back of his blue-eyed gaze. After all, it was one she was intimately acquainted with. She'd lived with her own fear for so long, ever since she'd learned a certain faction of the Protectors wanted children who were genetically like Hailey.

"What are you so afraid of?" she asked softly.

He recoiled as though he'd been stung. "I'm not."

The knee-jerk reaction had the effect of confirming her guess. Reaching for her wine glass, she twirled it around on the table before taking a small sip. She knew she should let the matter go. Drop it right now and leave it, along with her questions about his current life, for another day.

She was surprised to find a look of fierce hunger in his

eyes. Whether for her or for the knowledge she'd mentioned, she couldn't make out. As her inner beast stirred in response and she pushed it down, she realized she didn't want to know.

Doggedly, she continued. It was either that, or her mind would wander to a place it had no business going. "The Pack is not all that bad," she began, testing the waters.

"I'd rather not talk about it, if you don't mind." Grimacing, he took a large swallow of his wine. "It's difficult enough trying to wrap my mind around everything I've learned since I met you."

She nodded, deciding not to tell him that she'd only barely scratched the surface, including the truth about her own child. "I'm sorry," she said, meaning it.

"I've spent my entire life avoiding people, including your Pack, because I thought I was an anomaly. Weird, strange, put together differently from everyone else."

"Didn't the Pack representative—"

"I didn't let him talk much," he cut her off. "I figured it was pretty much the same story as the crap with my… with Jacob. If it wasn't some kind of con, they'd be trying to convert me or something."

"You don't trust anyone, do you?"

"Nope." The aching smile he gave her broke her heart.

"It's not wrong, you know. Being a Shifter." She resisted the urge to reach across the table and cover his hand, clenched into a fist, with her own. "We can't help what we are, in the same way that a sparrow can't decide to be an eagle."

He nodded, still silent behind his hastily erected wall.

Though she knew she should leave it alone, she'd already let too many questions go unanswered.

"You've never talked to anyone about what it means to be a Shape-shifter? Anyone at all?"

"I've never needed to." Anger vibrated in his voice. Mingled somewhere in his narrowed eyes, she thought she also detected a hint of shame. Even now.

"You sent away the Pack representative who contacted you, right?"

He nodded.

"I'm surprised he went that easily," she mused, half speaking to herself. "After all, they're supposed to be specially trained in dealing with Ferals?"

"With what?"

Inwardly cursing her slip of tongue, she gave him the truth. "Ferals are what we call Shifters who live outside the Pack. Some don't ever assimilate into human culture. Some, like you, for whatever reason, were never taught."

"Taught?" he scoffed. "That sounds like the sort of thing Jacob would condone. He was forever trying to teach me the true—according to him—meaning of what he called the good word."

Damn. So many layers of pain and mistrust. Could anyone get past them to the man underneath? Did she even want to?

Though she wasn't sure she did, because he was plainly suffering, this time she gave in to impulse and leaned across the table. Bypassing his hand, she reached for his face, briefly cupping the side of his cheek. "Listen to me. You can't honestly believe anything that man told you. You're not an abomination. Neither am I."

For the space of a heartbeat, he froze. Then, recoiling, he moved away from her touch, pushing back his chair so hastily it clattered to the floor. Standing, he glared down at her. The power and emotions radiating from his muscular body felt like flames, searing her.

"I'm… I don't know what to say," she began.

He waved her away. "I tried to find out what happened

to my mother," he said, again surprising her. "I figured if Jacob thought I was evil, he must have felt the same way about her. I believed he might have killed her, whether accidently during one of his cleansing sessions gone awry, or on purpose in a fit of self-righteous rage."

She held her breath and waited for him to finish.

"I couldn't find out anything," he finished. Despite the lack of inflection in his tone, she could only imagine how he must have felt. Believing his father was a murderer and then not being able to find proof. Without that, he'd never know the truth.

"I'm sorry," she said. "I can't help you with that. But I can help you with what it means to be a Shifter, if you want?"

One corner of his mouth twitched. "Hmm."

Again, heat curled in the pit of her stomach. Determined, she tried to ignore it. "I promise not to push."

Eyeing her, he didn't respond. Was it her imagination or had his eyes gone dark with matching heat? "Thank you. I'll tell you one thing. I spent my entire life fighting my own nature. Until you started talking, it never dawned on me that I could just accept it."

She wanted to lean into him, to rub up against him and help him celebrate his newfound self-acceptance. As her thoughts spiraled into passion, she forced herself to stop. Wondering if she'd lost her mind, she simply nodded.

They remained in companionable silence for a few minutes, there at the small kitchen table with their bellies full and the room growing warm from the heat of the fire.

Hailey continued to sleep, unmoving. Since she had no choice, at least until the morning, Blythe prayed she wasn't making a mistake doing as Lucas had suggested, by giving it time. Her daughter would wake, she had to believe.

By this time tomorrow, she'd be watching Hailey eat and listening to her chatter.

If not, they'd be finding a doctor first thing tomorrow.

Tears stung her eyes. Sipping her wine, she tried to focus on something else, anything else. She chose to study her surroundings, liking what she saw.

The cabin was small, true. But it appeared well made, the rustic appearance of the log walls matching the wildness of its surroundings. A braided throw rug sat in the center of the living room, in front of the couch currently occupied by Hailey. The fireplace was made of some kind of stone, maybe slate, and the small but functional kitchen appeared to have top-grade appliances. She marveled at the homey feel of the place. She felt comfortable here, at peace, which was odd, considering the circumstances.

Even stranger, though, was how close she felt to the man sitting across from her. She hadn't known Lucas Kenyon very long, but she felt as though she'd known him forever.

She'd need to be careful. That kind of attachment was something she could not afford. Taking care of Hailey already consumed her. She had no room in her life for anyone else.

Outside, the wind continued to blow. Occasionally, the gusts were strong enough to shake the cabin and rattle the windows. Inside, she was glad of the warmth and the company, overjoyed that she had her girl back, and prayed Hailey would soon wake up.

Lost in thought, she raised her head to find Lucas watching her.

She gave him a slow, friendly smile, hoping he'd see in it how thankful she was.

When he spoke again, it was to ask a question with a studied casualness that told her the answer was important to him.

"How much does Hailey know about this? Being a Shifter?"

His carefully blank expression made her smile. "She knows what she is, what I am. Though she's a few years away from changing, she's very aware of the wolf part of her nature. Where a human child might have an imaginary friend, our children have not-so-imaginary wolf pup friends instead."

He nodded. She couldn't tell what he thought by his expression, which had gone all granite again on her.

"Did you?" she asked, without thinking about it. The instant the question came out, she regretted asking it. "I'm sorry," she began, her words trailing away as he began to speak.

"I thought I was going crazy," he said. Though he still regarded her intently, his posture seemed to indicate he'd finally relaxed. "I knew the wolf was there, but I couldn't sense it in anyone else. The one time I tried to put out feelers with my father I was blasted by several angry biblical verses. He prayed over me and tried to make me feel guilty for even having the desire to change. I had no one I could ask."

"That's wrong." She ached to touch him, to try and do something to erase the awful memories put there by someone who should have protected and taught him. "I'm so sorry."

But she did nothing, because she had another, more pressing responsibility to her small daughter still unconscious on the couch. She could barely help Hailey, the person she loved more than anything else, so how could she even think she could assist Lucas?

"Don't be. I'm not asking for your pity," he said, sounding both resigned and angry. "I'm just trying to understand."

"I get it," she began. "Really, I do. And I promise I don't—"

"Mama?"

"Hailey!" Blythe jumped to her feet and rushed to her little girl's side. Though her heart felt as if it could pound right out of her chest, she had to appear reasonably calm so she wouldn't upset her daughter.

Lucas followed, but kept his distance.

"Hailey, you're awake!" Smiling, she reached down and gently gathered her baby in her arms, raining kisses on her head.

Immediately, Hailey began to struggle, pushing her away. "Stop it, Mama." Squirming, she scrunched up her face. "I don't feel so good."

Relaxing her grip, Blythe couldn't make herself completely let go. "I know, honey. You've been sick. But you're getting better now."

Hailey nodded. Then her caramel-brown eyes widened. "What about the bad man?"

"He's gone," Blythe said firmly, aware she needed to downplay Jacob Gideon as much as possible. "We went far away from him, to a place where he can't find you. My friend Lucas helped us."

At his cue, Lucas stepped forward into her line of vision. "Hi," he said softly.

Squinting at him, Hailey appeared uncertain. Then, she evidently spotted something that reassured her and she relaxed. "You're Pack," she said. "I can see your aura."

Instead of telling her what would be a confusing truth, Lucas nodded. "Pleased to meet you," he said, crouching down to put himself at her level. "I'm glad you're feeling better."

She nodded, then winced. "My head hurts." Before Blythe could respond, she peeked up at her through her long eyelashes. "Mama, you said you got me away from that bad man?"

"Yes." Blythe hastened to reassure her. "Far, far away. You're safe now."

Rather than appearing relieved, Hailey frowned. "What about the other kids, Mama? Did you bring them, too?"

Heart sinking, Blythe looked over her shoulder at Lucas, who appeared as stunned by the words as she'd been. "Other kids?" she asked carefully. "What do you mean, honey?"

Hailey sighed. "He had more kids—they let me play with them before they gave me the shot that made me sleepy. They're like me, Mama. Shifters," she said, her voice worried. "There's Erin and Susie and Jonathan."

"Is that all?" Lucas asked.

"I don't know." Hailey bit her lip. "There's probably more, but I'm not sure. I didn't get to play with them all. They kept us in different rooms, like at preschool."

Hellhounds. What on earth was Jacob Gideon up to?

Judging from the shock and horror Lucas tried to hide, whatever it was wouldn't be good.

"Why didn't you save them, too?" Hailey asked, looking from her mother to Lucas and back again.

Though she felt queasy, Blythe managed to sound normal, at least to herself. "We didn't know about them, baby."

"Oh." But Hailey persisted. "But you do now. And you'll help them, too, right?"

Blythe swallowed hard. How could she answer that? "Let me see what I can find out, okay?"

Content, Hailey nodded. Her eyes drifted closed, and she slid back into a deep sleep.

Swallowing, Blythe took a deep breath. How she wished she could simply fold her arms around Hailey's small body and go off to sleep, too. If she could, she might wake up to find that none of this was real.

Unfortunately, she didn't have that option. One glance at the tortured look in Lucas's eyes told her he realized it, too.

Things were worse, much worse, than either of them could have imagined.

Moving quietly, Blythe crossed to Lucas. He jerked his head, motioning her to move away from where Hailey lay slumbering on the sofa. "Not here," he mouthed.

She followed him back to a small bedroom. "Did you hear that? There are more children," she said, keeping her voice low, though it shook with her effort to keep from exploding.

Lucas looked as if he wanted to punch something. "I know. I can't believe that bastard. We've got to help them."

"But we can't save them all just by ourselves. We're going to need assistance."

He barely hesitated. "I agree. This has gone beyond the scope of anything I might have imagined. We have no idea what kind of experiments he might have run on those poor kids. We've got to get them out."

They stared at each other. "But how?" Blythe finally asked. "I can't endanger Hailey."

"Of course not." He swallowed. "We've got to let your Pack know. Even if it does involve those Protectors you seem so afraid of. Call them and arrange a meeting. We'll tell them everything we know and see what they suggest."

"Now?" she asked. This was huge and they both knew it.

"Yes, now. The sooner the better."

Hands shaking, she retrieved the number and used the untraceable cell phone to make the call. Rather than give elaborate details over the phone to a secretary, she simply requested a face-to-face talk with a Protector. Since Lucas had excellent Wi-Fi, she agreed that it could be on Skype.

"Eight o'clock tonight," she told Lucas. "I think you should sit in."

He gave her a quizzical look. "Is that allowed since I'm not Pack?"

"Who cares? This is urgent." Her voice rose slightly. They both glanced at the door, listening. Finally, Blythe went back to the den to check on Hailey, who continued to sleep.

Returning, feeling itchy and restless and uncomfortable in her own skin, she inhaled sharply.

"Are you okay?" he asked, staring at her.

"Sorry," she said. "I'm tense and tired." The instant she finished speaking, her wolf maneuvered to rise to the surface. For a moment, she battled her beast, finally pushing it back down deep inside her. This earned her a low growl from his, who obviously sensed what was going on.

Lucas, however, clearly didn't. "What the hell was that?" he asked, sounding shocked.

"Your wolf, reacting to mine."

He scratched his head. "Why?"

"Probably because I'm at the end of my rope. Out of sorts. This has all been… I need to go outside and change," she told him. "Blow off some steam."

He inhaled sharply, but didn't argue. Encouraged, she pressed on. "Do you mind keeping an eye on Hailey? She's still sleeping and I doubt she'll wake up for a little while. I promise I won't be gone long."

A look of such yearning crossed his handsome features that she stopped dead in her tracks. "Or not," she said.

"No, it's all right. No problem," he said quietly, once again expressionless. "Though my wolf wants to change and hunt with yours, I can manage until you return."

"I'll wait." Decision made, she pushed her wolf down. "I'll survive."

"It's okay, really." Hand on her shoulder, he steered her in the direction of the door. The feel of his large fingers seared her, even through her T-shirt, making her ache to turn and press her entire body into him.

Closing her eyes briefly, she took a deep, shuddering breath. The sooner she got out of here, the better.

"Fine. You talked me into it," she managed, reaching an instant decision. "We'll all be better after."

Then, before she could change her mind again, she handed him the cell phone. "I'll leave this here, just in case someone from the Protector's office calls back."

His impassive face revealed nothing. "Have fun," he said, pushing past her toward the kitchen. Once there, he turned his back, effectively dismissing her as he pretended to rummage through the pantry.

Finally, she turned away. She'd never felt such a connection—with a man trying with all his might to let her go.

Chapter 12

Moving quickly, she stripped off her clothing and strode to the door. She barely registered Lucas's harsh intake of breath at seeing her naked. In a second she'd moved past him, and stepped outside. The chilly night air hit her bare skin like a slap. She inhaled as she hurried down the porch steps, ignoring the cold on her unprotected human flesh as she headed out into the woods.

But until she vanished into the trees, she felt the heat of his gaze like a laser aimed at her back.

The forest was alive with night sounds. Standing absolutely still, she listened, well aware they'd all cease the instant she became wolf.

Finally, she had to let her wolf self free. Dropping to the ground, she began the process of the change, grinning savagely as her bones lengthened and her body changed. The pain was always fleeting, though she welcomed it. She'd always looked at it as a sort of rebirth.

When she rose, she was fully wolf. As usual, her view of everything had changed, led by scent rather than sight. And the smells! Her wolf heart skipped a joyous beat.

Crashing through the underbrush, heedless of what other creatures might hear that warned them of her presence, she ran. And ran, and ran.

Time—as humans knew it—had no meaning to her when she was wolf. It might have been several hours, it might have been less, but she gave her beast full rein and hunted, and explored, and ran some more.

Later, pleasantly exhausted, she returned to the spot where she'd started. This night, she'd filled the well inside her dual nature. Now her inner wolf was finally content.

The time had come for her to return to reality and hope the Protectors had called.

Pushing away the lingering resentment that her wolf nature felt, she began the process to reverse the change.

She shifted back to human, admitting that she felt a hundred times better. Despite the shocking rush of cold air to her unprotected skin, her entire body felt loose limbed, relaxed. Better.

As she strode in the direction of the cabin, she decided she'd send Lucas out with instructions not to return until he'd changed. Hopefully it would help him as much as it had her.

The night air carried a deeper, crisper chill as she walked back up the cabin porch steps. Leaves crunched underfoot, and the scent of wood smoke lent a holiday feel to the air, even though it was only mid-September.

She inhaled deeply, allowing herself to enjoy the peace as long as it lasted. Which wouldn't be long. The instant she went back inside, she had to start thinking about the Protectors and Jacob Gideon's Sanctuary.

As she opened the door and entered the cabin, Lucas

froze, staring. It appeared he'd been pacing. Her cell phone sat untouched on the table.

His gaze slid rapidly over her naked body, making her flush. The smoldering flame in his eyes made her flush all over, sending a dizzying current racing through her blood.

This would never work. While she was not blind to the simmering attraction between them, they'd both need to move past it.

It appeared he still hadn't developed the Shifter's lack of inhibitions. No matter. Being around her would help him with that. Trying her best to appear unabashedly unashamed, she strode to where she'd left her clothes and began getting dressed.

When she finally turned around fully clothed, she realized Lucas hadn't moved.

"No one called," he told her, his voice thick and unsteady. "Evidently whoever relayed the message in your Pack Protector organization assigned it a low priority."

Just like that, the feeling of peace vanished, to be replaced by a pit in her stomach. "I'll call them back."

"Good," he said, not looking at her.

As she moved close to him, she realized he was aroused. Completely and utterly aroused.

The knowledge sent a ripple of excitement through her. Forcing herself to remember that this was just because he'd seen her naked, she tamped it down. Though it was only physical, neither of them could allow something like that to get in between them. She suspected he knew this, too.

Once again, she'd forgotten he hadn't been raised with typical Shifters who take nakedness in stride. He reacted to her like a human male, visually aroused by the sight of unclothed femininity.

She might have smiled if she hadn't been so damn

turned on herself. Worse, to her shock, she had to fight the urge to brush her body up against him like a cat in heat.

Heart pounding, the flush of need, of desire, stunned and angered her. She had more self-control than this. So of course, she promptly shoved her attraction to him deep inside of her, to be taken out and examined when she was able to think clearly.

"I'll phone again while you go change," she managed, her own voice a bit husky. "Surprisingly, it really helped to let myself be a wolf for a while. A good run and hunt will do wonders for you." And your arousal, she added silently.

He shook his head. "Maybe later."

Since she didn't want to push, she simply nodded, unsure of what else she could say or do, other than the obvious.

He seemed to sense this. "I'll be outside, on the porch," he said, striding to the door and disappearing before she even had a chance to react. No doubt the cool night air would help him.

And she had to get herself under control. She had to make that call. No matter how badly her stomach knotted at the thought of contacting the Protectors.

Leaving her cell phone on the table, first she went to check on Hailey. She watched her daughter sleep all tucked up in her blanket. Blythe's feelings of tenderness were muted with a sudden, fierce rage. How dare someone like Jacob Gideon hurt her baby? And all those other children—where were their parents? Did any of them have any idea what the people at Sanctuary were doing to their children?

She'd find out soon enough.

Quickly, she returned to the kitchen and grabbed her phone. Punching redial, she waited impatiently for someone to answer. This time, instead of a live person, she got an answering machine.

Voice vibrating with frustration, she left a message.

"Did you get ahold of anyone?" Lucas asked from behind her, making her jump at the sound of his voice. She hadn't heard him come back inside.

She swallowed hard, raising her face and meeting his gaze. "No. I left another message," she said. "This time, I stressed that it was high priority. I'm thinking someone will realize that and call me back."

"Good." Dusting his hands on the front of his jeans, he moved closer. "I thought your Pack Protectors would at least be on the ball. What if someone was dying? How long would they take to do something?"

He had a point. "I don't know," she admitted. "I've never had to call them before. I never wanted to."

"You keep alluding to something about them. Don't you think it's time you told me?"

"Some things are better left unsaid."

The disappointment in his expression was almost more than she could bear. To cover, she continued. "I dialed the number for my local Pack representative and got the Protector's number from the recorded info. Maybe regular Shifters just don't ring them up. Maybe you have to be referred. I don't know."

"We need to find out," he grumbled, crossing his arms. Clearly, his mood hadn't improved. "We can't take a chance and involve human law enforcement, since we don't know who he's bought off."

His words made her realize something. At the thought, she gasped. "What if…" Feeling a bit paranoid, she bit her lip. "The woman I spoke with didn't sound all that concerned. Is it possible she might be…?"

"Working for Jacob?"

She nodded. "Exactly."

"That's highly unlikely. Aren't all the people who work for the Society of Protectors, or whatever they're called, aren't they all Pack?"

Just like that, that particular worry evaporated. "I'm jumping at shadows. Yes, of course they are. Jacob's not."

"And since there's no way a Shifter would ally himself or herself with a group like his, you're safe."

"*We're* safe," she corrected. "We're in this together, remember?"

He stared. "Are we?"

"Of course. You know that, right? We both want to stop your father, and we have to save any other children he might have taken."

Slowly, he nodded. "True," he said. She couldn't help but notice how studiously he avoided meeting her gaze. Why? Because she didn't trust him enough to tell him everything? How could he hold that against her, when she knew he kept secrets from her, too?

Maybe it was more simple—perhaps he worried his thoughts might show in his face. Did he really think she hadn't noticed his desire?

She wanted him, too. And when the time was right, she'd let him know. But this, this was far more important. There were children's lives at stake. They needed to be able to work together, as a team. For the first time, she wondered if they'd ever learn to trust each other.

"Trust has to be earned," she told him, speaking her thoughts out loud. "I get that. But you need to realize we're partners. That is, if you want to be. Honestly, I wouldn't blame you if you ran away from this as fast as you could."

He snorted. "Like I would. I'm the one who rescued you, remember? But you're right, trust does have to be earned."

True enough. And one of them had to make the first

move. "Speaking of trust…" She twisted her hands, finally jamming them in her pockets, and strode over to the window. "About the Protectors. I haven't told you everything. There's a good reason why I've avoided contacting them. I'm afraid they'll take Hailey."

"Why?" Clearly puzzled, he cocked his head. "I don't understand your logic."

"Because she's more than just a Shifter," she finally said, her voice low and full of the fear that had dodged her since she'd learned that the Protectors had issued a call for all parents of her daughter's kind. She didn't know how he'd react. "She's also a Griffon."

Though clearly, from the sound of her voice, this information was important, Lucas had never heard the word before. "What do you mean?"

"A Griffon is more than a Halfling. They're a cross between a Shifter and another species other than human. Like Vampire or Fae. Evidently, whoever made that donation at the sperm bank, er…didn't tell them the whole truth. Naturally."

While this might be mind-boggling to her, he still didn't understand why it would be such a big deal. "Is this common?"

"More than you might think," she admitted.

"Then why would your Pack Protectors take her?"

"To protect her." She swallowed hard. "Or so they say."

"From what?"

"Everything. Even among our kind—and other supernatural species—the Griffons are valuable. A few years ago a powerful Vampire Huntress did the same sort of thing as Jacob. She captured a bunch of Griffon children and tried to use their powers for her own advantage."

He still didn't get it. "Powers? What do you mean, exactly? Can they do things that other Halflings cannot?"

Expression solemn, she nodded. "We don't yet know the full extent of what they can do. There has been a lot of talk that they are the future of our people."

Dragging his fingers through his hair, he tried to understand, then shook it off. "You can teach me all this stuff later. We've got to focus on what's going on right now. You say the Protectors might want to take Hailey so they can protect her, right?"

Slowly, she nodded. "A law was passed a few years ago that said any Griffon child in danger should be turned over to them. I figured it'd simply be a matter of time before that was amended to any Griffon child, whether they were in danger or not."

"Well, can they?"

Expression miserable, she shrugged. "I don't know. Theoretically, I would suppose so."

Flinching, he tried to remain strong. "Once, I lost someone I loved because I couldn't protect her. Maybe you should consider it."

He saw in her face that she realized he'd begun to share his own secret with her. But she didn't press him. Instead, she considered his suggestion. "No," she finally said. "It's tempting, but after what just happened with Jacob, I don't trust anyone. I'd prefer to do my own protecting."

Her words brought him a rush of approval, mixed with fear. "I feel the same way," he said. Then, while she stared at him, he held out his hand. "Partners."

Moving forward, she took it, her grip firm as they shook, before they each let go. He'd felt a shock of current, but this time he'd expected it and braced himself. Evidently, this was only on his part, because she didn't react as if anything was out of the ordinary.

"Don't tell them," he said. "When you talk to the Protectors, just tell them she's a Halfling. They don't need to know the rest."

As she opened her mouth to respond, the cell phone rang.

"I'll handle this," he said, snatching it up and stabbing his finger at the answer button. "Hello?"

The man on the other end sounded bored, although courteous. "I've received two messages that a Blythe Daphne wants to speak with me."

So much for Skype. He supposed they should be grateful that at least someone had called.

"Are you a Protector?" Lucas asked, his voice verging on borderline hostile.

Evidently this startled the other man. "Yes. My name is Martin Hunter. Who are you?"

Without identifying himself, Lucas launched into an explanation of what had happened with Hailey. "And she says that he's got other children there, all Shifter. We feel their lives are in danger."

Martin was silent so long that Lucas began to wonder if he'd hung up. But then he cleared his throat and spoke. "Do you have proof of this? I mean, Jacob Gideon is a well-known preacher. Why would he want to harm little children?"

Barely keeping his frustration under control, Lucas answered. "Because he knows they're Shifters. He views Shape-shifters as evil, an abomination straight from the mouth of hell."

Martin made a sound that might have been either disbelief or disgust. "You sound adamant, but let me remind you that Jacob Gideon is human. There's no way he knows about our kind."

Taking a deep breath, Lucas knew he'd couldn't hold back anything just to keep himself safe. "Well, he does."

"Are you certain?"

"Yes."

He'd hoped Martin Hunter would take him at his word, but realized he should have known better. "Explain, please."

"He knows because I'm his son," he said. "And I'm a Halfling. When he found out, he tortured me, trying to beat the evil out of me. I escaped when I was fifteen, and stayed hidden for fifteen years. Until now."

Silence on the other end of the line. When Martin spoke again, his voice sounded grim. "Give me your coordinates and I'll be there as soon as I can."

Heart in her throat, Blythe watched as Lucas concluded the call. "Well?" she asked, the second he punched the off button on the phone.

"He said he'd be here as soon as he could." He looked and sounded grim.

"That's good," she said cautiously. "Isn't it?"

"I don't know. I didn't get a great feeling."

Alarm bells went off inside her at his words. She'd felt exactly the same way. Breathing deeply, she calmed herself by remembering what he'd said earlier. "Protectors are Shifters. I need to let go of my distrust and remind myself they're not on Jacob's side."

"I know." He didn't look any less worried. "I can't really say what felt wrong." Grimacing, he clearly made a determined effort to shake off his trepidation. "Either way, we need to see what he has to say."

"He's coming alone?" She found this off-putting, as well. "I'd think they'd send a team or something."

He shrugged. "I don't know how they operate. Maybe that comes later."

"Do you have any idea when?"

Again he shrugged. "Sometime tomorrow. He said he'd call me when he landed at Denver International. He's going to rent a car and drive down here. Is that how they usually do it?"

"I don't know. Like you, I've never dealt with them before."

A sound from the other room made her turn. She rushed over to the sofa to see Hailey trying to sit up, and failing.

"Mama?" Hailey held out her arms to be picked up, exactly the way she used to when she'd been a toddler. "I want to go in the kitchen. I'm hungry. Carry me?" She still appeared woozy from whatever drug cocktail had been administered.

Reaching down, Blythe scooped her up. Hailey clung to her, again reminiscent of when she'd been much smaller.

"I'm scared, Mama."

"It's okay, honey," Blythe murmured. "I've got you now. You're safe, I promise. I won't let that man near you again."

Face pressed against Blythe's throat, Hailey nodded. "He didn't like us. I don't know why, because he didn't even know me."

Kissing her daughter's forehead, Blythe tamped back the impotent rage and focused on giving comfort. She grabbed a blanket off the edge of the sofa and draped it over her daughter's small body. She carried Hailey past the roaring fire Lucas had built and into the kitchen.

Still holding Hailey like a baby, she sat, settling with her five-year-old in her lap. She glanced up at Lucas, who watched silently. Blythe managed a smile for her daughter's benefit. "Do you have any more of that soup?"

He nodded, coming into the kitchen and standing near the stove.

"Do you want some soup and crackers?"

Hailey's drawn expression brightened. "Chicken noodle?" she asked. "That's my favorite."

"Then chicken noodle it is," Lucas said cheerfully.

While he opened the can and poured it into a pot to heat it, Blythe soothed Hailey's hair from her forehead. "How are you feeling?" she asked.

Considering the question carefully, Hailey scrunched up her little face. "Okay, I guess. I'm really hungry."

That was a good sign. Smiling, Blythe exchanged a glance with Lucas. "Not too hot," she told him.

"I think it's perfect now," he said, ladling the soup into a bowl and then placing it on the table in front of Hailey and Blythe. He also got the saltine crackers.

After everything was ready, he smiled at Hailey. "Would you like something to drink?"

She nodded. "Apple juice?"

"You got it." He ruffled her hair before going to retrieve the juice from the fridge.

Still perched on Blythe's lap, Hailey picked up her spoon and began eating. She ate with a kind of determined doggedness that made Blythe happy. It looked as if her daughter was going to be all right.

After a few minutes, Hailey slowed. Finally, she placed the spoon on her napkin and yawned. "That was good." Squirming, she snuggled against Blythe.

"What do you say to Mr. Kenyon?" Blythe asked.

Sleepily, Hailey smiled. "Thank you," she chimed sweetly.

"Do you want to go back over to the couch?"

Hailey nodded. "Yes, please."

Hefting her daughter's small frame, Blythe stood and

went back into the other room. The fire continued to burn and while Blythe got Hailey situated, Lucas added a couple more logs to the fire.

After covering Hailey with the blanket, Blythe kissed her forehead. Then, settling back, she began singing in a low voice, just above a whisper, one of her daughter's favorite songs. Gradually, Hailey's eyes began to drift closed. In a few minutes, she had fallen back asleep. The deep sleep of a child with a full belly and no fear.

Heart full of love, Blythe gazed down at her child. *Safe.* For the first time since she'd met Jacob Gideon, she felt safe. When she looked up, she saw Lucas standing in front of the fireplace, bathed in an orange glow, watching her.

The instant their gazes connected, a slow burn started low in her belly. Inside, her beast woke, alert and hungry. Ready to mate.

As she had all the other times, she resisted. But this time, he didn't turn away.

Common sense urged Blythe to be the one to turn her back. But reckless curiosity, the kind that came from too many sleepless nights spent allowing self-doubt to cripple her, had her doing the opposite instead.

Stretching, she stood and, after one last glance at her sleeping child, crossed to Lucas. With her heart beating in her chest like a trapped hummingbird, she moved closer to him, with their gazes still locked.

In unison, they moved backward, around the corner and out of view of the sofa. No words were spoken as he took her hand and pulled her close, up against him.

She kissed him first, standing up on her toes and arching her body into his. He deepened the kiss, letting her feel the heat of his own desire. She was glad to learn it burned as hot as her own.

Knees weak, she clung to him. His heartbeat throbbed against hers. She felt the strength of his arousal, heavy and hard and hot, so hot pressed against her, even through the thickness of his jeans. Her corresponding rush of moist warmth told her she was ready for him, even now when all they'd done was kiss.

The way he held back left it up to her to take things a step further. If she wanted to, that is.

Truth be told, she did. Just not now.

She sighed, inhaling the masculine scent of him, pine and coffee and man. How easy it would be to sink into this, to let the fierce need that raged in her blood take over, a welcome distraction from the craziness that had become her everyday life.

Was that even fair? Not only to him, but to either one of them?

"Not like this," she said, reluctantly.

Releasing her and taking a step back, he nodded, letting her know he must have read something in her eyes.

"I want you, I need you, but…" She couldn't finish.

"It's all right," he lied, sounding like a man in pain. She could see why—the strength of his arousal was clearly outlined in the front of his jeans. Just the sight of this had her weakening, swaying toward him, before she once again mentally pulled herself up by her bootstraps.

About to attempt again to explain, she opened her mouth only to be stopped by the gentle press of his finger against her lips. "No need. I understand. The timing is off."

More grateful than she could say, she nodded.

"Come on. I'll show you the guest bedroom." He moved stiffly toward the door, half turning to face her before he'd taken more than a few steps. "Unless you want to bunk down with Hailey on the couch."

"I was hoping I could get you to carry her into my room with me," she said. "She and I can share the bed."

Still moving awkwardly, he led the way to another bedroom. "I'll, uh, need a few minutes."

"That's ok." Face hot, she moved past him and retraced her steps to go check on Hailey, who still slept deeply. She took the chair opposite, alternating between staring into the fire and watching her beloved child sleep.

Distantly, she heard the sound of water running, as though Lucas had decided to take a shower. From the size of his arousal, she guessed he'd taken a cold one.

The heat of the fire and the rhythmic sound of Hailey breathing lulled her into a sort of dozing state. The sound of the bathroom door opening snapped her awake.

Lucas strolled into the room, fully clothed, though his hair was damp. "Would you like me to move her now?" he asked in a low voice, glancing from her to where Hailey still slept deeply.

"You know what?" Blythe asked, making a snap decision. "I hate to disturb her. She looks so comfortable here on the couch. I'll let her sleep there for now. She's got the fire for warmth and if I really miss her, I can always come out here and sleep in this chair."

He searched her face. "Are you sure? That chair doesn't look like it'd be too great for sleeping."

"I'm positive." Giving him a tentative smile, she stood. "Actually, I almost fell asleep there just now."

After a moment, he nodded. "The guest bed isn't made up. Let me get you clean sheets and an extra blanket."

He retrieved these from a small hall closet and he turned as if about to take them into the room. She intercepted him, practically snatching the linens out of his hands.

"I'll take care of it myself," she said quickly, maybe a bit too quickly. "No worries."

Evidently he got the hint. "If you want to." Shoulders stiff, he turned away. At least he seemed to be walking a bit better. "Good night, then."

"Good night." Only after he'd closed his bedroom door did she let out the breath she had been holding.

She went through the motions of making the bed, the mindless task giving her a way to occupy her hands and keep her from thinking about what she'd almost done.

After she'd finished, she made one final check on Hailey, half hoping she'd be awake. Instead, Hailey still slept deeply, a slight smile on her face. Loath to wake her, Blythe returned to her room, slid between the sheets and turned out the light.

Then she willed her mind to shut off and hoped she'd fall asleep.

That night, though she wasn't sure until later whether it was a dream or reality, the wind picked up outside the cabin. Branches rattled, things went bump and once or twice, she drowsily thought she heard a boom of thunder.

Shifting restlessly in the bed, she got up at three to check on Hailey, and found her still sleeping peacefully beside the fire's burning embers. Blythe added an extra blanket and then, chiding herself for her unnecessary worry, went back to bed, sliding under the covers and sinking gratefully into a deep sleep.

When she next opened her eyes, morning had arrived.

Stretching, she flushed all over as she realized she'd been dreaming of Lucas, erotic dreams in which they'd come together in an explosion of passion. The images came flooding back, and she let herself enjoy them before tucking them away for another time. Making that a reality would have to wait for later. Right now, she'd take care of her morning necessities, and then she planned on heading toward the kitchen and whipping up something for breakfast. Either pancakes or eggs, she thought, humming happily. Maybe she'd do both. Hailey would love that.

A short while later, showered and dressed in clean clothes, she made up her bed and opened her door. The house was quiet, telling her no one else was yet awake.

Good. She noted that the fire had burned down to glowing embers and passed by the front of the couch. Taking care to move quietly, she sneaked a quick look at her still-sleeping daughter and froze.

The couch was empty. The blanket, the pillow and, most important, Hailey, were gone.

Chapter 13

A scream woke Lucas from an erotic dream featuring Blythe. He sat up in bed, heart pounding. He grabbed his boxer shorts from the floor, yanked them on, then tore off toward the living room.

Incoherent and on the verge of hysteria, Blythe stood shaking, pointing at the empty couch. "Hailey, Hailey, Hailey. She's gone."

"Hang on." He grabbed her, pulling her close. "Maybe she just went to the bathroom."

"I checked. I called her and when she didn't answer, I searched every square inch of this house. She's gone."

Releasing her, he crossed to the front door and tested the dead bolt. "It's unlocked, from the inside."

Blythe stared at him in shock and slowly shook her head. "She couldn't have left. Why would she?"

"Where would she have gone? It's cold outside."

"She didn't leave willingly," Blythe said, appearing unaware that there were tears streaming down her face. "She was taken."

Christ. Despite the growing certainty that she was right, they had to be certain. "You don't know that," he insisted, mind racing. "There's no sign of a break-in. Maybe she just took a peek outside and forgot to relock it. She's got to be here, somewhere."

Still violently shaking, she nodded.

"Come on." He held out his hand. "Let's check again, both of us. There's got to be some explanation."

Watching as she visibly pulled herself together, when she grabbed his hand, it was as if she grabbed on to a lifeline. He closed his fingers over her icy ones and found himself uttering a silent prayer that little Hailey was merely hiding and had fallen asleep.

Both silent now, they went through the cabin, room by room, which didn't take long at all. Beside him, Blythe grew increasingly more frantic, barely holding on to the edge of control, squeezing his fingers so tightly they went numb.

He didn't blame her. By all appearances, her daughter had mysteriously vanished. With the front door unlocked from the inside and all the rest of the cabin secure, she could have gone of her own free will.

To be certain, he began checking the windows. "Locked, locked and locked," he said out loud. "There's no way someone broke in here."

She nodded and then faced him, her expression blank. "Did you check the back door?"

About to tell her he had, he closed his mouth without saying anything. He had given it a cursory look, in passing. At first glance, the door appeared locked. Rattling the knob, he double-checked. But then as he was turning away, he saw the small, perfectly shaped circle that had been cut in the glass. Someone had cut it out and reached a hand in to unlock the door.

They'd come in through the back, grabbed Hailey and gone out the front.

"Blythe..." he began. "Come here."

All the blood drained from her face as she instantly assessed the situation. "Hailey, oh, my God." She swayed. "It has to have been Jacob. Somehow he found us. He's taken Hailey."

The outline of her body shuddered as her wolf wanted to force a shift. Fighting this, she swayed again, staggering so badly he thought she might fall. Then, just as he reached for her, she forcibly snapped herself out of it, as though a wire had been pulled from above to straighten her spine. Leaving him standing, empty-handed, wondering why he'd even thought he could help.

She yanked the front door open and rushed outside. Hurrying after her, he followed.

The sky had barely begun to lighten. The area around the cabin appeared virtually unchanged.

"Damn it all to hell," she said. Expression furious, she pushed past him and rushed back inside. Locating the cell phone, she snatched it up. Before he could ask what she meant to do, she'd scrolled through the recent calls, located a number and pushed Send.

Watching, he stood back, making no move to stop her. He knew she was either calling the Protector or calling Jacob Gideon. He wasn't sure which.

"Jacob," she practically spat the word into the phone. "What have you done with my daughter?"

Listening for a moment, she closed her eyes. "But—"

She mustn't have liked whatever else Jacob had to say, because she ended the call without saying another word.

Holding the cell phone, she stood motionless, a statue

with a downcast head. Whatever emotions she felt, he could only imagine.

Chest tight, Lucas moved closer. When she raised her gaze to meet his, the terrible bleakness in her eyes hit him like a punch in the gut. He coughed, to cover this. "Did Jacob admit to anything?" he asked.

"He claims he doesn't have her," she said, her voice shaking. "If he doesn't, then who does?"

"I don't know," he told her. "We'll find out, I promise you."

"It has to be him. It has to." She shook her head, her eyes wild. "Hailey," she cried, before crumpling. Somehow, Lucas managed to catch her, holding her against him and trying to soothe her.

"You're probably right. If Jacob took her, we'll get her back."

"And what if he didn't? What if it was someone else?"

"Who?" he asked, his tone fierce. "Who else would go through the trouble to locate us, all the way up here, and break in just to take a little girl? It has to be Jacob."

"He claims he doesn't know anything about her being abducted," she continued. "He also said he didn't order anything and as far as he knew, she was with me and that he had no idea where we are."

"Did you believe him?"

She shrugged. "I don't know. But he sounded pretty damn shocked."

The steel had come back in her voice. He admired her ability to snatch herself back from the edge and to try and think rationally, despite her fear and worry for her daughter's safety.

"Jacob is the type to boast," he said slowly. "He's supremely confident in everything he does. Look how he acted before, after you escaped. If he took her, why would he lie? I'd think he'd want to rub your face in it."

"Exactly." While he held her against his chest, she inhaled deeply several times, an obvious attempt to clear her head. "It doesn't make sense."

"Maybe he's afraid we'll come after her again," he offered. "That's the only reason for him to lie."

"No." She shook her head violently, still pressed against him, her shoulders shaking though she didn't make any sounds to let him know she was crying. "I believe him, hounds help me. I actually believe him."

Lucas let this sink in for a moment. "Once again, if Jacob didn't take her, who did?"

"I don't know," she said, pushing away from him to go stand in front of the window. "I have no idea."

Leaving Blythe in the kitchen with a warm cup of cocoa, Lucas did a walk around on his perimeter. The ground was too hard and dry to yield any clues, but the gravel on the driveway about halfway between the house and the road showed signs of a vehicle turning around. Obviously, whoever had driven it hadn't wanted to park too close to the house and take a chance of waking anyone.

That meant he must have been a large man—or more than one person—because they'd carried Hailey a good distance. Lucas figured they'd probably knocked her out, using chloroform or something, to make sure she didn't scream or put up a fight.

As he turned to head back to the cabin, he saw something else. The tires on Lucas's pickup truck had been slashed, all four of them. This had been done for insurance to make certain if they had awakened, they couldn't pursue Hailey's abductor.

Everything had the appearance of a well-planned, professional job. If Jacob hadn't ordered this, then who? And why? No one even knew they were here, other than the Protectors. He froze as a thought occurred to him. Blythe had said they'd take Hailey. What if they had?

Returning to the cabin, he told Blythe what he'd found.

Then, swallowing hard, he continued, "What if it was the Protectors? You said they might want to take Hailey."

She shook her head. "No one knows she's a Griffon. That would be the only reason they'd take her and, as far as I know, they haven't stooped so low to sneak in and abduct children in the middle of the night. I still can't let go of the idea that Jacob's behind this. He's the only one who would want her."

Listless, she sipped on her cocoa. "Unless it was some other sort of predator. One who preys on children." The darkness to her tone matched her expression.

"Don't think that," he ordered. "I need you sharp and focused. Do you think you can do that?"

Her eyes widened. Sitting up, she rolled her shoulders back and straightened. "I'll try." Her voice sounded much closer to normal. And, he noted with approval, the steel was back. Hopefully to stay this time.

"Good. If it wasn't the Protectors, then I don't understand how anyone was able to find us," he said.

"True, since the only one who knows we're here is that Protector you spoke with on the phone."

"Martin Hunter." He cursed. "Was he for real, or someone acting as a Pack Protector in order to learn our location?"

"It seems a bit far-fetched, but maybe you should call him again?" Blythe suggested, her voice vibrating with anger as she finally gave credence to the possibility that the Protectors had actually been the ones to steal her daughter.

Nodding, he pulled out his phone and scrolled to recent calls. After barely half a ring, the call went directly to voice mail. "His phone is off. He's probably en route."

She didn't respond. Because he didn't want her slipping back into whatever kind of self-protective purgatory she'd found, he moved closer and jogged her arm.

"We'll find out soon enough—if he doesn't arrive today."

While they waited, he went to his storage shed and located his snow tires. Jacking his truck up, he changed the shredded tires one by one until he had a drivable vehicle.

Inside, Blythe sat with her still-full cup of cold cocoa, staring at nothing. She put down her cup and stood. "I'm going to go outside and change. Maybe I can pick up her scent or something—I don't know."

"Would you like me to go with you?"

"No. But thank you. I need to be alone."

He nodded, aching for her but knowing there was nothing else he could do. This time, she walked out wearing her clothing. A short while later, he heard a mournful howl coming from the forest. The achingly bitter beauty of the sound made the hair on his arms rise. The sound continued, echoing off the mountains, for several minutes, before dying off into silence.

Throat tight, Lucas found himself listening for more. The grief-filled howl had touched something inside him, deep within his soul. His wolf had become agitated at the sound. Despite Blythe's request to be left alone, if he hadn't needed to remain to listen for the phone, he would have joined her. As wolf, not man.

Ninety minutes passed before she returned. Fully dressed, she seemed more tense than ever. Neither mentioned the howling. "Have you heard from this Protector guy?" she asked.

He shook his head no. He didn't know how he'd forgive

himself if it turned out he'd given information to someone who had been responsible for invading his home and stealing Hailey.

Together, they waited in apprehensive silence. He didn't have a television—there was no reception in these mountains without satellite, which he didn't want. He spent his nights reading or sketching, or walking in the woods. Always alone since Lilly's death, he'd become skilled at entertaining himself, even though he always felt his twin with him.

He wished he could think of something to distract Blythe. But then, he wasn't sure she wanted to be diverted.

Finally, three hours after Lucas had changed his tires, Martin Hunter called to let them know he was on the ground and about to begin the drive south.

Using a few terse words, Lucas explained the situation.

"She's gone?" Martin sounded stunned. "How is that possible?"

"That's what we wanted to know. Who did you tell?" Lucas demanded. "It had to be you."

"I told no one," Martin protested. "No one except my supervisor. Oh, and his secretary. She's the one who booked my flight."

"Where is your supervisor located?"

"I work out of the Dallas office," Martin said.

Texas. Jacob Gideon's home base. It was a long shot, but still…

Eyeing Blythe, who watched him silently, Lucas grimaced. "Sorry, but I have to ask. Is the secretary Shifter or human?"

"I don't know." Martin honestly sounded puzzled. "I've never met the gal. She just started last week."

Damn. Lucas would be willing to bet she not only was

human, but that she was a member of Jacob Gideon's church and Sanctuary.

"But I do have to ask you something," Martin said. "Is your phone line secure? You know cell phones are particularly vulnerable to being intercepted, with the right equipment."

Lucas cursed. The second possibility worked in theory—if someone even knew how to find his remote cabin.

"Check and make sure it wasn't your people who grabbed Hailey," he ordered.

"Will do," Martin promised.

"Good." Hanging up, he relayed to Blythe what Martin had said about their phone line being hacked by Jacob's people.

"I suppose that's possible," she said, still sitting as if there was ice in her spine. "But the only thing that doesn't add up is why isn't Jacob bragging about it."

Lucas considered. "Maybe one of his devout followers is trying to gain brownie points by surprising him with your daughter."

She winced, and then jerked her chin in a facsimile of a nod. "Stranger things have happened."

"At this point we have to consider all possibilities," he told her.

As he watched, her lethargy dissolved into rage. "This is ridiculous. We need to do something. I hate just sitting here and waiting, while Hailey is…"

"I know." Gathering her close, he simply held her while she wept.

As the day dragged on and the light faded, the air grew cooler and crisper. Full darkness fell and Lucas built another fire in the fireplace, unable to even look at the sofa where Hailey had slept.

Evidently Blythe had the same problem. She remained

in the kitchen, having exchanged her cocoa for a glass of wine, which again, she barely touched.

Unable to stand it anymore, Lucas went outside to wait. Finally, he heard the sound of a vehicle making the ascent up his long drive. A moment later, he saw headlights.

"Blythe." Just her name, but an instant later she joined him. "We have company," he said.

Blythe blinked twice, willing herself to find her focus. She couldn't fall apart, not now. Once again, she'd failed Hailey, true. But she refused to believe she wouldn't get a second chance to rescue her.

This Martin Hunter, Pack Protector, had better be good. Because she was counting on him to help her save her daughter.

Standing side by side with Lucas on his wooden porch, she watched the car—obviously a rental compact—approach. She stood unmoving, as did Lucas, while the driver parked the vehicle and shut off its engine.

A short, heavyset man climbed from the car. Opening the back door, he grabbed an overnight bag, then turned and made his way over toward them.

Every instinct went on full alert. He didn't look like any Pack Protector she'd ever seen.

Not that she'd actually seen one, but still. The Protectors were the law enforcers of the Shape-shifter world. She's expected someone along the lines of a toned, navy SEAL–type guy, not an I-ate-too-many-doughnuts-stereotypical cop.

Beside her, Lucas stiffened. Evidently he too felt that something might be off.

"Lucas Kenyon?" the man asked, his deep bass voice rumbling.

Lucas nodded. "And this is Blythe Daphne, the missing girl's mother."

Missing girl. Hearing the words out loud stabbed her heart. Determined, she lifted her chin and stepped forward, holding out her hand. "You must be Martin Hunter."

She waited until they'd shaken hands before clearing her throat. "I'll need to see your credentials, please."

Clearly surprised, Martin narrowed his eyes. Blythe sensed Lucas was ready to draw his weapon in the event there was trouble.

Evidently Martin noticed this, too. Letting go of his overnight bag, he raised his hand to his shoulders. "Easy, there. I'm getting my ID badge," he said.

Procuring this from a shirt pocket, he held it out toward Blythe. She took it, not entirely sure what to look for, and carefully studied it, before passing it over to Lucas.

"I suppose if he was here to try and kill us, he wouldn't have gone through all the bother of printing up a fake Protector badge," Lucas murmured.

"Fake badge?" Martin raised his rather bushy eyebrows. "Look, I've come a long way. I'm tired, hungry and cold. Plus I need to use your bathroom. Can we please take this inside?"

Ignoring him, Lucas continued studying the badge. Finally, he shrugged and handed it back to Martin. "Sorry. We're a bit suspicious."

The other man accepted his badge and stuck it back in his pocket and nodded. "Understandably so."

"Come on," Lucas said, touching Blythe's elbow, the gesture apparently to let her know it was okay. "Let's go in the cabin and talk."

Still unable to shake her foreboding, she led the way.

Just inside, Martin dropped his bag and excused himself to hurry to the restroom. The instant the door closed behind him, Blythe and Lucas looked at each other.

"Well? What do you think?" Lucas asked. "Is he for real?"

She shrugged. "I have no idea. I've never met a Pack Protector. It's a little early to tell."

"Let's give the guy a chance," Lucas said. "The first thing we need to ask him is if his organization is behind this."

Swallowing back impatience, she nodded.

When the Protector returned, Blythe fidgeted, waiting until he'd taken a seat. "Did your people have anything to do with this?"

"Not that I'm aware of," he answered. "I've put in a request for information, but haven't heard anything yet."

"Bureaucracy," Lucas muttered.

Martin nodded, his focus still on Blythe. "Why don't you tell me what you know?"

She glanced at Lucas before launching into the story. Martin took notes, which made her feel slightly better. He stopped her when she got to the part about other children.

"Pack children, you said?"

Glancing at Lucas, Blythe nodded and took a deep breath. "Not just Pack. At least one of the children is a Griffon."

This surprised him, she could tell. Though his expression remained for the most part unchanged, a quick flicker of interest flashed into his eyes before he looked down to shield them.

"How do you know?" he asked, his pen poised over the notebook.

Swallowing hard, she glanced at Lucas who nodded silently. "Because my daughter, Hailey, is one—she's a

Griffon. And I don't believe Jacob Gideon has any idea exactly what he has."

Grim-faced, Martin stood. "I'll have to call this in. Shifter children are bad enough, but Griffons..." He glanced at them both, frowning with preoccupation. "If you'll excuse me, I'm going to take a walk outside and make a few calls."

"Of course." Both she and Lucas watched him go.

"I don't get it," Lucas said, frowning. "What difference does it make if the children are Shifters, Griffons or *anything*? They're children, for Pete's sake. We've got to help them."

"I agree," she began, but he pushed to his feet.

"I hate to tell you this, Blythe, but I think your Pack Protectors are worthless."

Suddenly furious, she stood, too, crossing over to stand toe-to-toe with him. "First off, they're not *my* Pack Protectors. And right now, they're all we've got. They should be able to help. If not, we're no worse off than we were before we called them."

Though he narrowed his eyes, he didn't argue. But a muscle worked in his jaw, a hint of some strong emotion that might have been anger.

She knew exactly how he felt. All that emotion and nowhere to channel it.

Except, she knew exactly where she wanted to expend it and how. Rage and grief made her reckless. The moment she had the thought, electricity arced between them. She felt it, and she saw it affect him, too, in his deeper, faster breathing, his enlarged pupils and the way he flexed his hands as if he were stroking her overheated skin.

He took a step back, away from her.

"We've got to do something about this," he said, his expression pure pain. "Maybe not now, but soon."

The Protector's return saved her from responding. "Excuse me," Martin said, looking from one to the other.

"First up, I have good news."

Blythe narrowed her eyes. "About Hailey?"

"Yes." He glanced at Lucas. "Did either of you happen to meet up with a Shifter named Kane?"

"Yes," Lucas answered. "He's the one who hired me to work at Sanctuary as a guard. He also helped Blythe and Hailey escape."

Martin nodded, as though he'd expected no less. "He works for us. He's deep undercover. And it was hinted that headquarters is aware of the situation at Sanctuary."

"They know about what's going on and they haven't intervened yet?" Lucas said. "While Shifters are being tortured?"

"I'm sure they're working on getting them out," Martin said.

"What about my daughter?" Blythe grabbed his arm. "You said you had good news."

Martin turned to her, his expression relieved. "Yes. Your little girl is safe."

Blythe tightened her grip on his arm. "Where is she? What happened to her?"

Again, the other man glanced at Lucas before removing Blythe's fingers from his arm. "Kane's been tracking you."

"How?" Lucas interrupted. "I made sure we weren't followed."

"Best guess, some sort of GPS device." He took a deep breath, then faced Blythe fully, his resigned expression letting her know he expected an explosion. "I've been told his people were the ones who came and took your daughter."

Stunned, her first instinct was to punch him. Her second, outright disbelief. "That makes no sense. He helped us escape. If he wanted Hailey, why wouldn't he have taken her then?"

She had to give him credit. This Martin Hunter didn't back down. "He got new orders. He's trying to get the children out one by one. The Society wants to make sure they are all safe."

Clenching her teeth, conscious that she'd balled her hands into fists, she glared at him. "She was safe. She was with us."

"She needs access to medical facilities." Something flashed in his eyes—pity? concern?—and she knew he was about to tell her something she wouldn't like. "There is some concern that whatever experiments this Dr. Silva performed on her might have stressed her heart."

Just like that, all the air went out of her. Somehow, she made it to the couch and sank down. "How do you know this?" she asked quietly. "And how certain are you?"

"Ma'am, I'm sorry." Martin shook his head. "I can only report what I'm told."

"Fine." She struggled to understand. "But why take her this way? Without telling us? I'm her mother. I want to be with her."

"That's one reason why," Martin said promptly. "Kane has reported that Jacob Gideon has worked himself into a frenzy. He's vowed to get you and Hailey back, no matter what it takes. He also seems especially interested in your friend, Lucas, here. Of course, now that you've told me Lucas is his son, I understand."

Glaring at him, Blythe crossed her arms. "So the stories are true. The Protectors have gone beyond a simple request that Griffon children be raised by them. You've now resorted to stealing them."

Her statement appeared to anger Martin. "That's completely uncalled for," he said with quiet dignity. "This is a special case. Our job is to protect, not cause harm."

About to respond, she swallowed her words when Lucas squeezed her shoulder, giving her a gentle reminded that none of this was Martin's fault.

Martin grimaced, showing he understood her frustration. "Look, I know you love your daughter. Believe me when I say the best thing for her right now is to stay where she is."

"At least tell me that," she pleaded. "So I can go find her when this is all over."

But both Martin and Lucas were already shaking their heads. "It's better if you don't know. If Jacob finds you… We've got to take every precaution. When this case has been closed, you will of course be allowed to go to her."

Though Blythe nodded as though it all made perfect sense, as if she understood, her heart was breaking. If Hailey's condition was weakening, who knew how much time she had left? Blythe wanted to spend every possible moment with her daughter, right up until the end.

Chapter 14

Blythe took a deep breath. "There's something you need to know. Hailey's very ill. Though her heart condition alone could be enough to kill her, she mustn't be allowed to change into wolf. The Pack doctors I saw felt such a thing would destroy her already-fragile heart. She'll die, do you understand?"

Martin attempted a smile. "She's a bit young to even be thinking about changing, don't you think?"

"She's a Griffon," she reminded him. "You know they're different than other Halfling children. There's no telling what she might decide to do."

"I'll make sure to pass that on," he said.

"If I give you my phone number, can you have them let her call me? I really want to talk to her, to explain. A lot has happened to her in a short amount of time. I don't want her to be frightened or worried."

"I'll take your number," Martin answered. "But I can't

make any promises. I'm sure everything was explained to her."

"Right." Blythe couldn't keep the bitterness from her voice. Nevertheless, she scribbled down her number on a scrap of paper and handed it to him. "Just like Jacob Gideon explained everything. I'm sure that reassured her."

Martin frowned, but didn't comment. Taking the paper from her, he stuffed it down into his pocket.

"What about the other children?" Lucas asked. "Surely you're not relying on just one man to get them out? Kane helped us escape and had to fire two of the security detail. I'm afraid they're liable to talk. Even if they don't, I believe someone's going to notice."

"Others are also working behind the scenes." Now Martin smiled. "An entire team of Protectors out in West Texas are building a case against Sanctuary. Now that I'm involved, I'm being immediately reassigned. I'll meet them there."

Blythe exchanged a quick look with Lucas. "We'll go, too."

Martin's smile vanished. "That's probably not a good idea."

Lucas crossed his arms. "We have more reason than any of you to get those children out and stop Jacob Gideon."

"Your being there might endanger the other children."

For a second Lucas appeared taken aback. Then he grimaced. "Or we might be exactly the distraction you need. Have you thought about that?"

Passing his hand across his eyes, Martin suddenly appeared tired. "This is not my decision to make. I promise, I'll pass that on, too. But I've got to go. They're flying me out later tonight."

"All right then," Lucas said, sounding mollified though

Blythe knew him well enough already to recognize the fierceness burning in his eyes. He wasn't about to give up.

"For now, until I hear differently..." Martin gave them both a sharp look. "I'd like you two to stay out of the way and let us handle this."

Let them handle this. A quick glance at Lucas told her he shared her thoughts. That would be a cold day in hell. Wisely, Blythe kept that opinion to herself.

"We'll consider that," Lucas responded, his voice non-committal. Nodding, Blythe continued to keep her mouth shut, afraid of what she might say if she opened it.

"Well, then. Take care." Martin actually smiled, appearing to believe he'd contained the situation. After hand-shakes all around, he climbed back into his rental car and left.

Only then did Blythe exhale. Fist curled, she inhaled deeply, trying like hell to get herself under control. She wanted to punch something, a way of finding an outlet for the overflow of mingled emotions coursing through her blood.

"Hailey is safe with someone who risked his life to save her," Lucas said, no doubt trying to comfort her. "You'll see her again after we take Jacob down. And we will take him down."

"I know." While she did agree with him, she realized she needed movement. Something physical. A punching bag or...sex. Rough, hard and hot. Something to help her forget, if only for a few moments. A little relief in a world she no longer understood.

Glancing at Lucas from under her lashes, she debated going over to him and savagely ripping his clothes off. Instead, she swallowed hard and, hands still fisted, stalked to the window, aroused and fuming and aching as she watched Martin drive away.

* * *

Even with her back to him, ramrod straight, Lucas still shared Blythe's roiling emotions, which radiated off her in waves. Hell, her entire body vibrated from it. The air around her practically shimmered, as if at any moment, her body would begin the change to wolf.

Desire clawed at him, a given constant since he'd met her, but even more so after the passion that had flared between them earlier. Furious, he shoved that away. Not only was it out of place, but she was vulnerable. He could not, would not, take advantage of her in this state.

Yet that didn't keep him from burning for her.

He made a sound, low in his throat, completely involuntary. With her fist up like a boxer, she spun to face him.

"I can't believe this. The Pack—my Pack—broke in here and stole my child. Without even asking my permission, or at the very least letting us know what they'd done." Her eyes burned, green fire full of frustration and anger and the pain of betrayal. "How could they do such a thing? How could they not care that I'd be frantic with worry when she simply disappeared?"

Once, he'd told her that her Pack sounded similar to Sanctuary. Now, they'd proved it. Though he saw no need to point this out now—surely, she already realized that—he had no idea why these Pack Protectors thought he and Blythe would take orders from them. Especially after they'd high-handedly broken into his cabin and kidnapped her daughter.

Unless they planned to motivate Blythe and Lucas to action, manipulating them while appearing not to.

The idea seemed so bizarre, so impossible, that he kept it to himself. If Blythe independently reached the same conclusion, then they could discuss it.

"At least we know she's safe," he said, because he could

think of nothing else that might comfort this woman who mattered to him.

"True." But she didn't appear placated. "And this Martin Hunter. Does he really think we're going to sit around here and twiddle our thumbs?"

Lucas wasn't sure how to respond. Though he didn't like the idea of becoming the Pack's unwitting puppet, Blythe was right. They had to take action.

All through the years, he'd imagined getting his revenge. He'd thought so long that he had the details worked out, right down to the look of shock on Jacob's face. But he'd never imagined Jacob was crazy enough to amass a collection of other children. Knowing the scope of Jacob's hatred toward those he considered demons, Lucas couldn't help but wonder how many of them had already been killed.

Looking down so Blythe couldn't read his thoughts in his eyes, he swallowed hard at the thought.

Forgotten children, suffering untold torture before they were murdered and unceremoniously tossed in some sort of communal burial pit like wild animals.

The image broke his heart. Unfortunately, he knew from experience the scenario was not only possible, but extremely likely. Because Jacob Gideon, fanatical preacher of a church he called Sanctuary, was pretty damn close to murderously insane.

"These other children," he said slowly, considering his words. "How in the hell did Jacob get away with it? Surely someone had to have reported their children missing. They couldn't all be in the same situation as you and Hailey, convinced to join his church for a promise of healing. Someone in the media would have picked up on that."

"Good point," she agreed. "But Hailey has no reason to lie. She had to be telling the truth."

"Agreed. We've got to do something. We just need to make sure it's the best possible move. No matter what your Pack thinks."

"Quit calling them my Pack." She grimaced. "I can't shake the feeling that they're manipulating us. They took Hailey because they want us to do something. What exactly, I'm not entirely sure. And why the heck they couldn't just ask us rather than take such extreme measures...."

Instead of finishing her thought, she rounded on him, shooting him a look of such blatant heat it felt as if a bolt of lightning went straight to his gut.

At first, he didn't respond. He could barely think, never mind speak. Every instinct he possessed had him aching to touch her, curling his fingers against the urge.

"You probably think that's paranoid, don't you?" she asked, her restless movements impossibly sexy.

Clenching his jaw, he tried to clamp down on his overheated senses. "Actually, I don't," he managed, his voice rough. "The thought had already occurred to me."

She nodded, sweeping her hair away from her neck, the sensuality of the movement drawing his gaze. "Then what do you think we should do?"

Do. If he didn't get out of there and away from her, he didn't know how much longer he could resist yanking her up against him and covering her mouth, hard, rough and dangerous, like a beast making his claim.

This was something he definitely needed to get over. His body ached to make promises he couldn't keep. He wasn't going to stop being a loner. Problem was, even his inner wolf could smell the desire in the air, see the electricity arcing between them.

Surely she had to sense it, too.

When she raised her head and looked at him, he saw

from her enlarged pupils that she did. The passion of the kiss they'd shared, with the promise of so much more…

Damn. A shudder, strong as an electric shock, ran through him. He needed to look away, turn away. Instead he stood frozen, as though shared desire had cast some sort of spell on him.

She swallowed, the movement drawing his gaze to her slender throat. "About last night," she began, her voice husky with traces of sex and sin.

"That was a mistake," he cut in, letting her hear his frustrated fury. He teetered so close to the edge of losing control, he didn't think he could survive discussing the heat that constantly simmered between them.

"No." Apparently undeterred, she moved closer, her stride sure and confident. A blatant invitation, sexy as hell, making his body thrum.

"It wasn't," she continued. "Like I said, the timing was off. And I'm glad we didn't. I'd never have forgiven myself if I'd been making love with you when my daughter disappeared."

Making love. Not having sex. A fresh surge of arousal had him harder than he'd ever been.

He somehow managed to nod, hoping now that she'd said her piece, she'd go. "Yeah, well, it's late. Maybe we should both try to get some sleep before heading out. I figure we'll leave in the morning." Despite his best efforts at sounding normal, he knew he didn't.

"Okay." But instead of leaving, she came closer still, making his heart skip crazily. She stopped when she was only a few feet from him, close enough so that he couldn't breathe without her scent filling his nostrils. "I'd rather have sex."

It took a major effort to keep from groaning out loud. "You don't owe me anything," he managed to say, attempting to sound casual in spite of the edge of desperation that had crept into his voice. Sex. Every throb of his heartbeat seemed to be repeating the word.

She made a sound, husky and sensual, that went straight to his groin. "I don't use my body as a form of payment. The truth is, I want my daughter back so badly it hurts. I can't turn off the screaming in my head. I need to do something to erase the pain."

Heat suffused him, making him sway. Even his inner wolf sat up and took notice. Though he recognized she wanted to use him, he understood. "You're playing with fire," he warned. "Don't start something unless you have every intention of finishing it."

"Oh, I promise you, I do." She reached up and pulled him to her. As her lips touched his, he gave up the fight and let go of restraint and threw caution to the wind.

They came together like a forest fire, raging in the vortex of pine and stone and mountain, consuming everything in its path. Parched, he drank her in, while she devoured him as though every fiber of her being had been starved.

Mouth to mouth, skin to skin, they impatiently tore away the unwanted barrier of clothing, craving closeness and refusing to allow even the tiniest bit of space between them.

They clutched each other as they tumbled backward onto his bed. Mindless with passion, he let them fall, knowing he would cushion her. Riding him down, the half-lidded droop of her eyes fierce and unbelievably arousing. When she took him inside her, sheathing him in her hot wetness, he nearly lost control.

No. He desperately needed this to last. More than that, he wanted them both to find equal pleasure. Gripping her tightly to keep her from moving, he somehow managed to rein himself in.

"Slow," he ground out.

"Fast," she countered, struggling to move and damn near driving him insane in the process.

"Not yet." Guiding her with his hands, he kept her movements much slower than the frenzied rush she wanted.

With a sigh, she shimmied, almost causing him to lose it again, and then she began to settle down. The instant she relaxed her defenses the tiniest bit, he gave a savage grin and rolled them both over, taking the dominant position.

"Now," he growled, nuzzling her neck. "I will show you how to do this taking our time."

And so he did.

Killing her slowly: that was what he was doing. Blythe moaned, arching her back as Lucas entered her, inch by fully engorged inch. Using what had to be phenomenal self-control, he withdrew equally slowly, torturing her and filling her with a mindless need.

She needed *more*. Fast and hard, she wanted him to drive into her until they both reached mindless oblivion. Not like this. This languid exploration felt far too intimate, too personal.

So she fought him, struggled against his hands on her wrists, writhing and using her body to entice him to abandon his Herculean command.

Instead, her attempts only shattered the small remains of her self-control. With a wild cry, she let herself go, her world exploding as he brought her to the peak again and again. Each time, as she began the dizzy descent back to reality, he teased her body back to life, sending her spiraling to release again and again.

Finally, her body slick with sweat, spent and weak, she sagged against him. And then, he finally let himself go, driving into her with all the power and passion she'd craved earlier.

Unbelievably, she came to life again, glorying in the sensation, her spirit joining his as they fell into a perfect rhythm, dancing to their own music. She sensed it as he neared the peak, thrilled as she joined him there.

They both cried out, clutching each other close, her body clenching around his as he spent himself, buried deep inside her.

There were no words she could say, nothing that would even come close to letting him know the magnificence of the experience they'd just shared. But then, as she gazed into his eyes, she saw no words would be necessary. He already knew.

Knowing that, she let herself drift off into sleep with a smile on her lips.

As he cradled Blythe in his arms, Lucas reflected on how many changes had occurred in his life since seeing her on the evening news. He'd never spent the night with a woman before. But she was sleeping, spent from the amazing intensity of their lovemaking. He'd never experienced anything like it with any other woman. Truth be told, he doubted any other woman could come close to making him feel this way.

This worried the hell out of him. Briefly, he contemplated trying to ease out of her arms and leave her slumbering in his bed. Oddly, he couldn't tear himself away.

He didn't want to leave her. Ever.

With that thought foremost in his mind, he closed his eyes and willed himself to sleep.

In the morning he woke with a raging hard-on. Gazing down at Blythe, who still slept in his arms, he tried to understand. Was this only his body's natural response to the stimuli of a beautiful, naked woman in his bed, or was it something more?

As she murmured in her sleep and wiggled up against him, he grew even harder. Whatever the reason, he wanted to wake her with kisses and then bury himself deep inside her.

Wrong. More than wrong. By every rule of logic, the hours he'd spent exploring every inch of her body should have slaked his hunger, quenched his thirst. Instead, if anything, making love with her had only made him crave her more.

He needed to back away or he was in deep trouble. Anything more than a casual involvement would be a major mistake. Guys like him never ended up with women like her.

Somehow, he managed to force himself to get out of bed and head on into the shower. When he finally emerged, both his mind and his body clean, his bed was empty.

Down the hall, the other bathroom door was closed. A moment later, he heard the sound of the shower starting. Telling himself it was all good, he decided to get packed. They could grab something to eat on the road.

As he gathered some things to toss into a duffel bag, she appeared in his doorway, wrapped in a towel, her hair wet. Again, unbelievably, his body stirred.

"Morning." He tried to sound casual.

"Good morning." Her smile sent a jolt of heat straight to his groin. "I know you said we were leaving this morning. What's the plan?"

Thankful they were on more solid ground, he attempted a smile. He wished his body would stop throbbing. "I'm just about packed," he said. "If you are, we can stop for breakfast on the way."

Though she nodded, she didn't move. "I'm not, but it'll

just take me a few minutes. What I meant was, have you come up with some ideas about what we're going to do once we get to Sanctuary? Should we get in touch with Kane?"

Slowly, deliberately, he concentrated on folding one last T-shirt and placing it in the bag. "I don't know. What do you think?"

Her expression darkened. "We can't try to figure out what the Pack wants and doesn't want. We really shouldn't let them figure into our plans at all."

"I don't know." Abandoning the attempt to focus on packing, he forced himself to meet her gaze head-on. Again, he experienced that jolt of lightning that bound them. Pushing past it, he continued. "Still, I don't want to do anything that might jeopardize getting the children out. Since he's got an operation already in place, we need to let him know."

Her frown let him know she wasn't happy. "I agree," she finally said. "Who knows, maybe Kane will be glad of our help."

"That way, he can focus on rescuing the children while we distract Jacob."

At his word, her gaze sharpened. "Keep talking."

"We've got to draw him out, and occupy him while Kane and his people find out where he's hiding the children, and stop him for good. We've got to publicly expose him. He needs to be arrested and put away." *Or killed,* he added silently. "That's the only way to stop him."

"I agree." Her towel slipped, allowing him a tantalizing glimpse of her breast.

Desire slammed him, heavy and hot. He cursed under his breath. They'd get nothing done if they spent all their time in bed. "Listen," he said. "Would you mind continuing this discussion after you've put some clothes on?"

She cocked her head, appearing startled, before a slow, knowing smile spread across her face. "No problem." Giving him one last considering look, she dropped her towel to the floor. Then, completely naked, she bent over, picked the towel up, and marched away, down the hall to the guest room.

He nearly tackled her. Instead, he kept his feet rooted to the floor and watched her go. Only when she was out of sight was he able to breathe a sigh of relief. Again he wondered what the hell was wrong with him?

A few minutes later, she returned. Wearing jeans and a T-shirt, she seemed relaxed, at ease, comfortable in her own body.

Unlike him. He felt as if his skin was stretched too tight.

Arms crossed, she eyed him. "Have you thought about how we're going to deal with the Protectors?"

"You know more about them than I do. What do you suggest?"

"I like your idea. We work with them, but separately."

"As in, they don't give us orders." He smiled back, finally feeling as if he was back on solid ground. "We'll coordinate with them. As long as we don't get in each other's way, we should be fine."

He could tell from her expression that he hadn't fooled her in the slightest. "You do know we're in this together, don't you?"

Restless, he began to pace, wishing he had more room to stretch his legs. She followed him out into the living room, waiting silently while he gathered his thoughts.

Watching him, her beautiful cat's eyes narrowed.

"You're not going to hand yourself over to that monster."

"How do you do that?" he asked. "It's like you read my mind."

Instead of answering, she continued, "I couldn't live with knowing you were killed because of me."

He refused to let her words touch him. "I'm the perfect distraction. Me. I'm pretty sure he'd give just about anything to get his hands on me again."

"Why? Because you're his son? I know it's not out of any sense of fatherly love."

Snorting, he didn't bother to conceal his derision.

"I'm the one who got away. I'm sure he's spent years plotting what he'd do to me if he ever got his hands on me again."

Again he remembered what Jacob had done to Lilly. How battered and bruised her poor slender body had looked the last time Lucas had seen her. And how badly he still craved revenge.

He looked up to find Blythe staring at him. For an uncomfortable second, he wondered if she actually was able to read his mind.

"Are you okay?" she asked.

"Sure." He gave a flippant shrug. "I'm fine."

She continued to eye him. "What are you hiding?" she asked, her perceptiveness reinforcing his earlier suspicion about her psychic ability.

Lilly. A sister he'd failed so badly that Jacob had been able to kill her. But Blythe must never know, or she'd lose her trust in him, too. Rather than lie to her outright, he again gave her as much of the truth as he could offer. "We all have our secrets, don't we?"

To his relief, she didn't press. "I'll go pack. It should only take me a few minutes."

"Great." He turned back to his own bag, making a show of checking the contents. "I'm almost done, myself."

He felt her absence the same way he would have felt

the loss of one of his lungs, as though he couldn't catch his breath.

Just what he did not need. Worse, this burgeoning connection between them had her sensing he was holding part of himself back from her. As if he'd ever share what had happened to his sister with anyone. His single greatest failure, with a cost too great to bear.

He should have been the one to die instead of Lilly. Instead, he had to go on living, trying to find a way to atone for what he'd done.

After so many years, he couldn't bring himself to even say her name out loud. He could still see her face, perpetually fifteen in his memory, her upturned eyes alight with mischief and the joy they'd shared when they'd learned to change together.

He'd thought they were freaks.

She'd believed they were sinners.

But as wolves, they'd hunted and explored and gloried in simply *being.* Wolves. A miraculous, youthful kind of wonder.

Odd that such a joyous time always brought back such pain. And guilt. Always the ever-present guilt.

Lucas blamed himself for allowing Jacob to find out. He'd been on the trail of an elusive, tantalizing scent. Lilly had nuzzled him twice, warning him that they had to shift back and return home. Jacob would soon be returning from his church in town, and they had to appear presentable for the formal evening meal he insisted on every night.

He'd whined, intrigued and exasperated, wanting to finish off a spectacular day with a snack of some small creature. Finally, she'd raced off, teasing him as she noisily flushed out any hidden prey.

Now that any chance he might have had of tracking his quarry had vanished, he'd been furious. So, so furious.

Uncharacteristically so. Rather than returning to the area where'd they'd left their clothing, he'd taken off at a full-out run to try and burn off his frustration.

Lilly hadn't followed.

By the time he'd located her, their father's car was making its way up the long drive.

Beginning the process to change back to human, they rushed through the transformation. Dressing hurriedly while each kept their eyes averted, they dashed back to the house, hoping to make it to their rooms without encountering anyone.

They were not so lucky.

"Hold it right there." Jacob, appearing more enraged than Lucas had ever seen him. He held a pair of black binoculars.

Lucas had thought his heart would stop.

"I saw you," Jacob had snarled, his face so swollen with rage it was almost unrecognizable. "Demon spawn. Something has taken over my two children." He called for his guards. If the beefy men thought their boss had lost his mind, they didn't show it.

It took two men to contain Lucas. Though he was only fifteen, he was strong and he fought them. Lilly did not. Perhaps she believed this to be a game—probably she felt she could easily charm Jacob out of his rage, as she so often had done in the past.

But that was before Jacob had considered them minions of hell.

Chapter 15

In retrospect, Lucas knew he should have recognized the madness. Jacob had been growing more and more fervent, spewing vitriol against anyone who thought differently than he. But fifteen-year-old Lucas had been a typical teenager—self-absorbed and involved with only what was going on in his life.

His and that of his twin sister, Lilly.

Even now, so many years later, his chest constricted at the memory of her. They'd been close, as only twins can be. He missed her with an ache that never entirely eased.

How Jacob had killed her Lucas never learned. He just knew the man he'd once called Father had locked them up away from each other. Left in the dark without food, without water, Lucas had grown progressively weaker. That was when the torture—referred to as tests—had begun.

Fifteen years later, Jacob had no doubt refined his techniques, perfected his cruelty with a laser-sharp focus.

Lucas had never understood what Jacob had been trying to learn from them, and with his bruised and battered body screaming for it to end, eventually he hadn't cared.

Until the day he'd seen his sister's lifeless corpse as they dragged her down the hallway past his cell. "Dead," one of the guards had sneered after noticing Lucas watching. After that, nothing could contain him. Jacob had killed Lilly. Lucas had plotted and planned. First he'd make his escape, get away from the madman. He'd regain his strength, grow up and then he'd be back to get his revenge.

The next time they brought him out for more tests, he'd broken free. Though he'd had to attack the man who'd escorted him, even stealing his weapon, he hadn't killed. No, that particular sin he planned to hold in reserve to commit against Jacob Gideon. Because one day, he would avenge his sister's death.

"Hey." Blythe's voice reached him from the doorway. "Are you all right?"

Startled, he jumped. Glancing at Blythe, he swallowed hard, wondering at the fierce sense of rightness, of a circle coming complete. He'd always known Jacob would pay for what he'd done. It would seem that day had finally arrived.

He forced his thoughts away from the past, focusing on the future. This time, he could not fail. There was more than one child's life at stake now.

He'd talk to Kane. Find out if the other man would welcome his and Blythe's help in finding the children and getting them to safety. Once that had been accomplished, he would make sure Jacob paid dearly for what he'd done. No matter what the cost.

Right now, though, he needed to clear the air. "This…" He waved his hand, struggling to find the right words, something he'd never been good at doing. "Changes things between us."

She froze, as if she instantly understood what he meant, and then slowly shook her head. "No, it doesn't. Not unless you want it to."

With two sentences, she'd succeeded in placing everything neatly back with him. His choice. His decision.

Hope seized him, a bright spark, which he quickly extinguished. He thought of Lilly, her vivacious spark gone, her body lifeless. And once again faced the truth. He wasn't worthy.

More than anything he dreaded seeing Blythe reach that same conclusion. She must never know.

He managed a casual shrug, while his insides churned. "No, I don't."

She nodded. "Good. I don't want anything to change, either."

He couldn't look at her as he zipped his duffel and hefted it onto one shoulder. "Are you ready to go?"

"Give me five minutes," she said, sounding way too cheerful. "I'll meet you in the kitchen."

He nodded, wondering why he felt such an awful, aching sense of loss.

Walking away, Blythe grimaced, stretching out her sore body. It had been far too long since she'd shared herself with a man, especially another Shifter. Their lovemaking had been…vigorous, to say the least.

She swallowed hard. Explosive, insane and absolutely glorious was more like it.

Honestly, she was perfectly okay with Lucas's decision to keep things casual between them. She certainly didn't need any distractions at this point in her life.

Still, the man fascinated her. She knew he had secrets—maybe that was why. Whatever he was hiding from her must be extremely personal. As she'd watched him a moment ago, lost in his memories of the past, she actually felt his pain, a visceral ache deep in her heart.

She knew he'd been unaware of the emotions flickering across his rugged features. Grief and regret and anger. Those were to be expected. But what she found the most intriguing was the guilt.

Why did he feel guilty? Surely he didn't blame himself for what Jacob had done. Or for what had happened between them last night.

All of her meager belongings were already packed in the plastic bag they'd left the store in. She was as ready as she was ever going to be. She could only hope this car trip wouldn't be a form of slow torture, since she wanted him as much or more than she had the previous evening. She found herself missing his motorcycle.

When she returned to his room, carefully avoiding even glancing at the still-rumpled bed, she found him motionless in the exact same spot as when she'd left him a few moments ago.

"Are you all right?" she asked again, softly.

Lifting his head, he met her gaze straight on. The darkness in his blue eyes stunned her. "I'm fine. How about you? Are you ready to go?"

She nodded, pushing away the desire that still coiled slow and heavy in her body. "Did you check the truck to see if you could find a tracking device?"

"No. I don't care if Kane knows where we are. Now that he has Hailey, I doubt he'll be monitoring it anyway."

She nodded. "Good point. How about we take turns driving?" Holding out her hands for the keys, she tried to project confidence. "I'll take first shift."

The look of masculine outrage he gave her made her smile. "I'm driving. Come on."

Following as he led the way to the truck, she wished

she could place her finger on what exactly was wrong. This was more than awkwardness after a night of intense lovemaking. But, as good as she'd gotten at picking up on his moods in the short time she'd known him, she couldn't figure this one out.

As he unlocked the truck, she decided to ask once more. "Really, if something is wrong, you can tell me."

Irritation laced his expression when he swung around to face her. "For the love of… Stop. Just stop. I'm fine. You're fine. We're heading back to Texas to try and stop a monster from hurting children. How about you focus on that instead of me?"

He had a point. Still…

Studying him as he faced her, bristling with anger, so large and male and damaged, a sudden flash of insight showed her what might be the reason for his hesitation. Whatever his father had done to him had caused irreparable damage. She was forcing him to face his past, to revisit the horror of his warped and ruined childhood, asking him to leave his safe place, possibly the only location where he felt truly protected.

"You don't have to go," she said, crossing her arms as she absolved him of any lingering obligation. "You've done enough—more than enough—and you barely know me. I can drive myself. You stay here."

The look he gave her told her he thought she'd lost her mind. "Why would you think I'd do that?"

Choosing her words carefully, she glanced back over her shoulder at the rustic and beautiful cabin in the woods. "This is your refuge, your…"

"Sanctuary?" He sounded grim. Furious, too.

She blanched. "Well, I wouldn't use that word, exactly."

"Then don't." Shaking his head, he stared at her, the coldness in his eyes making him appear a stranger. "And don't ever insult me that way again. I'm leaving now. With or without you."

That said, he climbed up inside the truck and started the engine.

Blinking hard, she wondered at the sudden tightness in her throat. Attempting to shrug it off, she hurried over to the passenger side, yanked open the door and got in. As she secured the seat belt, feeling as though every nerve ending was raw, she knew she needed to consider a few things, as well.

First and foremost would be to stop butting her nose into places she wasn't wanted. Most specifically, Lucas Kenyon's life.

Lucas drove without looking at her. Teeth clenched so tightly his jaw ached, he wanted to lash out at her. Yes, she'd insulted him. But worse, the fact that she'd, even for a second, believed him to be such a…coward, rankled him to no end.

He'd grown used to despising himself. And while he'd known it would hurt to have someone else look down upon him the same way, he hadn't expected it to be quite so painful.

Because it was Blythe.

Ever since they'd shared their bodies, the atmosphere between them had felt charged, like a powder keg about to explode. Lucas didn't understand how this could be so. Sex was supposed to calm wildness, not enhance it.

Blythe's cell phone rang. Though her eyes widened as she checked the caller ID, her voice sounded expressionless as she handed it to him. "It's Jacob."

Punching the accept call button with his thumb, he held it up to his ear. "What do you want?"

Jacob laughed, sending a shudder of revulsion through Lucas. "I've missed you. Why don't you come for a visit?"

"A visit." Lucas managed a half-assed chuckle. Jacob was fishing for information. No doubt he was trying to find out how much Lucas knew. Still, now would be the perfect opportunity to set the trap. "Can you imagine why I'd want to do that?"

Jacob went quiet for a moment. His next words made a chill skitter along Lucas's spine.

"I can think of thirty-four reasons," Jacob said.

Whatever Lucas had expected, it hadn't been this. "Thirty-four?" he said, letting the horror he felt come through in his voice.

In the seat beside him, Blythe covered her mouth with her hand.

"Yes." Jacob's voice sounded calm and matter-of-fact.

This, more than anything, alarmed Lucas. "You seem awfully confident that I know what you're talking about."

"Don't pretend you don't. I might be amendable to a trade."

"Why?" Lucas asked. "What do you want? Let's hear it."

On the other end of the phone, there was silence. Hesitation?

"I'm going to hang up," Lucas warned. "I'm not in the mood to play games."

"Fine. I'm simply not achieving the results I wanted with the subjects I have," Jacob said. "Maybe because they're so young. Either way, I'm very interested in seeing if there will be something different about you two."

Two. Again Lucas flashed back to Lilly. Again, as the familiar rage filled him, he had to fight the powerful memories. "I don't understand," he drawled, though he thought he might. "What kind of results do you mean? Explain."

"No explanation is necessary." Whatever control Jacob had been exerting to keep himself reined in vanished. "I wasn't successful with either you or your sister. This is my greatest regret. I'd like another chance."

"Don't you *dare* mention her," Lucas snarled. His inner wolf growled at the rioting tangle of emotions surging through him. "And you should know by now, there's no way to exorcise it out of us. We're born this way and we die this way. It's a simple fact of nature."

There was the briefest of pauses as Jacob digested Lucas's words, and then the explosion came, exactly as Lucas had known it would.

"Demonic possession," Jacob hissed. "I won't listen to your lies."

"Gee." Lucas didn't bother to keep the sarcasm from his voice. "You sure know how to inspire people with your love and acceptance and really make them want to visit." And with that, he disconnected the call.

Wide-eyed, Blythe watched him.

"He'll call back," he said, after relaying the gist of the short phone conversation. "After all, he's playing right into our hands."

Grimacing, she appeared doubtful. "Either that, or we're playing right into his."

Listening to the raw emotion in Lucas's voice as he'd tried to reason with the man he refused to call Father, Blythe had battled her own wolf.

Fight instincts. Something she'd only read about but never before experienced. Her wolf sensed his inner beast, had his back and was ready to join him in a fight. Like pack members, a team. Or…like *mates*.

The thought made her blush. She chanced a glance sideways at him, finding him grimly focused on the road ahead. Luckily, he couldn't read her mind. He'd made it quite clear he didn't want any romantic entanglements.

Neither did she, no matter what her inner wolf thought.

She settled back into her seat, waiting for her turn to drive.

With only the monotonous sound of the tires against pavement and the low-key music on the radio station, she must have dozed off. Because it seemed as if she blinked and then opened her eyes to find the sun had traveled nearly all the way to the horizon.

Stretching, she sat up straight and rubbed the back of her neck. Lucas glanced sideways at her, a half smile curving one corner of his mouth.

"I thought you needed to rest," he said. "You've been asleep for a couple of hours."

"Where are we?" Blinking, she tried to shake off her grogginess.

"New Mexico. I'm thinking we'll stop before we cross over into Texas."

"Do you want me to drive some?" she offered, ruining it with a wide yawn.

"Not yet," he said. "We haven't got too much farther to go."

There was curiosity in her expression. "I don't remember it taking this long to get to the cabin from Texas."

"That's because you slept the entire way."

"Now you sleep and I'll drive."

He shook his head. "I'm not tired. Plus, I've still got to get ahold of Kane." Pulling out his phone, he dialed the number. When Kane answered, he put the call on speaker and outlined what he and Blythe wanted to do.

"You're asking me to authorize an illegal operation." Kane sounded disgruntled.

"Do you have a better idea?"

"That's just it," Kane said, frustration showing in his voice. "We don't. The place is like a fortress. We tried to get a search warrant, but that was denied. Not enough evidence."

"Even though you have a little girl willing to testify that Jacob is holding other children prisoner?" Blythe's face mirrored the disbelief in her tone. "What more do they need?"

"He's a respected television preacher," Kane said. "And apparently very well connected. I'm guessing his organization makes sizable political donations. No one wants to touch him. We're in limbo right now."

Blythe cursed.

Lucas touched her arm. "You saw how he had the entire town in his pocket. We're not going to get him legally."

"Then we have to do something illegal in order to bring that monster down. End of story." Blythe jammed her hands into her pockets, no doubt to keep her from hitting something. Lucas could definitely relate.

With a sound, Kane acknowledged her point. "Fine. Though I have to tell you, we don't usually allow civilians to help."

"You're already about to operate illegally," Lucas pointed out. "Might as well go for the gusto."

"Try not to get hurt, okay?"

Lucas nodded, unable to suppress a quick grin. "I take it that's a yes?"

"Would it matter if it wasn't?" Then, without waiting for an answer, Kane continued, "Yes. In this instance we'll take all the assistance we can get."

"Thank you."

"I need a little time to get organized," Kane said. "Don't show up here until tomorrow."

Agreeing, Lucas concluded the call. "Looks like we're

in. Might as well stop for the night, since we don't want to be too early."

Full darkness had fallen by the time they stopped. They spent the night in a tiny motel in Raton, New Mexico. Though her legs felt hollow when she finally stepped from the truck, Blythe marched into the room without going anywhere near Lucas.

Normally, she would have found maintaining such resolve difficult, but exhaustion trumped everything.

The place was old, verging on ancient, but clean. There were two double beds, side by side, and Blythe simply climbed into one, curling up on her side without comment. Though überconscious of Lucas moving about the room, her entire body ached. She let exhaustion claim her and closed her eyes.

When she opened them again, dawn peeked around the edge of the short curtains over the lone window. Lucas sat fully dressed on the other bed, watching her, blue eyes dark and unfathomable.

She stretched, blinking sleepily at him.

"Good morning," he said.

Just the sound of his husky voice sent desire spiraling through her. Inside, even her wolf whimpered. Determined not to give in, she pushed up on her elbows and managed a distant smile. "Hey."

"Hey," he said back. And then she remembered where she was.

"Have you already showered?" she asked, praying she could manage to sound completely detached.

His nod had her scrambling from bed, snagging her bag of clothing on the way. "I need thirty minutes," she told him, already on her way to the bathroom.

Twenty-eight minutes later—she'd noted the time on the bedside clock before she went—she opened the bathroom door and emerged. Showered, fully dressed, teeth brushed and hair dry. And, she thought as her stomach rumbled, starving.

While she was showering, Lucas had opened the curtains. He stood with his back to her, peering out, though he turned as she entered the room.

"I'm ready." She gave him her best perky smile, though she was careful not to hold his gaze too long. "Along with a large cup of coffee, I'd really like to get something to eat as soon as possible."

He nodded his agreement, apparently finding nothing wrong with her completely fake attitude. "Grab your things and let's go."

Once again the day fell into the now-familiar routine of driving, broken up by the occasional pit stop. When they crossed the Texas border, her entire body went from relaxed to alert, as though Jacob and Sanctuary were sending out some sort of telepathic signal warning them away rather than welcoming them.

She swore under her breath.

"You feel it, too?" Lucas asked, noting her rigid posture. "Just a few minutes after we left New Mexico?"

Reluctantly, she nodded. "What do you think it is?"

"Honestly, I don't know." He didn't sound alarmed, so she tried to relax. "I didn't notice it the last time I was here, but I'm guessing it's some sort of instinct."

"Like a heightened sense of intuition?"

He nodded. "My wolf is on full alert."

Hers was, too. She didn't comment. Instead, she turned her head to gaze out the window.

Keeping distance between them made her feel off-kilter. Wrong. She wanted to lean close, rest her head on his shoulder and draw strength from his touch.

She almost said to hell with it and did it anyway. Only

she couldn't bear it if he rejected her again—not now, when more than anything they needed to work as a co-hesive team.

Pushing her jumbled thoughts out of her mind, she tried to focus on the task ahead: the children. In her mind's eye she kept seeing Hailey's precious, freckled face. The chil-dren were more important than her infatuation with a man who didn't want her completely.

She felt energized. Maybe because they were travel-ing with a purpose, bolstered by a sense of determina-tion. They *would* rescue those children. Jacob would pay.

Good always won out, right? Staring at the boring flat-ness of the landscape as they drove, Blythe wished she felt more certain. Once, she would have been able to make such a statement with unshakable faith.

These days…not so much.

When they stopped at a gas station, she went inside. By the time she emerged, Lucas was on the phone. As she ap-proached, he concluded the call.

"I talked to Kane. He's going to pretend to be unaware of our involvement. Remember, he can't officially sanc-tion it."

"That's fine with me."

"Me, too." He smiled, looking wolfish. "However, read-ing between the lines, he's waiting for us."

Before long, the sign heralding the city limits came into view.

"Almost there," he said. Again she felt her entire body react to his voice, which made her jittery. She hated to admit it, but he'd been right when he'd said making love had changed things between them. More than that, their coupling had changed *her*. She didn't think she could ever go back to the way she'd been before.

In truth, she didn't even know if she wanted to.

Finally, they turned down the road that led to Sanctuary.

"There it is," he growled, coasting to a stop before the huge wrought iron gates. "Hell on earth. Sanctuary."

Eyeing the gates, Lucas wondered at his complete lack of emotion. He'd expected to feel anger, sorrow, anything. Instead, all he felt was an overpowering sense of urgency.

Good. He'd be able to think clearly. He pulled over to the shoulder, put the truck in Park and turned off the engine.

Beside him, Blythe, too, had fallen silent. The slight hitch in her breathing exposed her reaction to the sight of Jacob Gideon's Sanctuary.

"What do you want to do?" she asked, staring at the silent house.

Handing her a pistol, he gave her a savage smile. "First, I text Kane. Then, we'll go in with our guns drawn."

Nodding, she checked the safety, which was on, then to make sure her weapon was fully loaded. Satisfied, she once again met his gaze. "And then what?"

With his own pistol ready, he lifted one shoulder. "And then we'll play it by ear."

Moving in unison, they exited the truck. Though he knew he could die, he felt no hesitation. No matter what the cost, he had to protect Blythe. Jacob could have him killed or tortured, but Lucas would give his life to make sure nothing happened to Blythe.

This time, he would not fail a woman he loved.

Loved? The thought nearly stopped him in his tracks. Steeling his resolve, he pushed the shocking notion away. He'd examine it later, assuming he survived. After he owned his own soul again, he could think about being the right man for a woman like Blythe.

For now, he had two purposes. Free the children and then…he'd find a way to make Jacob pay.

No one stopped them as they walked up the driveway. Lucas figured since Jacob had to be expecting them, they might as well take the most direct approach.

When they reached the front door, he touched Blythe's shoulder. "Stay behind me, okay?"

She started to speak, then shook her head. "We're partners, remember?"

And she pushed past him and yanked on the door handle.

Apparently it was unlocked, as it moved.

They stepped inside.

Four men stood blocking the entrance. All were holding pistols, aimed directly at them.

Blythe must have watched the same movies Lucas had, because she never faltered.

"Really?" Lucas said, bringing his gun to bear on one man, and then another. "So we're going to have a shoot-out. Which means at least a couple of you are willing to die."

Gesturing at Blythe to stay with him, Lucas moved forward. "Even better, I'll bet old Jacob gave you strict orders to make sure neither of us gets hurt. Which makes your guns pointless. Now move out of our way."

He snarled the last two words. When none of the men stepped back from the doorway, he fired, hitting one of the men in the kneecap. He crumpled, screaming as he went down.

This was enough to send the other three back, stumbling in confusion and shock. Lucas guessed they hadn't expected a serious attack. Hell, even though they were armed, he was betting Jacob had given orders not to harm Blythe or Lucas. This effectively made their weapons useless.

And they knew it.

"Come on," he told Blythe, already moving. They were halfway down the hall before any of the remaining three guards pretended to care.

"Stop," one of them shouted, halfheartedly.

Blythe turned and fired another shot, purposely shattering a large, decorative mirror next to him. "It could have been you," she yelled.

Lucas admired her marksmanship as he ran for the elevator. At the last minute, he realized they'd do better taking the stairway. They wouldn't take the big, curved ornate one that led to the upper floor, but the hidden one meant to be used when the elevator failed.

"Let's use the stairs. That way they can't stop us. We'll try the labs first," he said.

Behind them, near the foyer, came sounds of disorganized confusion, which meant Jacob's people were trying to mount some sort of defensive attack. Which would be pretty pointless, since Jacob's objective appeared to be to get them inside and trapped.

If everything went according to plan, Kane and his team would now begin getting the children out.

The first corner was up ahead. As they approached it, a voice came over the intercom, loud and commanding.

"Stop," Jacob shouted, his tone reverberating with authority. Despite everything, Lucas froze. The man himself. Exactly who they'd come to see.

Chapter 16

Though the sound of Jacob's voice brought Lucas the familiar reaction—fury—he refused to let it affect his judgment.

"Come on," he urged Blythe. "Make them come after us. We want the showdown to be in his office, away from the children." They tore around the corner, passing the elevator and heading for the stairs.

Heart hammering, Lucas glanced at Blythe. She was balancing on the edges of her toes, ready to sprint. "Let's go."

Taking off, he hit the stairs two at a time, Blythe thundering up right alongside him.

When they reached the top, two men appeared. Skidding to a halt, Lucas braced himself for a fight.

"Look at their auras," Blythe murmured. "I think they might be on our side."

One man jerked his head in a barely perceptible nod. "Come with us," he ordered.

The other man mouthed the words "Play along." Then, raising his voice, he spoke again. "We're taking you to see Jacob."

The other Shifter made motions for them to hide their guns. Lucas jammed his into the waistband of his jeans, pulling his T-shirt down over it. Blythe did the same. As hiding places went it was less than ideal, but would have to do.

The men moved to flank them. One grasped Lucas's arm and the other took Blythe's. "Come with us."

They went willingly, only pretending to be reluctant.

Finally, they stopped outside the familiar double doors. Jacob's office. The other man's place of power.

The guards knocked once. At Jacob's command to enter, they opened the door, stepping aside as Lucas and Blythe entered together. Jacob waited, seated behind his massive desk like a king holding court. He steepled his hands in front of him, eyeing them with an odd combination of disdain and eagerness.

Standing there, finally facing down his own personal demon, Lucas realized that Jacob, the monster, was only Jacob, a man. One who clearly thought a lot of himself and hurt small children. But he wouldn't be powerful without the thugs and brainwashed sycophants in his congregation.

He'd be nothing. Nothing but pure evil.

"It's about time you came back." Voice triumphant, Jacob stared at Lucas. "The prodigal son, finally returning to repent his sins."

"No." Lucas didn't even try to hide his contempt. "I've done nothing wrong. And, as far as I'm concerned, I'm no longer your son. I haven't been since I was fifteen."

Heaving a sigh, Jacob glanced at Blythe. "No, I suppose not." He leaned forward, malice lighting his eyes.

"Are you ready for a truth? You never were my son. As if such abomination could come from my loins." He snorted.

Beside him, Blythe made a strangled sound low in her throat. Lucas felt her support, giving him strength.

Jacob's words made no sense. "What do you mean?"

Jacob's smile sent a shudder of revulsion up Lucas's spine. "Though I raised you, you weren't my son by blood. Your actual father was a member of my church and had been completely blindsided to learn his wife—and the mother of his children—was a werewolf."

Though Lucas kept his face expressionless, inwardly, he winced. The man—his actual human father—had confided in the wrong person. "Where is he now?"

Jacob sighed. "He had an unfortunate accident when you were an infant."

"What about my mother?" Lucas asked. "What happened to her?"

"She was evil," Jacob spat, pounding the desktop with the flat of his hand. "That bitch trapped a human with her succubus ways, got him to impregnate her and then left him with her devilish spawn."

Despite the jumbled mixture of words, Lucas focused on one thing. "My mother is still alive?"

"Of course not." Again the satisfied smile. "Do you truly believe God would suffer a harlot such as that to live? She died in a house fire a few weeks before your father. An unfortunate accident."

Hands clenched, Lucas had to forcibly restrain himself from leaping over the desk and taking Jacob by the throat.

"Was it?" he asked. "That sounds like it might have been another one of those things you engineered for your own benefit."

A pleased smile played around the corners of Jacob's mouth as he continued, "Being the kindhearted pastor I am, naturally I stepped up and took over the care of his children."

"Why?" Lucas asked. "Why would someone like you do such a thing?"

"For the pleasure—and fame—of exorcising your demons. I knew what your mother was, so I followed her. The moment I learned she was a werewolf, I knew she had to die. Then, only your father stood in the way of me taking her demon spawn."

An inferno of fury engulfed Lucas. Not only had Jacob murdered his twin sister, but also their parents. And Jacob called *them* demons?

Lucas nearly started when Blythe slipped her hand into his and squeezed. He glanced at her, saw the steely determination in her beautiful green eyes and felt his own resolve strengthen.

"Jacob, all of this is history, in the past, and can't be changed." He flashed his own smile, aware of the savage ruthlessness welling up inside him. "I didn't come here to hear your explanations. I knew they'd be skewed in such a way that they'd sound rational to your evil, twisted mind."

At his words, Jacob recoiled, his malicious smile slipping. Noting his advantage, Lucas took a step closer.

"Here and now, right now, there's only one bit of knowledge from the past that I care about."

"Your sister?" Jacob guessed, once again clearly enjoying himself.

Lucas tensed. Beside him, Blythe turned and stared. Suddenly, Lucas realized she needed to know the truth about everything. About him.

He took a deep breath. Again, Blythe squeezed his hand. Unflinching, letting every bit of his hatred show in his eyes, he met Jacob's gaze. "What did you do with Lilly's remains?"

For a split second, shock flashed across Jacob's aristocratic features. Then, as he schooled them back to indifference, he let one silver eyebrow rise. "Remains? What exactly do you mean?"

Tamping down a blazing flash of anger, Lucas stared at the other man, aching to reach across the desk, haul him up by his tie and wrap his hands around his neck. "Did you bury her? Cremate her? Either way, I'd like to know where she is."

Jacob leaned back in his chair, craftily narrowing his eyes. "Now why exactly would I tell you that?" he drawled.

A man could only take so much. Lucas started forward. Only Blythe's grip on his hand pulled him back. Glancing at her, he saw empathy in her expression.

"Breathe," she murmured, drawing Jacob's amused look.

Ignoring the evil incarnate across from him, Lucas did exactly that. He took one deep breath, then another. Finally, when he had himself under control, he responded.

"Why would you tell me what you've done with Lilly?" he asked, his tone cold and level. "Because if I only do one thing before you kill me, I'd like to honor my sister."

Jacob laughed, the guffaws more insulting than any word could ever be.

Lucas couldn't help it. He saw red. His inner wolf snarled. He let his own lip curl back in response as he felt his body begin the change.

Not yet. Not only did he need to make sure Kane had enough time to get the children out, he wasn't finished with Jacob.

"Do you miss Lilly?" Jacob taunted him, sounding amused. He looked at Blythe, speaking to her. "He and his sister were very close. The two of them were twins, as alike in every way as they could be."

He sounded fatherly, like a kind, loving man reminiscing about the past. Even Lucas might have bought into it if he hadn't been there. He knew what kind of horrific acts the older man was capable of.

"We were." Clenching his teeth, Lucas tried to force himself to stay cool as he eyed Jacob again. He lost the battle.

Blythe at his side, he faced Jacob, waiting. "I should kill you now," he snarled. "You've single-handedly destroyed everything I had. Give me one good reason why I shouldn't." Jacob's instinctive recoil brought Lucas a violent sort of pleasure. "Now, you have one more chance. I asked you a simple question. Where are my sister's remains? I have a right to know how she was laid to rest."

In response, Jacob puffed himself up, trying on his bravado like a suit. "So that's it. That's what you're willing to exchange for your freedom?"

Lucas narrowed his eyes. "Let's not forget the children. You said you were willing to make a trade. Us for them."

"That was before I had all the cards." He gestured to his guards. "Handcuff them and get them out of here."

"Just a minute," Blythe said, advancing toward Jacob. "Lucas is not the only one with a beef against you. You tried to kill my daughter," she snarled. For the briefest second, Lucas swore her wolf visage showed through her human face. "For that alone, I should rip your throat out. I don't have a single reason not to."

Standing, Jacob nearly stumbled over his chair in his haste as he took a step back. For the first time since they'd entered the room, he seemed uneasy. "Guards, cuff them," he ordered.

The two guards, Shifters both of them, didn't move.

Watching the woman he now knew was his mate, Lucas felt a savage sort of joy.

"I should join you," he told Blythe, letting Jacob see his teeth.

For a man who believed them to be demons, apparently Jacob didn't have a lot of faith in the protection of his God. This deity, whoever he was, bore absolutely no relation to any Christian god, as far as Lucas was concerned.

"What's the matter? Cat got your tongue?" Lucas took another step closer, chuckling as Jacob shot a nervous glance toward the door, as though contemplating flight.

Blythe moved to block it.

Lucas growled, low in his throat.

Again, Jacob tried to order his guards to protect him. When they didn't move, he matched Lucas glare for glare. "You wouldn't dare."

"Maybe I will." Lucas made a slow circle around the older man, like a wolf stalking hapless prey, while Blythe watched. "But I suggest you tell me what I want to know. Now. What did you do with Lilly?"

Instead of answering, Jacob made one last attempt to command his men. "Guards, seize them!" he ordered, managing to sound both autocratic and desperate.

When neither man showed the slightest indication of obeying, Jacob's face became mottled with rage. "Do you want to lose your jobs? Do as I say! Immediately!"

After exchanging a look, the two guards moved slowly forward, one on each side of Lucas and Blythe, each taking an arm in a grip that was not meant to confine anyone.

"Well?" Jacob demanded impatiently. "What are you waiting for? Get them handcuffed and throw them in one of the holding rooms."

At that moment, one guard's walkie-talkie crackled. "All clear." Kane's voice, confident and sure. "We're done here. Proceed as planned."

While Jacob was still frowning in puzzlement at this,

the two guards withdrew their weapons and pointed them at him. One of them glanced at Lucas before handing him a pair of metal handcuffs. "You need to cuff him, not kill him, all right?" he asked, smiling.

Accepting the cuffs without another word, Lucas grabbed Jacob and shoved his hands behind his back. Once he was cuffed, he pushed him back against the wall. "One last chance," he snarled. "What did you do with Lilly?"

But Jacob only pressed his mouth tight. Ignoring Lucas, he faced his two employees. "What is this? You're here for *my* security. Release me this instant."

One of the men flashed a badge. "FBI. You're under arrest for the unlawful kidnapping and holding of minor children. Anything you say can and will be held against you in a court of law. You have the right to an attorney—"

"Yes," Jacob interrupted. "I demand you let me call my attorney."

"Come on." Shaking his head, Lucas led Blythe from the room. He could feel her anger, mingling with his own impotent rage. "I wanted to kill him."

"Me, too," she said. "I've never felt anything like that blinding rage. The only thing that stopped me—"

"Was the knowledge that I didn't want to become just like him," he finished.

"Exactly," she said, her mouth tight and grim.

"He's evil incarnate," he said, unable to keep the bitterness from his voice.

The long, careful look she gave him reminded him she now knew his innermost secret.

"Listen, about my sister," he began.

She blinked, focusing on him. "I understand."

Though he wasn't certain she did, that explanation would have to wait for another time. "As soon as possible, I swear I'm going to find out what that bastard did with her remains."

She nodded. While it would never be enough, it was a start. Eventually, maybe he could let go of the bitterness and the anger entirely.

"Hey, you two." Heading toward them at a brisk walk, Kane called out from farther down the hallway. "All the little ones are out safely."

"Good." Lucas squeezed Blythe's hand once before letting her go. "That's all that really matters."

"Yep." Reaching them, Kane clapped Lucas on the back. "Several of them are listed on the missing children database. We should be able to get him—and his people—on numerous charges."

"I'm so glad," Blythe said. "Now he'll never be able to do this again to anyone."

"Exactly." Kane shot Lucas a look. "Actually, he had more than children."

"Adults?" Lucas shouldn't have been, but for some reason he was taken aback.

"That's not so surprising," Blythe put in, shaking her head. "Considering what he did to me. He would have kept me prisoner here, too, if I hadn't escaped."

"Yeah, well..." Kane's expression went grim. "I think the two of you need to see this. We found a woman... she's in bad shape. It looks like she's been here awhile. She won't speak." He glanced at Jacob first. "Maybe you might recognize her."

Then at Blythe. "Considering that you've been through something like what this woman apparently has, you might be able to reach her."

Though weariness had soaked Lucas to the bone, he nodded. "Of course," he said. Blythe also agreed, her voice soft.

"I knew you'd help," Kane said. "Follow me."

Lucas took Blythe's arm and—amazingly—realized he drew strength from the touch. The sharp glance she gave him told him she felt the same sensation.

They headed toward the elevator. As Kane pressed the button that would take them to the lower level, Blythe shuddered. "I hate this place."

Lucas pulled her into her arms, hoping he was right and she could draw on his strength, too. "I know," he said, kissing her cheek.

Seeing this, Kane smiled. "I always suspected you two were mates."

Mates. The word settled around them as the elevator doors opened on the floor that had once meant terror to so many. Lucas's nostrils flared at the smell. Still the same. Vile and repellent.

As for Kane's supposition, that had no place in this hall of horrors.

Head up, Blythe stepped out of Lucas's embrace and faced Kane. Only Lucas could see the tiny quivers she tried so hard to hide. "This woman. Where is she?"

"This way," Kane said, heading past the lab. As they reached another door, one that had been locked the last time Lucas had been here, he paused. "I should warn you, there's no way to prepare you for her condition. There's no telling how long she's been here, but from the looks of her, I'd say a pretty long time. I was thinking maybe if another woman…"

Blythe nodded. Only Lucas, standing close in case she needed him, felt the shudder that racked her body. "I'll do my best," she said, sounding so brave and determined that he wanted to kiss her.

"That's all you can do," Kane said. He opened the

door and stepped inside. Blythe followed, Lucas right behind her.

Inside the small, windowless concrete room, it took a few minutes for his eyes to adjust to the dim light. Blinking, Lucas tried to see. As things came into focus, he went very, very still, almost afraid to breathe.

A slender woman, emaciated and filthy, sat hunched on a cot. Long, dark hair lay lank and tangled around her thin shoulders. Her sallow skin and the dark circles under her faded blue eyes told of ill treatment and poor health. She looked up at their approach, her face blank, a complete lack of interest in her dull gaze.

Until she saw Lucas. The instant she registered his face, she let out an incredulous cry.

For Lucas, all time stopped at that instant. Moving forward, he fell to his knees in front of the cot, reaching out his hand to gently touch her thin arm. "Lilly?" he asked, shock and wonder, horror and joy coursing through him. "How is this possible?" he managed. "How can it be you?"

Weeping, his sister covered her face with her hands. When he reached for her, she pushed him away. "No," she croaked. "Don't touch me. I'm dirty, I stink and I'm sick."

"I don't care." Lucas pulled her close, holding her with care. Skin and bones, she felt brittle and breakable. His sister, his twin. Not dead, but oh, what had she suffered? And how had he not known?

His throat ached as he smoothed her hair.

"I thought you left me here," she sobbed, her tears soaking his shirt. "At first. Then Jacob told me he'd killed you. All these years, I've blamed myself for not protecting you."

Incredulous, he could only stare. "Blamed yourself?"

"I'm your big sister. I should have done more."

An old joke between them, when they were younger. She'd been born first, thus she was older by minutes.

Gently, he continued to hold her. "I thought the same. For fifteen years, I've blamed myself for not protecting you. I believed you were dead—that Jacob had killed you."

She sniffed. "I'm so glad you got away."

"I would have taken you with me if I'd known…" Words failed him. All this time. She'd been a prisoner here all these years and he hadn't even known.

"Don't." Lilly gazed at him fondly. "You're here now and that's what matters."

From the doorway, Kane spoke. "We're going to get you to a hospital to be checked out, okay?"

Still watching Lucas, Lilly slowly nodded.

"The paramedics are on their way now."

He'd barely finished speaking when three paramedics arrived, bearing a stretcher.

"Let's get out of their way and let them do their job," Kane suggested. "Your sister will get all the help we can give."

Lucas stood, giving his sister's hand one final squeeze. "We're going to wait outside, all right?"

"Lucas?" Though she nodded, Lilly sounded panicked. "Don't go too far."

"I won't," he said. "I'm not going to lose you again, I promise."

Shooing them out into the hall, the paramedics began to check over Lilly. Kane closed the door to give them privacy as they worked.

This worried Lucas. "Are you sure they can be trusted?" he asked. "You know Jacob had just about everyone in town on his payroll. I don't think we should take a chance that they might do something harmful to Lilly."

"No worries." Kane clasped his shoulder. "We've had our own people in place for some time now. We've got this covered."

"It's over," Blythe said, sagging against him as he gathered her close. "It's finally over."

About to cover her mouth with his, Lucas gave her one more truth before he kissed her. "Actually, I'd say for us, it's about to begin."

As Lucas kissed her, Blythe felt a sense of relief, of rightness, of coming home. Her life was finally on the right track. Except for one hugely important part.

The kiss was brief, but powerful. When they broke apart, Blythe looked for Kane. The other Shifter had gone to the end of the hall to give them a semblance of privacy.

Apparently, instinctively understanding the direction of her thoughts, Lucas took her hand and they moved toward him.

Kane met them halfway. "What's wrong?"

"I want my daughter. Can I have her back now?" Clutching Lucas's hand so hard it probably hurt, Blythe didn't bother to hide her eagerness.

Kane's smile was full of understanding. "We'll be taking you to her once we finish wrapping up this investigation. It won't be too long now, I promise."

Smiling back, Blythe nodded. Then, as she studied Kane's face, she thought she saw…*something*. With her heart skipping a beat, she faltered and let her smile fade. "What are you not telling me? How is Hailey? Is she all right?"

Kane looked past her to Lucas, shaking his head. "How does she do that?" he asked kindly. "It's almost like she can read minds."

Lucas shrugged. "I don't know. She's pretty intuitive. If there's something she needs to know about Hailey, just tell her."

"And stop speaking about me as if I'm not in the room."

Blythe inhaled, trying not to panic. "Please tell me the truth." Lifting her chin, she tried to brace herself for whatever must have happened to her baby girl.

"I see." Kane scratched his head.

"I remember when you said you weren't sure how Jacob's experiments affected her heart. Is that it?" Blythe clutched Lucas, terror squeezing her chest so tight she wondered if she could breathe.

"No, not at all." Kane spoke in a soothing voice. "She does have some health issues—"

"Believe me, I'm well aware of her health issues. That's why I sought out Jacob Gideon and Sanctuary in the first place—out of desperation." Struggling to stay calm, she reminded herself to breath normally. "What happened with her heart? Is she all right?"

"She's fine." Kane shook his head. "I'll let her tell you herself."

Fine. Though she wanted to sag against Lucas in relief, she knew she had to be strong for her daughter.

Refusing to let the sinking feeling overwhelm her, Blythe eyed Kane. The kind compassion she saw in his face let her know he wasn't messing with her, or even trying to shield her from something terrible. In the end, she realized if Hailey was well enough to tell her, things couldn't be so bad.

"Kane, I've been through a lot," she managed. "Don't play games with me. Hailey is my world."

Instantly, the other man looked contrite. "I'm sorry. It's good news, I promise."

She refused to let herself believe him entirely.

"Are you okay?" Lucas asked, solid and strong with his arms still wrapped around her, his breath tickling her ear.

Resolutely she lifted her chin and nodded. "Yes," she said. "Yes, I am."

"Good." Kane's smile widened. "Then I have a surprise for you. Wait right here."

Exchanging a look with Lucas, Blythe nearly melted into the tenderness in his eyes. "Whatever it is," he said. "You won't have to face it alone. I'm right here with you."

The door to Lilly's cell opened and one of the paramedics came out. "We're going to have to transport her to the hospital," he said.

A moment later, the other two men emerged with Lilly on a stretcher. Her eyes were closed and she appeared to be asleep.

"Is she all right?" Lucas asked, his voice alarmed.

"We gave her something to help with the pain. It knocked her out, which is good."

"Pain?" Lucas frowned. "What's wrong with her?"

The two men exchanged a look and then continued moving down the hallway, leaving the third paramedic to explain. "She has numerous broken bones, to begin with," he said. "In addition to being malnourished and extremely weak. We need to have her thoroughly checked out. It'll be a few hours until you can see her. Kane can give you the hospital address." With that, he hurried off to catch up with the others.

Blythe could sense the rage boiling within Lucas. As she gripped his hand, she saw his wolf, fueled by adrenaline and fury, fighting to break free.

Chapter 17

"Lucas," Blythe said urgently. "You've got to hang on. We're surrounded by humans and Shifters."

The moment her words registered, she saw it in his gaze. Slowly, he nodded. "The legal system had better make sure that bastard pays for what he did to her."

"And for what he did to the little ones," Kane said, joining them again. "Just be glad you didn't have to see that."

Blythe swallowed hard. "I don't know how anyone could have done such a thing to children. Are they going to be all right?"

Grim-faced, he looked away. When he met her gaze, his own was bleak. "We hope so. We had to round up several ambulances from nearby towns. All of them will have to go to the hospital to be checked out, just like your sister."

Blythe blinked back the sting of tears. Seeing the condition of Lucas's sister was horrible enough. She didn't know how she would have reacted if she'd seen little children in similar shape.

"What about the others? The adult members of Jacob's church? What will happen to them?"

"They've all been taken to a safe house for questioning and evaluation. Charges may be filed if we learn they knew something about the kidnapping and torture of minor children."

"Did you find Dr. Silva?" Blythe put in. "That woman definitely knew what was going on. She was a major participant."

Kane gave her a grim look. "Not yet. Evidently she didn't live on the premises. But I promise you, we will find her. And when we do, she will be charged."

Blythe nodded. "Fair enough."

"You two can come with me," Kane said, his expression once more professional. "We'll need to take your statements, and then there's one more thing I'd like you both to do."

Blythe didn't ask what that might be. Neither did Lucas. Instead, they followed Kane down the long hallway to the elevator, stepping inside and riding back to the main floor.

Kane took them through the kitchen, which was completely empty, and into a huge pantry. There, he pushed on one of the shelves, and an entire side slid open.

"Our base of operations," he said. "This house had several hidden places like this."

Lucas nodded. "Lilly and I used to explore them when we were kids."

Glancing around the room, Blythe was reassured to see so many men and women with their auras proclaiming they were all Shifters. She recognized surveillance equipment—admittedly only because of what she'd seen on television rather than personal experience.

"Are they all Pack?" Lucas asked, telling her that he, too, recognized the auras.

"Most of them." In his element now, Kane seemed buoyant and completely at ease. "Several, like myself, work for the Society of Pack Protectors. We've worked very hard to integrate our operations with those of the FBI and Texas State Police."

Lucas nodded. "Impressive." He took Blythe's hand, and she drew on his strength.

"What now?" she asked.

"We'll have some questions for you, but first I want to show you something." Kane motioned them to follow him. "This way, please."

He led them to an oversized monitor and gestured at two office chairs. "Take a seat. It'll be just a moment," he said. Once they were seated, he began fiddling with the switches on a control panel.

Blythe glanced at Lucas, who shrugged. "No idea," he mouthed. She eyed the back of Kane's head and settled back to wait, still holding Lucas's hand.

"Here we are," Kane exclaimed. He sounded happy and excited, which seemed odd, at first.

A second later, a blurry image appeared on the screen, gradually coming into focus. "Mommy?"

"Hailey!" Blythe nearly jumped up from her chair, pulling Lucas with her. Instead, she let go of his hand and scooted closer, until she was only a few feet away from the monitor. She gripped the edge of the desk, fighting to maintain control of her emotions. "Baby girl, I have missed you so much."

"Me, too." Hailey's freckled little face looked so solemn. "Are you all right, Mommy?"

"I'm better now," Blythe answered honestly, pushing the words out past the knot in her throat. "How are you feeling?"

Hailey pursed her lips while she considered the question. "Really good. I'm all better now, Mama! I can do a lot of things that I couldn't before, thanks to Samantha."

Blythe glanced at Kane, finding him grinning broadly. "Samantha?" she asked, almost afraid to hope. "Who's that?"

"My new friend," Hailey shrieked. "She's a lady like you, but she's a Healer. She put her hands on me and fixed my heart."

The Healer. The news almost sent Blythe to the floor. Luckily, she was sitting. Her grip on the front of the desk became painful. "Are you…are you sure?" she managed, tears streaming down her cheeks. "You're all better? The doctors said so?"

"Yep. So did Samantha." Leaning closer to the monitor, Hailey's eyes widened as she studied her mother. "Mommy, why are you crying? This is good news!" Dismayed, her lower lip trembled and she appeared on the verge of tears herself.

Immediately, Blythe reined in her emotions. Swiping at her eyes, she smiled. "These are happy tears, sweetheart. Is the Healer still there with you?"

Hailey shook her head. "She couldn't stay. She said she was busy, sort of like Santa Claus only she doesn't have any elves."

Behind her, Blythe heard Lucas snicker. She looked up to find both him and Kane grinning ear to ear.

Looking back at the monitor, she saw Hailey leaning closer, her lips pursed to give a kiss. "I miss you, Mommy."

Scooting forward, Blythe did the same. "I miss you too, baby."

Someone beside Hailey spoke, causing her to swivel her head. "Okay," she said, sounding sad. "Mommy, I have to go. When can we go home?"

"Soon," Blythe promised, her eyes stinging from holding back a fresh spate of tears. "Very, very soon."

"Bye…" Hailey said and waved. Blythe waved back, just as the screen went black.

"That was something," she murmured, again swiping at her eyes. "My baby girl, all healed. You don't know how hard I tried to get Hailey moved up on the waiting list."

Lucas squeezed her shoulder reassuringly. She glanced gratefully at him before turning her attention to Kane.

"Who did this for us?"

Kane's smiled widened. "The Society of Pack Protectors might have had something to do with it."

She nodded. "Give them my heartfelt thanks. If there's ever anything I can do to repay them…"

"You already have." He winked. "Getting between Jacob and the children, giving us time to get the victims out… That was payment enough."

Taking a deep breath, Blythe tried to adjust to her new reality. Despite all that they'd gone through, the possibility of her daughter having a future made everything worth it.

"When can I see her?" she asked, not bothering to hide her eagerness.

Both Lucas and Kane laughed.

"It won't be too much longer," Kane said. "We've got to ask both of you a few questions, and then you'll be free to go. I'll have a driver take you to your daughter."

"A driver?" Lucas put in. "She's that close?"

Kane nodded.

Barely able to contain her excitement, Blythe pushed to her feet. "Then let's get this questioning over with. The sooner I can get on the road, the better."

In the end, what should have taken thirty minutes ended up taking over two and a half hours. First the FBI and then the state police. They questioned Blythe and Lucas separately, and finally went over the same set of questions together.

Twice.

By then, most of the FBI and the state police joint task force had headed into town for a planned news conference. A few were left to finish up the interrogation and then help Blythe reunite with her daughter.

Near the end, during the final interrogation where the officers questioned them together, Blythe struggled to control her irritated impatience. Looking up, she caught Lucas watching her with a reassuring smile.

Suddenly, she wondered if, once this was over, she'd ever see Lucas again. While they were still working as a team right now, comforting each other, celebrating together, even kissing, she remembered how intent he'd been on keeping it casual.

It wasn't casual for her anymore. She couldn't expose Hailey to a man who wouldn't be in her life for good, and she couldn't expose her own heart to the pain of keeping it casual with her one true mate. She'd shrivel up and die bit by bit.

Abruptly, she stood. "I need to use the ladies' room," she said. "And if you tell me I have to be escorted, I'm going to start wondering why you're treating me like a criminal."

At this, the officer conducting the questioning cracked a smile. "No need for an escort."

Relieved, she smiled back. "Do you have any idea where it is?"

He shook his head.

Lucas stood also. "I know. I can show you."

"I'm not finished with you yet," the officer said. "It'll just be a few more minutes."

"Just tell me where it is," Blythe told him. "I'm sure I can find it."

"The closest one is near the foyer." He gave her step-by-step directions.

"That doesn't sound too difficult," she said. "I'll be back in a few minutes."

Stepping out of the room, she took a deep breath. Amazing how things could turn on a dime. From feeling as though all hope was gone to this, having received an answer to her most fervent prayer—the gift of her daughter's health. She'd certainly had a wild roller-coaster ride.

Exiting through the pantry into the kitchen, she looked around in surprise. Sanctuary was strangely empty, as it always was every time she'd been here. This shocked her, as she'd expected to see the place swarming with law enforcement personnel.

Ah, well. Jacob's reign of terror was finally over.

The large bathroom was exactly where Lucas had directed, right off the foyer. In keeping with the rest of the entryway, it was efficiently elegant, with understated opulence. She stepped inside and reached for the handle to pull the door closed.

She never made it. Too late, she realized someone else was already inside the bathroom. Something heavy slammed into the back of her head. She went down without being able even to scream.

Lucas glanced at his watch for the second time. The officer had finished the questioning, dutifully recorded the answers and was packing up his equipment. Blythe still had not returned.

"I'd better go look for her," he said, standing. "I know she's eager to get on the road."

The other man looked up, appearing unconcerned.

"You know how women are. She's probably reapplying her makeup or something."

"Not Blythe." Lucas spoke with certainty. "She's been gone nearly twenty minutes. That's far too long."

The man yawned, not nearly as worried as Lucas. "Then I'll go with you."

There was no sign of Blythe—or anyone else—on the way to the bathroom. This felt a little unsettling, and Lucas's feelings of unease grew when they reached the foyer without seeing Blythe. The bathroom was empty, too.

"Maybe she got lost heading back to interrogation."

Every instinct on high alert, Lucas shook his head. "She knows how to find the kitchen. Something happened to her."

"I doubt that." The officer yawned again. "All the cult members have been rounded up. There's no one here but cops and feds."

Heart racing, Lucas pulled out his cell phone. "I'm going to call Kane."

Looking at him askance, the officer didn't appear convinced. "And tell him what?"

Swallowing, Lucas struggled to control his fury. "I'll let him know I believe one of Jacob's people—maybe even Dr. Silva herself—was hidden somewhere in the building. And that I believe they've taken Blythe."

With that, he punched in the number and made the call.

The instant he'd been reassured that Kane was on his way, Lucas began searching every square inch of Sanctuary. Obviously, Dr. Silva or one of Jacob's other people had managed to hide from the joint searches of the FBI and Texas State Police.

But they wouldn't stay hidden from him. If he had to, he'd shift to wolf and use his efficient lupine nose to sniff them out.

They had Blythe. Damned if he was going to let them hurt his mate.

His mate.

Stunned, he said the words out loud. Earlier, Kane had intuited the truth. Blythe truly was Lucas's mate, the other half of him. He'd heard somewhere that Shifters, like their wild counterparts, mated for life.

He could well believe this. He refused even to consider the possibility of a life without Blythe.

Gut instinct told him she hadn't left Sanctuary. Whoever had taken her hadn't had time to get her past the authorities and off the compound. He'd find her, before anyone caused her further harm.

Weapon drawn, he began searching the top floor. That was where Kane found him, cold determination fighting off panic, a scant thirty minutes later.

"I've called my unit back in," Kane said. Lucas appreciated the way the other man moved right back into search-and-rescue mode without questioning.

"Thanks. I've been doing a search, room by room. I'm reasonably sure they haven't left the building."

Kane nodded and drew his weapon. "Sounds good. We need to see if we can find blueprints of this place. I know there are a ton of hidden rooms, much like the area we used for a base."

"There are."

Kane snapped his fingers. "Did you say you and your sister used to explore them as kids?"

Lucas nodded. "We did. I can even remember a few of them. I've been looking for hidden entrances while I searched the obvious places."

"Let me help you finish up on this floor. I'll take the west side of the hall, you take the east."

They'd nearly finished searching the top floor by the

time the rest of Kane's team arrived. Kane barked out their orders, letting two of his men check the last few rooms on that floor. "Lucas and I will take the bottom floor. Several of you need to search the basement," he said.

Taking off, his team skipped the elevator and went for the back stairs.

"Do you remember any hidden rooms down there?" Kane asked. "Other than the labs, that is?"

Lucas thought for a moment. "No. The basement wasn't used much back then. Other than where Jacob locked up me and Lilly once he found out what we were."

Shooting him a considering look, Kane grimaced. "My men will still check it out," he decided. "And while we're searching this floor, how about if you try to remember the location of some of those secret rooms? We'll start there."

Lucas took a deep breath, trying to settle the mounting sense of urgency building inside him. He needed to keep cool, calm and collected to have the best chance of saving Blythe. "I can remember two. Let's try and find the entrance to the one that used to be my favorite. It's here on the main floor, so whoever abducted Blythe could easily have taken her there."

"Fantastic," Kane said and grinned at him. "I'm assuming it's like the pantry, with a hidden switch that opened an entrance?"

"Exactly."

Kane touched his arm. "Show me."

Lucas led the way. Taking the steps two at a time, he then hurried down the hall. "There's a seldom-used study at the very end of the hall. I remember a secret entrance inside the closet door," Lucas said, yanking it open and pressing hard against the baseboard until he heard a click.

There was a sigh of air as the door opened.

"Here we are."

"Excellent." Once again, Kane had his weapon up. "We go in together. Be ready for anything."

Head aching so badly the pain made her want to vomit, Blythe struggled to open her eyes. She couldn't remember what happened—not exactly—though her intuition told her it wasn't good. She came to in the dark, her eyelids fluttering as she woke. Her first thought was to wonder how she'd gotten this splitting headache; her second was to gradually realize what had happened.

She'd been attacked. But why? And by whom?

Slowly, she opened her eyes, letting them adjust to the lack of light. When she tried to move, she realized she'd been strapped to a metal table, similar to those in hospital operating rooms.

Immediately, she thought of Dr. Silva.

The only body part not tied down was her head. As things came into focus in the dim light, she knew she had to do something. Moving painfully from one side to the other, she tried to get a better idea of her surroundings.

What she saw made her gasp. Dr. Silva perched cross-legged atop a tall counter, unmoving and staring at her.

Blythe cleared her throat. The sound caused no change to her captor's unblinking regard. In fact, the other woman seemed totally out of it, as if she'd gone into some sort of trance.

With all the weirdness that kept happening in the place, this possibility seemed entirely feasible.

Blythe tried to determine exactly how securely she'd been tied, wincing as she attempted to raise her neck and shoulders up off the table. Judging from the tightness of the straps at her wrists and ankles, pretty securely indeed. She couldn't move except to wiggle her hands and feet.

"It's pointless to try and escape," Dr. Silva spoke,

sounding robotic and lifeless. Either she'd gone into a deep, deep depression, or—more likely—had taken some kind of drug.

"Why are you doing this?" Blythe asked. "Everything is over. Jacob Gideon is in federal custody and the children have been freed."

"They cannot stop me," Dr. Silva said, with a complete lack of enthusiasm or energy.

"What's wrong with you?" Blythe figured she may as well ask. Nothing ventured, nothing gained.

The longer she kept the other woman talking, the more chance she had of being rescued before the doctor took it upon herself to finish Blythe off.

She could only hope. Eventually, Lucas had to realize she was missing. He would find her. She had to believe it wouldn't be too late.

"I know what you are. Tell me how you do it." Dr. Silva spoke again, her voice ragged and hoarse. Still unmoving, her eyes burned with a feverish intensity as she stared at Blythe. "Before all this ends, tell me how you do it."

Aware she had to tread carefully, Blythe eyed her back. She didn't immediately reply, afraid the wrong answer might send the other woman into a furious frenzy.

Dr. Silva began rocking in place, her slight shoulders hunched. One hand crept up and began pulling at her short hair. Clearly, the recent events culminating in Jacob Gideon's arrest had been too much for Dr. Silva's sanity.

When Blythe didn't answer, Dr. Silva began muttering to herself under her breath, an anxious and breathless sound.

Dread began building in Blythe, making perspiration trickle between her breasts. What should she say, how could she respond? Though she felt 99 percent certain she knew what the other woman was asking—the mechanics of how Blythe shape-shifted—she wasn't sure exactly how to explain a complicated genetic process.

And with this woman, clearly driven mad by her sadistic research, the wrong answer could have dire consequences.

"Tell me," the doctor screamed, spittle flying. She slid down from her perch and stalked over to Blythe, circling, eyeing her with an off-the-charts intensity that was horrific.

But Blythe remained calm. Dr. Silva's entire belief system had to be grounded in the science she'd studied in medical school. Therefore, she had to understand there was no magical answer.

"It's how I'm made," she said, her voice steady and sure. "Isn't that what all of your…experiments revealed?"

The other woman's eyes narrowed. "I found nothing. No anomalies. Oh sure," she waved her hand in a jerky motion. "The genetic code was a bit off. But not enough to indicate how such a thing is possible. Your bones change shape! How can that be?"

Sensing the question was more than rhetorical, Blythe knew she had to proceed with caution. Rather than take a chance with the wrong answer, she lifted her shoulder in a shrug, then winced at the sharp stab of pain.

Dr. Silva slapped her hard across the cheek. If Blythe hadn't been tied down, the force of the blow would have propelled her backward. Blythe bit her lip to keep from crying out.

"There has to be something to indicate how you are able to change from human into wolf. I need to learn the secret before I am arrested. Tell me. Now."

Blythe said. "You're asking me to explain the unexplainable. That's like asking a bird how it learns to fly."

Dr. Silva slapped her again. This time, Blythe saw stars. As the edges of her vision grayed, she thought she might pass out. In truth, she'd almost welcome going unconscious if it would stop the pain.

But she fought to stay awake. She didn't dare let down her guard. Who knew what the crazy doctor might do then?

When she could see again, she licked her cracked lip and tasted blood. "Why?" she asked, her voice a croak. "Why is this so important to you?"

Her question appeared to startle the other woman. Tilting her head, she watched Blythe with a cold eye, all the while continuing to yank on her hair. "Because I want to become a wolf," she finally said, and bared her teeth in a menacing snarl.

Blythe's inner wolf responded in kind. For the first time, Blythe realized she might have a chance to escape her bonds if she shape-shifted.

As Blythe watched in horrified fascination, Dr. Silva snarled again, then got down on all fours and howled. Did she think somehow magic would strike and change her into a wolf?

Blythe inhaled deeply. This was her chance. Despite the pounding ache in her head and the throbbing of her split lip, she had to go for it.

Closing her eyes, she willed herself to change and set her inner wolf free.

As the tingling began, she saw the familiar sparkle of the fireflylike lights. At the sight, the doctor only howled louder, the sound filled with an insane mournful longing.

Glad she made no move to stop her, Blythe felt her bones begin to lengthen, her face begin to change form. The shackles fell from her now much more slender body parts, long before they could stretch her into an unnatural shape.

Free, fully wolf, she bounded from the table. Crouching over the now groveling doctor, Blythe as wolf contemplated ripping out her throat.

At that moment, Lucas and Kane burst into the room.

Lucas took in the scene, immediately realizing what must have happened. With her clothing torn and left behind on a steel table, Blythe had become wolf, most likely in self-defense. She'd gone on the offensive. And Dr. Silva had rolled onto her back with her belly exposed, adopting the submissive posture known to all wolves and dogs. Except she was neither. She was human.

Still, she'd clearly surrendered.

Though Blythe, with her fur bristling on her back, seemed to be so enraged that she didn't care. In fact, it appeared to Lucas that she was on the verge of slaughtering the other woman, who clearly appeared terrified.

"Stop!" Lucas shouted, the voice of authority and reason. "Back down, Blythe! Right now!"

Though the huge she-wolf froze, she didn't move away from her stance over Dr. Silva.

Chapter 18

"Blythe," Lucas said, his tone much calmer and full of all the love he felt for her, love he'd never known would be his. "Don't kill her. You aren't like that. Let Kane arrest her."

At his voice, wolf Blythe raised her massive head and looked at him, her curled lip and snarl disappearing. Then, moving gracefully, she backed away from Dr. Silva. Not retreating, not at all.

"Thank you," Kane said. Turning, he went over to the doctor, keeping his pistol aimed at her. "Dr. Silva, you're under arrest."

Sitting up, she hung her head and didn't respond. Kane helped her to her feet and cuffed her, before beginning to read her rights.

Both Lucas and Blythe—as wolf—watched this in silence. Then, he went to her. Crouching low, he buried his hands in her fur, his heart full of relief and love. "You can change back now," he said. "You're safe."

At his word, she lowered her head. Then she backed away. Turning a circle, wolf Blythe found a spot and lay down. And then she initiated the change back to human.

As soon as the thousands of firefly lights disappeared, he went to her, snagging her torn and ruined clothing on the way. "These are mostly destroyed, but they're better than nothing."

"Here." Kane passed him Dr. Silva's white lab coat, which he'd evidently taken from her. "She can wear this."

Lucas took it, appreciating how the other man, even though he was Pack, kept his back to Blythe's nakedness.

Clearly drained, Blythe allowed him to help her put her arms into the lab coat. Then, once she'd buttoned it, he brought her to her feet, keeping her up against him for support.

Gently he held her, hoping she couldn't see how his hands trembled.

"Are you all right?" he asked.

Slowly, she tested out how each leg would bear her weight. "I think so. Yes."

Still treating her as if she might break, he tenderly brushed the hair back from her face, sending a shiver through her. Her lip was split and swollen, with a small trickle of blood at the corner. "I thought I'd lost you."

She smiled. Though a bit wobbly, the enchanting curve of her mouth made his heart skip a beat. "No, you didn't. You always find me."

Smiling back, chest tight, he tried to speak past the odd knot in his throat.

"I hate to interrupt," Kane said. "But we're all done here."

Eyes narrowed, Lucas shot him a look of warning, before turning his gaze back to Blythe.

Kane continued as if he hadn't noticed. "Blythe, why

don't you get cleaned up and get ready to go? I know you're eager to see that little girl of yours."

Lifting her chin, Blythe stepped away from Lucas and nodded. "Definitely. Though I need to find something else to wear. I can't travel wearing only a lab coat."

"I'm pretty sure we can dig up something," Kane told her.

"Great." For whatever reason, she wouldn't meet Lucas's gaze.

Confused and, damn it, hurt, he watched her pulling away from him. In a way, he understood. By not protecting her from the crazed Dr. Silva, once again, he'd failed her.

"Lucas?" The sharp edge in Kane's voice told Lucas he understood. "I can give you a ride to the hospital to see your sister."

Chest tight, he nodded. "Thanks. I'd like that."

Though she'd already turned away, Blythe paused. Glancing back over her shoulder, she gave him a tentative smile. "I guess this is goodbye, then? At least for now?"

Though he knew she really meant for forever, he dredged up a smile in response. He held out his arms and pasted his best impersonal look on his face. "Come give me a hug."

With a wordless sound, she crossed to him and wrapped her arms around him. Holding on so tight she nearly cut off his breath, she kissed his cheek. He hugged her back, closing his eyes and inhaling her feminine scent one last time.

When she released him, he had to blink rapidly to keep his eyes clear. Swallowing, he hoped he didn't make a fool of himself as he faced her. "Goodbye, Blythe. Say hi to Hailey for me," he managed.

She waited, as though she expected him to say something more. When he didn't, she finally nodded, her green eyes alight with what looked like pain. "I will. And you do the same with your sister." Her tender smile seemed genuine, which oddly enough made it hurt even more.

A knock at the door had them moving quickly apart, as though they'd been caught doing something wrong.

Kane cleared his throat. "The rest of my team is here." He raised his voice. "Come on in."

Silent, Lucas and Blythe watched as he handed over custody of Dr. Silva. Once she'd been escorted away, he holstered his pistol and turned back to them. "All right, then. Are the two of you ready?"

Exhaustion warring with exhilaration, Blythe followed the officer down the hall to one of the sleeping quarters. Inside, she would be given clean clothing and then whisked away to begin the several-hour journey to be reunited with Hailey.

Lucas, on the other hand, had gone with Kane. While she understood the temporary separation was necessary, she'd expected…more. Not promises, not exactly. But something. Maybe exchanging phone numbers. Or a quiet *I'll be in touch.*

The abrupt dismissal hurt. Clearly, he'd done his duty, helped free the children, and she was on her way to being reunited with her little girl. With his insistence on keeping things casual between them, apparently he considered his role finished. She wondered if he was glad to finally wash his hands of her. She wondered…

Stop.

Disgusted with her restless uncertainty, she pushed away the thoughts and emotions. She'd been granted a miracle: her daughter had been healed. She'd focus on the joy of that. Though she knew she'd always wonder what might have been, she had been given Hailey back. No one could take Hailey from her now.

Resolutely, she opened the closet door and grabbed a long dress. Shapeless and plain, it would more than adequately cover her until she could get to her own clothing or a store to buy something in her size.

A pair of flip-flops completed her outfit.

Now she was ready.

Dusting her hands off on her dress, she squared her shoulders and told the officer she would like to get on the road.

This time, she made the trip in a navy blue unmarked police cruiser. She elected to ride in the backseat and fell asleep an hour into the drive.

Stirring, Blythe groggily opened her eyes. According to the dashboard clock, she'd slept over three hours. Sitting up, she dragged her fingers through her hair and leaned forward into the front seat.

"How much farther?" she asked.

The driver smiled. "A couple more hours. How about we stop and stretch our legs? You can get something to eat if you want."

Though what she really wanted was to see Hailey, she also couldn't remember the last meal she'd had. "There," she pointed ahead where a huge sign for a popular hamburger chain beckoned.

The short break helped more than she'd expected. She ate then cleaned up in the restroom, and they were back on the road before thirty minutes had passed.

Finally, just as the sun had begun to set, they pulled up in front of an ordinary ranch-style house. The car had barely stopped before Blythe opened her door and jumped out. Since she wasn't sure of the protocol—as in, if they'd let her in—she ran up the front steps and turned impatiently to wait for her escort to catch up.

The front door opened. Blythe turned and there she

was! Hailey! She scooped her daughter up, hugging her so tightly. Hailey laughingly protested.

"Mama!"

"Sorry, baby." Covering her baby girl's perfect little face with kisses, Blythe noticed two people standing in the foyer.

"Come in," the tall, slender woman said, smiling. "I'm Samantha Herrick. This is my husband, Lucaine. We're here on a short break from my work."

Still clutching Hailey, Blythe shook the redheaded woman's hand, warmed by the genuine kindness in her caramel eyes. "I can't thank you enough," she began. "I've been on your waiting list for what seems like forever and—"

"It's all right." Samantha dipped her head, as though embarrassed by the praise. "And actually, I should apologize to you for even *having* a waiting list."

"But it's unavoidable," her dark-haired husband said, slipping his arm protectively around his wife's shoulder. "There's only one Healer for millions of Halflings."

"Miss Sam made me all better." Hailey bounced on Blythe's lap, her five-year-old energy in sharp contrast to the wan, listless child Blythe had seen last. Love and gratitude made Blythe feel alternatively weepy and giddy.

"You look exhausted," Samantha said, her soft voice full of sympathy. "Hailey's been staying in our guest room. Why don't you spend the night there with her?"

Appreciative, Blythe shook her head. "You've already done enough. I owe you a debt of gratitude for healing Hailey. I couldn't possibly impose any more."

"It's not imposing." Lucaine's deep voice carried a hint of authority. "Especially since we insist."

With a sigh of gratitude, Blythe gave in. "Thank you," she said.

"Yes, thank you," Hailey echoed, snuggling into her

mother's side with a big grin. "Mommy, I missed you sooo much."

"I missed you, too." Holding her daughter, breathing in the baby-shampoo scent of her hair, Blythe wanted to feel completely content. A few weeks ago, this, holding her healthy child safe in her arms, had been her only dream. But now she wondered for the hundredth time what Lucas was doing and how he was holding up.

While Kane drove him to the hospital, Lucas allowed himself to close his eyes and rest. His physical fatigue could be cured by a good night's rest.

The exhaustion in his soul went a lot deeper. He had no idea how long something like that took to disappear. Went to show what happened when he actually let someone in, he thought ruefully. A world of hurt.

"Your sister is special," Kane said, the bemused certainty in his voice making Lucas open his eyes in confusion.

"Yes, she is," Lucas agreed, wondering where Kane could possibly be going with this. "For fifteen years, I've blamed myself for her death, and she's considered herself responsible for mine."

Kane shook his head. "She must be a strong woman to survive so long under those conditions." A thread of anger underscored his tone. "I'd like to personally wring Jacob Gideon's neck."

"Me, too." Gut twisting, Lucas eyed the other man. "If I'd known, I would have rescued her a lot sooner. I hate knowing that he's kept her locked up and subjected her to his damn experiments and torture." He cursed, blinking back tears for the second time that day.

Damn. Turning his head to face the window, he pretended to study the passing landscape while trying to get his emotions under control.

He nearly jumped when Kane squeezed his shoulder. "Hey, man," Kane said. "Don't blame yourself."

Tired of pretending, Lucas didn't even bother to try and summon a smile. "How can I not? She's been through hell, and all because I ran away without her."

"Let me get this straight." Kane's expression was equally grim. "First you beat yourself up because you think she's dead and then when you find out she's not, you *still* feel responsible."

"Don't you understand?" Lucas snarled. "I didn't save her. I should have saved her." Fist clenched, Lucas wanted to hit something.

His wolf growled, earning a similar response from Kane's.

"You were fifteen. A kid." Kane gave him a fierce look, one without the slightest trace of pity. "So was she. Neither of you can spend the rest of your lives blaming yourself for the actions of a criminally insane man. You need to get your head straight so you can help her."

Slowly, Lucas nodded. Kane was right. Lilly needed him now more than ever, and he couldn't—hell, he damn sure wouldn't—let her down. Never again.

When they arrived at the hospital, Kane escorted him to Lilly's room. At the door, he clapped Lucas on the back. "I'll wait out here so you two can have privacy. Just yell if you need anything."

Grateful, Lucas nodded. Though he couldn't find the words to express his gratitude, he felt sure Kane understood.

As if he'd read his mind, Kane dipped his chin and jerked his head toward the room.

Lucas took a deep breath and pushed through the door.

Looking tiny and far too battered, in the hospital bed, Lilly appeared to be sleeping. Yet, as Lucas quietly approached, she opened her eyes as if she'd sensed him.

"Hey." She held out a hand. Gently, Lucas took it.

"Hey, yourself. How are you feeling?"

Lilly's wan smile broke his heart. "Okay, I guess. You'll never believe it, but all these doctors are like us. Shapeshifters. Pack, they call it."

He nodded. "I know. I found out about them recently, myself. Have they told you what they think is wrong?"

As her smile faded, her eyes filled with tears. "It appears my wolf is damaged. All those times they forced me to change, all the painful experiments…" Her voice broke down. She turned her head into her pillow and began to sob in earnest, shoulders shaking.

Dropping into the bedside chair, he leaned over and awkwardly tried to comfort her. All he could do was rub her back and just be there.

Gradually, the intensity of her sobs faded and she drifted off into sleep. Sorrow warred with fury. How could someone, especially a man who proclaimed himself a man of God, do this to another being, human or not?

Exiting the room, he found Kane leaning against the wall, waiting. Kane took one look at him and cursed. "What's wrong?"

In a few, clipped words, Lucas revealed what his sister had told him. "I'd like to find that son of a bitch and make him pay," he finished.

"I'm right there with you," Kane replied, surprising him. "But don't give up hope. We brought Samantha—the Healer—in to heal Hailey. I'm sure we can bring her up again to help Lilly, if necessary."

Lucas nodded, drawing comfort from the knowledge. "Have they done a complete analysis of her condition?"

"Not yet. They'll need a bit more time. How about I buy you a beer and something to eat?"

Glancing back at the hospital room, Lucas grimaced. "I don't want to leave her."

"Completely understandable. But I'm pretty sure she's going to sleep for a while. You've got to take care of yourself, too. How long has it been since you've eaten?"

Trying to remember, Lucas finally gave up. "All right, let's go eat. I'm guessing since you mentioned beer, you're not thinking the hospital cafeteria?"

Kane grinned. "Absolutely not. I've got just the place in mind. And tonight, you can bunk with me."

When Lucas started to protest, Kane waved him away. "I live all by myself in that house. The guest bedroom can use a visitor. Stay as long as you want. Once you know more about your sister's condition, you can make other plans."

Stunned at the kindness of a man who was essentially a stranger, Lucas decided to go with the flow. His only regret, as he followed Kane out to the hospital parking lot, was that Blythe wasn't with him. He already missed her more than he would have imagined possible. Not merely a regret. His longing for her was an ache, a keening howl inside his mind.

With her little girl asleep in the soft bed next to her, Blythe slept better than she had in weeks. Her deepest prayer had been answered: Hailey had been healed. If she had a new empty spot inside her, she and Hailey would now be able to live a life that would fill them both to overflowing. She couldn't demand all the joy the Fates had to offer. She burned at the memory of Lucas and his "give me a hug." Time to focus on what she had rather than on what she did not.

Yet, she couldn't help but wonder what Lucas had done after she left: where he'd slept, and if he and his sister were getting reacquainted with each other and were making plans for the future.

She missed him with a visceral ache that made her feel hollow in the midst of all her joy. His presence, however unlikely, would truly make her happiness complete.

In the kitchen, she and Hailey sat down to breakfast with Samantha and Lucaine. The other couple clearly were in love, as evidenced by their tender looks and constant touches. Thinking of Lucas, Blythe found herself envying them. She could only hope that once everything settled down, Lucas would be willing to take a chance on love. On her. On them.

"You look sad, Mama," Hailey observed.

"I'm just thinking." Ruffling her baby's hair, Blythe looked up to catch Samantha's knowing stare. She managed a wan smile back before turning her attention to making sure her daughter ate her breakfast.

After they'd finished eating, Lucaine grabbed his briefcase. "Feel free to stay as long as you need," he told Blythe, before giving Samantha a kiss that must have curled her toes. He left for work and Hailey went into the den to watch television, leaving Blythe and Samantha alone in the kitchen.

"So what are your plans?" Samantha's easy smile invited Blythe to share. "You must be so relieved to have your daughter back."

"Yes. Having Hailey back and healthy is the greatest gift anyone could ever have given me. I'm so lucky Lucas decided to help me."

Again, Blythe saw Lucas's face, and she nearly doubled over from the pain of his absence. Inhaling sharply, she got herself together. "As for my plans, I'm ready to go home to Houston," she said. "Now that Hailey is well, I'm hoping we can ease into a normal life. She hasn't had much of one so far."

Samantha nodded. "How about you?"

Glancing toward the other room, where her daughter watched a cartoon with a dancing yellow sponge, she smiled. "Me, either. Ever since Hailey was born, I've devoted my life to getting her well."

"What kind of work did you do?"

Since Samantha seemed genuinely interested, Blythe relaxed, enjoying the rare camaraderie over steaming cups of coffee. "Mostly I've been living off the money my mother left me when she died, as well as doing some freelance website work and ebook formatting. The only thing that's kept that business from taking off was the fact that I've had limited time."

"I guess you'll have time now, especially once Hailey starts kindergarten in the fall."

School. Blythe smiled. "She's been so ill, I hadn't even thought about that. But you're right, I definitely will have more time on my hands."

Again, she thought of Lucas, wishing she could call him, just to hear his voice and ask him how he was doing.

"You're missing a man?" Samantha asked softly.

Surprised, Blythe studied the other woman. "Are you psychic, too?"

"No." Samantha chuckled. "It's just written all over your face. When Luc and I were trying to hash things out, I remember feeling as if the world had ended."

"Did you know for certain that he was the one?" Blythe couldn't help asking. "I mean, from what I've always understood about mates, when two find each other, they both know there can never be anyone else."

"Is that how you feel?" Samantha's gentle smile inexplicably made Blythe want to cry.

"Yes." She sniffed back tears. "The thing is, I'm pretty sure he feels the same way. I don't understand why he beat such a hasty retreat."

"Then give it time," Samantha advised. "He'll come around. If it's meant to be, it will happen."

Though Blythe nodded, she knew the unspoken part of that would haunt her. "I keep thinking of all that was taken from him. The awful man who raised him actually murdered his real parents. At least he has his sister back."

"I wonder…" Samantha looked thoughtful. "If he has any other family alive who he doesn't know about. Aunts and uncles, cousins, grandparents."

Stunned, Blythe grimaced. "If there were, surely they would have taken Lucas and Lilly in and raised them after their parents' deaths."

"Maybe they didn't know." Picking up the phone, Samantha eyed Blythe. "If it's okay with you, I'll call my Luc and have him check it out. He works for the Pack Protectors. Since at least one of Lucas's parents was Pack, he ought to be able to find information."

"Sure, why not." The rightness of the idea made Blythe feel better. "Lucas helped me get my daughter back. If I can help him reunite with his real family, that would be a way to repay his…kindness." She choked on the last word.

Too kind to remark on this, Samantha nodded and punched a number into the phone. She spoke briefly to her husband and disconnected the call. "Done," she said, giving Blythe a satisfied smile. "He'll call me back if and when he finds out anything."

"Thank you." Again, to her consternation, Blythe's eyes filled with tears. "I miss him so much."

"Have faith." Samantha covered Blythe's hand with hers

before getting up from the table and carrying the dishes over to the sink. "It definitely will help you get through all of this."

Faith. Slowly, Blythe let the word sink in. She'd refused to give up on Hailey, and look how that had worked out. Samantha was right. How could she do any less for the man she truly believed was her mate?

"Let me wash those." Swiping at her eyes, Blythe jumped up and attempted to nudge Samantha away from the sink. "You've already done enough."

"I've got this." Samantha refused to move. "All I'm going to do is rinse them off and put them in the dishwasher. Go spend time with your kiddo. When you're ready, I'll call the Protectors and let them know you're wanting to go home. Personally, I think you should take another day or two. Whenever you choose to leave, I'm sure they'll send a car for you."

Once again, the other woman's kindness had Blythe's eyes pricking with tears. Sniffing, she nodded her thanks and went to watch cartoons with Hailey.

Chapter 19

The popular bar was in a dilapidated building called, appropriately, "The Shack." From the crowded parking lot to the absence of available tables, everything about the place screamed "good times."

Exactly what Lucas was not in the mood for at all.

"I think this is just what you need," Kane said, as if Lucas had spoken his thoughts out loud. Hell, for all he knew, maybe he had.

"Look around." Kane strode through the crowd to the bar area, where he snagged the last two available stools. "Tell me what you see."

It took a moment—foggy brain and all—but Lucas finally realized what the other man meant. Judging from the array of auras, The Shack was chock-full of Shifters.

Lucas took a seat, elbows on the bar. He briefly debated summoning up a smile, and then decided he was too damn exhausted to bother. "I see what you mean," he said. "Shifters."

"Yep." Grinning, Kane ordered them both a beer. Despite the crowd, the bartender brought them instantly.

Grateful, Lucas took a long drink of his before asking for a menu.

"No need," Kane told him. "This place has the best burgers in town." Raising his hand, he placed their order.

Lucas nodded his thanks.

"So what are you going to do?" Kane asked, his voice kind.

"About what?" Distracted, Lucas stared into his half-finished beer mug and tried to ignore the mournful strains of the country music playing on the jukebox. The last thing he needed was another reminder of what—who—he was missing.

The skeptical look Kane shot him left little doubt that Kane felt Lucas knew exactly what he meant.

"About Blythe?" Lucas finally asked, since Kane was right.

Arms crossed, Kane nodded.

"Nothing," Lucas replied with a shrug. "She'll be all right, now that her daughter has been healed. And I accomplished what I set out to do. Helped her and her daughter and in the process, saved a bunch of other children. Once my sister is well enough to travel with me, I think I can head back to Seattle—or even my Colorado cabin—with a clear conscience."

At first, Kane didn't respond. He took a long drink of his beer and regarded Lucas with a sharp gaze. "Running again, are you?"

Lucas couldn't even summon the energy to be offended. "How is going home 'running'? I've got my sister back and Blythe has Hailey. It's all good. There's nothing left unfinished."

Kane's knowing smile flat-out called Lucas a liar. "We

only get one mate," he said. "I know you aren't all that familiar with Pack lore, but most of us would give anything to meet our mate."

At the word, Lucas dropped his false bravado and winced. "There it is again. That word. *Mate.* I'm not sure I even believe in such a thing."

Slowly, Kane shook his head. He finished the last of his beer and signaled for another before he spoke again. "Come on, man. Cut the bull. You know she's yours. And you're hers. Any Shifter who gets within a few feet of the two of you can tell. So what are you afraid of?"

About to protest, Lucas bit back the words, well aware the other man was right. He had nothing left now but truth.

"Blythe deserves a hell of a lot better than me."

Kane's incredulous expression paid Lucas the highest compliment. "You can't be serious."

Lucas's casual shrug fooled neither of them. "Look at what happened to my sister. I wasn't any good at protecting her. Blythe needs a man who can take good care of her and of Hailey. Someone better. End of story."

To Lucas's shock, Kane actually bared his teeth. "Then you're more of a fool than I took you for." He turned away, giving Lucas his back while he surveyed the interior of the bar. When his second beer arrived, he slid it over to Lucas without even looking. "Here. You need this more than I do."

Because he suspected Kane might be right, Lucas accepted the drink. He couldn't help but wonder if Kane could be correct about everything.

"You'll never know unless you try," Kane pointed out, swiveling back around to face him, nearly making Lucas spill his beer.

"Will you stop that," Lucas demanded. "Damn. It's like you're reading my mind."

"Well, hell, your thoughts are plain on your face." Apparently undeterred, Kane continued to stare, grinning.

The burgers arrived and talk was momentarily suspended while both men dug in. True to Kane's promise, Lucas thought this might be the best hamburger he'd ever tasted. He nearly rolled his eyes in bliss as he chewed.

Neither of them spoke until they'd both destroyed their meals.

"I told you," Kane said, leaning back in his chair with a satisfied smile. Then, before Lucas could respond, he tossed a few bills down on the counter. "My treat. Come on, let's get out of here."

"Thanks. I owe you one."

Halfway to the door, Kane shot him an exasperated look. "There you go again. You've got to stop that." His cell phone rang and he stopped to take the call.

Glad to be outside in the parking lot, Lucas continued on to Kane's vehicle. Ears still ringing from the loud interior of the place, he leaned against the door while waiting for Kane to finish his call.

"Hold on," Kane was saying. "I'll let you tell him yourself." He held the phone out. "Someone wants to talk to you."

Curious, he accepted and held the phone to his ear. "Hello?"

"I have some news for you." It was Blythe, sounding oddly breathless. At the sound of her husky voice, his stomach did a flip-flop.

He managed some sort of response, ignoring Kane, who stood a few feet away, grinning.

"I know Jacob said both your real parents were dead, but it turns out you and Lilly aren't completely alone in the world. I had Samantha's husband do some checking and I found out you have an aunt and uncle, another uncle and several cousins still alive."

She took a deep breath, her voice wavering just the slightest bit as she continued, "I'm not sure what the circumstances are, or why they didn't take you in when your parents passed away, but the information will be forwarded to Kane in case you want to contact them."

Stunned and oddly humbled, he cleared his throat. "Thank you. That means a lot to me."

"You're welcome." Her voice an odd combination of happy and sad, she continued, "I know I can never pay you back for all you've done for me, but this is at least a start."

"Pay me back?" He couldn't believe she'd say such a thing. "You don't have to…"

"Lucas," she interrupted him quietly. "No matter what happens, know this. I am grateful. Thankful. You gave me back my family. Now, I've given you back yours." She laughed, a strangled sound of relief mingled with sorrow. "I hope you and Lilly forge a wonderful relationship with your newfound family."

Then, before he could articulate his reaction to her words, she ended the call.

Stunned, he wordlessly handed the phone back to Kane. "Let's go," he managed, his voice breaking. Waiting while Kane unlocked the door, he got inside, buckled up and waited for the other man to start the ignition.

He couldn't think, couldn't feel, couldn't…damn him. What the hell was wrong with him?

He loved her. Loved her with everything inside of him.

Closing his eyes, he braced himself, trying to weather the pain the knowledge brought. Once again, without even trying, he'd managed to mess everything up. The question was, could he fix it?

"Hey." Kane's voice was infinitely kind. "Are you all right?"

Though he wasn't, Lucas nodded.

Kane's phone pinged, indicating he'd received a text. "I've got the information on your relatives," he said. "I'll write it down for you later."

Though he knew he had to formulate a response, Lucas couldn't force words out past the huge lump in his throat.

Apparently, Kane understood anyway. He started the car and put it into Drive. They rode the entire way back to Kane's place in silence.

As they pulled into the driveway, Lucas turned to his new friend. "How far away is Blythe?"

"A couple of hours." Kane watched him closely. "I could drive you there, if you'd like."

Torn, Lucas considered. "I've got to see Blythe. But I don't want to leave my sister for too long."

Checking his watch, Kane grimaced. "Visiting hours are over in thirty minutes. I'm sure she's going to need her rest. We have just about enough time to pop in there on the way out of town.

His heart suddenly light for the first time in ages, Lucas agreed. So this was what hope felt like.

Lilly was still sleeping soundly when they arrived, and since the nurse advised them not to wake her, Lucas left without telling her where he was going.

"If we drive straight through, we can be there by midnight," Kane advised. "I don't know about you, but I think if we stay a few hours, and then take turns driving, we can each catch a bit of sleep before heading back to the hospital in the morning."

Again Lucas felt his heart expand. "You don't have to do this," he began.

Kane silenced him with a look. "Don't start that again."

Understanding, Lucas nodded instead. "All right, let's go. It sounds like a plan to me."

Once they were on the road again, Kane broke every speed limit, claiming he'd radioed ahead to alert the local authorities.

"I'm going to call Samantha and let her know you're coming," Kane told him.

"As long as she doesn't tell Blythe." Lucas smiled, feeling almost giddy with hope. "I want to surprise her."

Kane made the call, keeping it brief. Lucas could tell from the light banter that his newfound friend truly was happy for him.

They pulled up in front of an older ranch house shortly after midnight. The porch light was on in what Lucas chose to believe was a welcome.

Kane pulled up to the curb and left the motor running. "Good luck," he said.

Surprised, Lucas turned to look at him. "Aren't you coming in?"

"Nah." Kane yawned, and then smiled a sleepy smile. "I'm going to take a nap in the car. Wake me when it's time to head back and I'll drive while you sleep."

Again Lucas found himself choking up. To cover it, he nodded once and got the hell out of the car.

Heading up the walk, he debated whether to ring the doorbell or not. Luckily, the door swung open as he approached. A willowy redhead stood framed in the light, smiling warmly.

"You must be Lucas."

He nodded, trying to see past her, hoping for a glimpse of Blythe. Now that he'd actually arrived, with his heart hammering and his palms sweaty, he had no idea how she would react.

His wolf, having been asleep until now, stirred. The

yearning came from within, both the beast and the man, longing to be reunited with the one who was his mate.

Samantha laughed. "So it's like that, is it? Well, come on in. Blythe is in the kitchen. She and Hailey fell asleep earlier watching TV. I just woke Blythe so she could put Hailey to bed."

Heart in his throat, he tried to find the words to express his thanks, but the sight of Blythe in the next room crowded out any other thoughts.

Staring at him, she'd gone white, as if she'd seen a ghost.

He started forward. Behind him, Samantha closed the door.

"Lucas?" Appearing stunned, Blythe didn't move. "What's wrong? Has something happened to Lilly?"

"She's fine," he reassured her, taking both her hands in his. "I came to see you."

From the slight frown between her brows, he could tell she still didn't understand. Gently, he pulled her into his arms. She didn't resist, but still she held herself aloof.

"I've missed you," he said. He had to choose his words carefully, but he didn't want to. He wanted to let them burst out of the hidden place inside his heart, and tell her everything.

Finally, she buried her face in his neck, clinging to him. "I've missed you, too. I've been trying to wrap my mind around the prospect of life without you."

"Don't," he growled.

She pulled back, surprise and consternation plain on her lovely face. "Don't what?"

"Don't even consider living without me." He spoke with fierce tenderness. "Because you won't have to. I was foolish to leave you. I've come back to rectify my mistake."

At her gasp, he took a deep breath, suddenly realizing

that he might be assuming an awful lot. "That is, if you want me."

"Want you?" She laughed and he realized she was crying. "I've wanted you for so long."

He kissed her then, a long, drugging kiss full of savage wonder and love. "I love you, Blythe. You heal me. Complete me. Somehow, you make me forget…"

Gazing at him, her heart shining in her eyes, she looked so beautiful he couldn't continue.

When he didn't finish, she tilted her head, a half smile tipping one corner of her lush mouth. "Forget what? The past?"

"Everything," he said, drowning in sensation, his emotions and desire and existence all so closely tied up in her that he could scarcely breathe.

The slow smile that blossomed on her face had his heart lurching madly. "You are everything to me," he whispered, kissing her face, her neck and finally her mouth. "I love you."

She gave a glad cry. "I love you, too."

He took another deep breath, gazing deep into her eyes. "Will you and Hailey consider going back with me?"

"Back where? To the cabin in the mountains?"

"No." Realizing he'd told her next to nothing about his life, he smiled. "To Seattle. I have a condo there, but I'm going to need to find a larger place anyway, probably at least three bedrooms. Because as soon as Lilly gets out of the hospital, she's coming home with me, too."

"Of course." She kissed him then, a kiss full of promise and passion. It was a kiss strong enough to make a lonely soul whole once again.

When they finally came up for air, he rested his head against hers, forehead to forehead, noses touching. Mates. No longer apart.

"What about your family?" she asked, her clear gaze searching his face. "Are you going to contact them?"

"I thought we could do it together." He swallowed hard, wondering if she could hear the way his heart threatened to explode from his chest. "And maybe once we've gotten to know them, we can invite them to our wedding."

She gasped. "Our...?"

Taking advantage of her parted lips, he kissed her once more. Caressing her, loving her, claiming her as his.

"Wedding." Firmly he spoke the word. "I don't have a ring, but I'd like to ask you to marry me." Still holding her hands, he dropped to one knee. "Blythe Daphne, will you do me the honor of becoming my wife?"

Green eyes sparkling, she dropped down to her knees with him and took both his hands. "Of course," she said, smiling. "As long as you promise to kiss me again."

And pulling her close, so he did.

* * * * *

Don't miss Karen Whiddon's next romance,
TEXAS SECRETS, LOVERS' LIES,
available October 2013 from
Harlequin Romantic Suspense!

COMING NEXT MONTH FROM

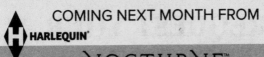

HARLEQUIN®

NOCTURNE™

Available October 1, 2013

#169 CLAIMED BY THE DEMON
by Doranna Durgin

Michael MacKenzie is a man fighting to maintain his sense of self. He follows his bonded demon blade's influence from place to place and has learned to assume that the blade is manipulating his feelings, twisting or manufacturing them, even when it comes to love. When Gwen Badura meets Mac in Albuquerque, she is stunned by her connection with him—and horrified to realize he not only wields a demon blade as her father did, but that he's fast tumbling down that same wild road to disaster. Gwen must decide between running from her past or running toward her future...with Mac.

#170 OUT OF THE NIGHT
by Trish Milburn

When diner owner Olivia DaCosta narrowly escapes an attack perpetrated by rogue vampires, the last person she expects to save her is sexy vampire cop Campbell Raines. But as humans start being targeted and kidnapped one by one, Olivia realizes that she is in more danger than even *he* poses. And despite knowing that Campbell can feed from her, since they share the same blood type, Olivia somehow feels safest in his embrace. But can Campbell's lust for blood be overpowered by his lust for *her*?

YOU CAN FIND MORE INFORMATION ON UPCOMING HARLEQUIN® TITLES, FREE EXCERPTS AND MORE AT WWW.HARLEQUIN.COM.

HNCNM0913

REQUEST YOUR FREE BOOKS!

2 FREE NOVELS FROM THE PARANORMAL ROMANCE COLLECTION PLUS 2 FREE GIFTS!

YES! Please send me 2 FREE novels from the Paranormal Romance Collection and my 2 FREE gifts (gifts are worth about $10). After receiving them, if I don't wish to receive any more books, I can return the shipping statement marked "cancel." If I don't cancel, I will receive 4 brand-new novels every month and be billed just $22.76 in the U.S. or $23.96 in Canada. That's a savings of at least 17% off the cover price of all 4 books. It's quite a bargain! Shipping and handling is just 50¢ per book in the U.S. and 75¢ per book in Canada.* I understand that accepting the 2 free books and gifts places me under no obligation to buy anything. I can always return a shipment and cancel at any time. Even if I never buy another book, the two free books and gifts are mine to keep forever.

237/337 HDN F4YC

Name _____ (PLEASE PRINT) _____

Address _____ Apt. # _____

City _____ State/Prov. _____ Zip/Postal Code _____

Signature (if under 18, a parent or guardian must sign)

Mail to the Harlequin® Reader Service:
IN U.S.A.: P.O. Box 1867, Buffalo, NY 14240-1867
IN CANADA: P.O. Box 609, Fort Erie, Ontario L2A 5X3

Want to try two free books from another line?
Call 1-800-873-8635 or visit www.ReaderService.com.

* Terms and prices subject to change without notice. Prices do not include applicable taxes. Sales tax applicable in N.Y. Canadian residents will be charged applicable taxes. Offer not valid in Quebec. This offer is limited to one order per household. Not valid for current subscribers to Paranormal Romance Collection or Harlequin® Nocturne™ books. All orders subject to credit approval. Credit or debit balances in a customer's account(s) may be offset by any other outstanding balance owed by or to the customer. Please allow 4 to 6 weeks for delivery. Offer available while quantities last.

Your Privacy—The Harlequin® Reader Service is committed to protecting your privacy. Our Privacy Policy is available online at www.ReaderService.com or upon request from the Harlequin Reader Service.

We make a portion of our mailing list available to reputable third parties that offer products we believe may interest you. If you prefer that we not exchange your name with third parties, or if you wish to clarify or modify your communication preferences, please visit us at www.ReaderService.com/consumerschoice or write to us at Harlequin Reader Service Preference Service, P.O. Box 9062, Buffalo, NY 14269. Include your complete name and address.

PARA13R

At first glance, he was all distracted gray eyes, a faint frown between dark brows, tension along high cheekbones and lean jaw, and a set of mouth with a quirky upper lip that looked as though it was crafted to carry a wry smile. Glossy dark hair was as scruffed as the rest of him, his one shoulder carried slightly higher than the other, with his movement not quite even and yet still full of its own strength.

On second glance, she saw the worse-for-wear jeans and shirt and jacket—but by second glance, he'd seen her.

His eyes narrowed. "Who are you?"

She'd lived her life with the uncanny ability to see through people, to anticipate them.

From him, she felt nothing.

No, not true. She felt that which she couldn't unravel—a slow, humming throb that both called to her and terrified her.

"Who—" he said.

"I don't know you," she snapped, suddenly breaking free

of that spell. "I want you to stay back, please." Blunt words, straight to the point.

He only frowned at her. "It's been a long day. Whatever you're up to…don't do it where I have to deal with it."

Those eyes—even in this uneven illumination, perfectly clear. Perfectly focused. Shadowed not by lighting but by expression and mood, and so pinned to her—

I'm not breathing.

No wonder her lungs ached.

Or that her voice sounded not quite so assertive when she said, "Please get out of my way."

She'd been right. That mouth…born for a wry smile. He said, "As soon as you stop blocking the only way out."

She took a sharp and hasty step aside—clearing the path, leaving as much room between them as possible.

He took a moment—she wasn't sure if she'd ever felt so looked at—and then he strode away with not so much as a glance back, that wry smile lingering.

Gwen touched the chain at her neck, fine platinum rope and always, always there. Her fingers ran to the flat disk hanging beneath her shirt—the habit of touching it so instilled that she rarely did it consciously. Her father's gift.

Now she found her fingers on it…and, through her shirt, closed her hand around it. Looking for…

She had no idea. But she thought maybe something had already found her.

**Will Gwen get the answers she's looking for?
Or will she give in to temptation?**

**Find out in CLAIMED BY THE DEMON
by Doranna Durgin
Available October 1, 2013,
only from Harlequin® Nocturne™!**

HARLEQUIN®
NOCTURNE™

A cop is torn between duty and unholy desire

Since the death of her fiancé, Olivia DaCosta is the one who continues his good work feeding the homeless. Every day is a lone struggle to keep her diner open after the plague that devastated the human population. Now, amid the chaos, a vampire race has begun stalking the survivors.

Because of her rare blood type, Olivia has learned to avoid vampire contact—until she meets one she can't resist. After Campbell Raines saves her life, it's clear there's no ignoring their potentially fatal attraction.

OUT OF THE NIGHT

by

TRISH MILBURN

Available October 1, 2013, only from Harlequin® Nocturne™.

www.Harlequin.com